ON THE 2

FELICE STEVENS

Published by Good Man Press

ISBN: 979-8-88949-006-7(eBook)
ISBN: 979-8-88949-008-1(Paperback)

First Edition, August 2023
Printed in the United States of America

Cover Art by Reese Dante
Cover Photography by Wander Aguiar
Model: Clever
Edited by Keren Reed
Copy Editing and Proofreading by Flat Earth Editing
Additional Proofreading by Lyrical Lines

DEDICATION

To the NYC MTA....

Just kidding.

To my family. Now and for always.

ACKNOWLEDGMENTS

Thank you, Keren, for always pushing me to make my stories the best that they can be. To Hope and Jess from Flat Earth Editing, I couldn't and wouldn't do this without you. Dianne from Lyrical Lines, you get the golden glove for all the spectacular catches. And to Reese, you never cease to amaze me with your brilliance.

To my wonderful readers, I owe you everything. Thank you for allowing these characters into your lives.

CONNECT WITH FELICE

BOOKBUB
https://www.bookbub.com/profile/felice-stevens

NEWSLETTER
https://tinyurl.com/y85e69ab

READER GROUP
https://www.facebook.com/groups/FelicesBreakfastClub/

FACEBOOK AUTHOR PAGE
https://www.facebook.com/felicestevensauthor/

INSTAGRAM
https://www.instagram.com/felicestevens

TWITTER
https://twitter.com/FeliceStevens1

WEBSITE
felicestevens.com

CHAPTER ▶ 1

"Sorry. Didn't mean to bang into you."

Irritated at being squashed, I glanced up from my newspaper and was instantly…interested.

Windblown and grinning, the man smoothed the errant strands of dark hair that landed over his brow, and then he settled into the empty seat next to me on the Uptown Number 2 train. Green eyes framed by ridiculously long, thick lashes sparkled at me, and a charmingly crooked smile crept over his face—a face chiseled by the gods of fabulous cheekbones and perfect chins. Twin dimples winked at me.

What the hell? The first rule of survival on the subway was not to stare directly at anyone, but damn, I couldn't help it. I reassured myself it was only because he was so good-looking that he'd startled me. I wasn't used to seeing model-like perfection on the Uptown 2 during Monday morning rush hour. Or at any time, for that matter.

"Am I naked?"

I blinked, brought back to reality by his low chuckle of amusement.

"Excuse me?"

"You're staring at me, so either I'm naked"—he paused, and I sensed he had a flair for the dramatic—"or you'd like me to be."

Heat flared in my belly and shot up to my face. "I-I don't know what the hell you're talking about. No, you're not naked, and no, I'm not interested in seeing you get to that point."

Dirty liar. Yes, you are.

"Pity."

Now he was the one staring, and though I returned to my newspaper, the words blurred before me. I sensed his probing gaze and finally set my paper on my lap.

"Do you mind?"

"I don't know. Do I?" That cheeky grin returned. "Guess it all depends on what *you* have in mind."

"You're staring at me. It's…annoying." I waved my hand in the air between us. "It's fucking with my concentration, and I'd like to read my morning paper."

"It's Monday. Didn't anyone ever tell you it's important to ease into the week?"

"No." I lifted the paper again, effectively ending our conversation.

I'd been taking the train to work for over fifteen years, and never had I engaged in a conversation with a stranger. This was New York City. You paid your overpriced fare, waited forever for a train, hoped you could find a seat, and if you did, you sat and either listened to music, read the news, or stared off into space, having perfected looking without seeing. God forbid you caught the wrong person's eye; there was a chance you'd end up a statistic on the evening news.

All I wanted was to be left alone so I could figure out how to quash this instantaneous unwanted attraction that had sprung up with regard to this man. I shifted, a vain attempt to put extra space between us, but the seats were too narrow, and neither of us was small. The way he filled out that sleek suit he wore, Mr. Gorgeous had to be six two and two twenty.

So here I sat, trapped with Chatty McChatterbox, and I still had over eight stops to go. Given that I had no desire to leave my coveted seat and stand squished between a man who thought brushing one's teeth was a weekly occurrence and a teenage girl on her way to school who'd decided this was the perfect morning to eat her McGreasy breakfast on the train, I knew I'd have to suck it up and stay put.

We lurched to a stop, and of course the banal, useless announcement came on the loudspeaker that there was traffic ahead and we'd be moving shortly.

Lies. All lies.

Minutes ticked by, and as we continued to wait, I became acutely aware of the man's warm, firm thigh pressed to mine. Why couldn't it be winter, when we'd be all bundled up and I wouldn't be able to zero in so easily on his musculature?

Perfectly sculpted muscles at that.

Dammit, why is it so hot in here?

Sweat trickled down my spine.

My seatmate frowned. "I hope it's not going to be like last week. It took them over half an hour before we got to the next station."

"It better not," I muttered. "Someone better be sick for them to screw up the trains like that again."

My neighbor's brows rose high. "Well, aren't you a merry ray of sunshine? And such a caring New Yorker. It's because of people like you that we have a reputation for being rude."

My face flamed. "I didn't mean it like it sounded. Just, I have meetings and I can't be late. I'm sure everyone else has to get to work as well. Even you. So hopefully it's not just because the conductor needed to take a piss and stopped on a whim."

"What do you mean, even me? You don't think I could have a job that's as important as yours?"

No. As the deputy chief financial officer of a huge private hospital, I was responsible for deciding how and where to spend the hundreds of millions of dollars we received yearly. I was certain Gorgeous George did not top me in the my-job-is-bigger-than-yours department.

"I don't know what you do. I'm assuming it's modeling or something."

That charming smile appeared again. "Why thank you. But alas, no. I'm not a model. Merely a shop boy." When I didn't respond, he explained, "I work at Macy's Herald Square in the men's department."

"Oh. My apologies. That sucks." My grimace was real. "Must be tough dealing with customers all day." The less I saw anyone, the better. I was much better with numbers than people. Numbers were definite. People were messy. Emotional. Needy.

"I love it. I find people fascinating." He propped his chin in his hand and gave me the benefit of those luminous, grass-green eyes.

Already frazzled by the conversation, I uncharacteristically stumbled over my words. "Uh, well, uh, lucky you, then."

"I bet I can guess what you do."

Another uncomfortable bead of sweat ran down the back of my neck. Not because the train was ridiculously overheated, but because the proximity of this stranger was doing all sorts of weird things to my breathing and pulse rate.

Get a grip, Nash.

"Doubtful," I told him.

A corner of that generous mouth kicked up. "Wanna try me?" The tip of a pink tongue peeked out—and for fuck's sake, I was getting turned-on in the middle of rush hour on the filthy 2 train.

What the hell was happening?

If anyone from my office could see me, my reputation as The Iceman would be shot to hell, as I was burning up from the inside out. But I managed to pull it together and not lose my shit.

"Sure." It was the only word I could manage.

He tapped his artfully stubbled cheek with a long, elegant finger. "Corporate exec. Probably something to do with numbers, and big ones at that. You're close to forty, give or take, and live alone in a high-priced condo. You have issues with your family."

I didn't want to react but couldn't help it. My jaw dropped. "That's…pretty damn close."

He lifted a shoulder. "It's a talent. One of many." He winked.

I ducked my head, pretending to try and read the paper that thankfully covered my lap. How did this person pull such a visceral reaction from me that no one else—man or woman—had ever managed to achieve? I wanted to know what he tasted like from top to bottom.…My fingers tightened on my paper.

I found both men and women attractive. I mean, sex was sex. No big deal. Fun and occasionally pleasurable. Like the other night. Julia from Legal came home with me and rode my dick like a fucking pogo stick. She was beautiful, brainy, and slightly terrifying. We'd been casual bed partners for a while, neither of us looking for permanence, but when one of us had an itch, the other was happy to scratch it. She always seemed to enjoy it more than I did, though. For me it was…it was fine. I didn't need fireworks. That shit was for books and movies, anyway, not real life.

But with this guy…this stranger…my reaction went way beyond finding him attractive, and I needed to think of something, anything, to stop the crazy thoughts tumbling in my brain. What could take my mind off grabbing this man and dragging him off the train to have filthy, hot sex?

The crotchety board of directors of the hospital popped into my mind, and my erection instantly deflated. I breathed a sigh of relief. Visions of flabby, naked old men would do that.

"Are you dating anyone?" He nudged my shoulder, and I grimaced, shifting slightly.

"Are you aware of a thing called personal space?"

The train wheezed and squealed, picking up speed as we rounded a curve. To my mortification, centrifugal force pushed me up against the man, and for a brief moment, I caught a whiff of his aftershave and wanted to eat his face. Another half inch, and I'd be tasting his lips. Lips that looked soft and kissable and…evidently, my coffee hadn't kicked in to start my brain functioning. That had to be the reason I was lusting over a stranger on the 2 train.

"Speaking of personal space…usually men buy me dinner first," he murmured, and I grabbed the seat bar on my left and pulled off him.

"Sorry. I couldn't help it."

He winked. "That's what they all say." He nudged my shoulder, the push of his hard muscle sending my pulse spiking once again.

Would this train ride never end?

Maybe if I answered his earlier question, he'd shut up. "No. I'm not seeing anyone."

"Why? You've obviously got money—I can tell your suit is Armani, and your tie is this year's Fendi. I'm a fan of Hermès and Gucci, myself." That simmering gaze traveled at an excruciatingly slow pace over my body, leaving me aching with…something. "Bad divorce?"

Oh, for God's sake.

My control snapped. "Listen, I paid for a train ride, not a therapy session. I just want to sit here, read my paper, and be left alone." I stuck my face in the pages and prayed we'd reach our destination soon. But of course the train crept on the track like a burglar through a pitch-black living room, and we weren't getting very far uptown at all.

"No wonder you're not getting any."

I ignored him.

"I mean, you're very attractive, but who wants to play in the sheets with an ogre?"

I huffed and rattled my paper.

"Unless you *were* married and you've sworn off relationships. *Hmm*. That seems more likely."

"I have not been married," I gritted through clenched teeth. "I don't want to get married."

"Why not? Are you a player? One of those guys who bangs a different woman every night?"

A snicker had me setting the paper down. Again. Curious George's face was alive with laughter. He was going to get a punch in the nose if he didn't shut up.

"First of all, I'm not a frat boy. I don't use terms like '*bang*.' I've grown well beyond that terminology."

"Well, excuse me, your highness. Fine. Do you have sexual relations with many different women?"

Pretty-boy didn't have to know I was bisexual. He'd never leave me alone.

"I—" About to answer him, I stopped myself. Why the hell was I continuing to engage with a stranger about my life? And if he could be nosy, so could I.

"What about you? Do you have a boyfriend? Or a girlfriend?"

He seemed taken aback that I'd asked him a personal question, and those expressive green eyes widened. For the first time, he paused. "I did. But he cheated on me."

Having grown up with a father who could've taught a master class in adultery, I could sympathize. "I'm sorry. That's never fun to deal with."

The train hiccuped and began to move at its normal speed.

For someone as voluble as this man, the subject of his life proved to be the one topic that shut down his spark. "He was getting calls late at night and acting shady. I'd check out his Instagram and see him tagged in pictures with some guy who looked like a party boy. I didn't think Oscar was like that. He was a manager at Applebee's, and he wanted to own a franchise one day. I thought he was someone steady who had his head on straight."

"Sounds like a smart businessman."

He pursed his lips as though the betrayal still tasted as bitter as a lemon. "So I thought, until I found out the truth. One night after I came home from work, he was off, saying he had to go out and interview potential employees. No idea what made me suspicious, but I tracked him on his phone, followed him to a club in the Village. When I went inside and searched, I found Oscar getting his dick sucked in the bathroom. Dirty bastard."

A discreet cough sounded above us, and I glanced upward into the disapproving face of an older man. I shrugged. "Get some earphones if you don't want to hear."

His face flamed, and he turned away from me while other people snickered. Obviously, my seatmate's story was providing salacious early morning gossip fodder on the way to work for some commuters. But since he had no reservations about spilling his guts to a total stranger, I had no qualms about continuing the conversation.

Who was I kidding? I wanted to satisfy my own need to know the details. Equally stunned and repulsed by his story and the thought that shit like that went on in public places, I prodded him. "Damn…that's awful. The cheating was bad enough, but sex in public?"

I must've looked as shocked as I felt, because he grinned. "Oh, I don't mind that. Sometimes the mood hits, and you just need it. A dressing room, bathroom stall, under the table…quick, fast, and deliciously naughty." He licked his lips. "Know what I mean?"

No. I hadn't a clue what the hell he was talking about. I could never rationalize being so out of control and desperate to have sex that I'd take a chance and go at it in a public place. Sex belonged inside. Behind closed doors. In the bedroom. I ignored his question and countered with one of my own to ferret out more info.

"How long had you been together?"

"Three years. I don't even know when the cheating started 'cause he keeps denying it and saying he loves me and it was a one-off mistake, but I don't believe him. Why should I? If he lied about one thing, how can I trust anything he tells me to be the truth?"

Something didn't sit right with what he'd said, and despite the fact that I'd never been in a relationship, I knew that if someone had cheated on me, their ass would've been right out the door.

"You aren't still with that loser, are you?"

He stared at the filthy floor. "No. I mean, I told him we were done, but he keeps coming around, trying to get me to forgive and forget. He says he never meant for it to happen and that he loves me, but in my book, you don't cheat on someone you love." The fun and flirtiness had vanished from his handsome face. "I don't answer his texts or calls. I deserve better than a liar."

"Everyone does."

My mother had failed to see that, and my father, bastard that he was, had been adept at pulling the wool over her eyes.

The train pulled into 34th Street–Penn Station, and the doors opened. Without another word, my seatmate jumped up and darted out.

I was left bemused and bewildered, realizing I had no idea what his name was or if I'd ever see him again.

And wondering why I cared.

CHAPTER ▶ 2

Another morning, another day at the grind. I raced down the steps, hearing the rumble of the train in the tunnel. If I was late again, I'd get in trouble. It didn't matter that my manager liked me. He'd have to write me up, and I couldn't afford to lose my job. I was lucky as hell to have found the tiny shoebox of an apartment I lived in. No bigger than four hundred square feet, I barely had room for myself, a sofa, and the futon I slept on, which I'd crammed in a corner. The racks of clothing might have had something to do with the lack of space, but I had to keep up the appearance of a stylish trendsetter if I wanted a job in fashion. My life might be small, but I tried to live large.

I tapped my phone and pushed through the turnstile, then dashed to my usual car—second from the last, where it tended to be less crowded at this early point in the ride—and my heart kicked double-time.

He was there. In the same seat as yesterday. Grumpy-faced as Scrooge before Christmas, but I'd take it.

I'd noticed him for weeks—who wouldn't? All that delicious goodness wrapped up in fine worsted wool and discreet but expensive ties. In the spring, the trains were too crowded to get close, but by summertime the city cleared out, and there was now room to position for maximum viewing pleasure. Getting a seat next to him two days in a row was a bonus. My lucky day indeed.

My breathing steady, I strolled over to where he sat and put my ass into the seat. That sharp-as-a-knife jaw flexed, and his full lips sagged in a frown.

"Good morning," I chirped out in a perky tone I figured would set him on edge, but I wanted to poke the bear since I couldn't poke anything else. I was right. He was tighter than a virgin and moved his leg away from mine, saying nothing. That so wouldn't fly with me. "Don't you remember me? From yesterday?"

"No."

"Oh, come on now." No way in hell was I letting him get away with such a blatant lie. "Not only did I guess what you did for a living, I can also tell you're not the type to talk to strangers on the subway. So I'm sure you remember our little *tête-à-tête*." I smirked. "Besides. I've been told I'm unforgettable."

"Annoying as hell is more like it." He huffed out a sigh but still hadn't looked at me. "Do you mind? I'm—"

"Trying to read the paper. Yeah, I can see that, and really? Who still does that? You said the same thing yesterday until you decided to interrogate me about my ex."

That finally got to him. Dark brows raised, he set his paper in his lap. "Interrogate? I asked a few questions because, just like now, you won't be quiet and leave me in peace."

"So you do remember me." I smirked with triumph. "I knew it."

A dull-red flush crept up his neck. "Obviously, it was

the highlight of your day, but not mine."

That stung. "Damn, you're rude."

He folded his paper in half. "Seems like you can dish it out but not take it."

"Wow. Playground comebacks. I'm impressed."

He grunted and returned to reading. I allowed the train to rock me into a half sleep, but my phone buzzed with several texts. I dug it out of my cross-body bag and grimaced. Oscar.

I'm coming by tonight. We need to talk.

I'm sorry. It'll never happen again.

Make sure you're home. I'll be there at 8.

"Fucking asshole," I muttered to myself, shoving the phone away.

Grouch-face set his paper down. "Your ex?"

I blinked. Twice. "I'm sorry. Were you talking to me? Unprovoked?"

The slight uptick of his lips transformed his face from grouchy to oh-my-God gorgeous. "Shocking, isn't it?" Those icy eyes warmed, and I wanted to drown in their ocean-blue depths. "But you were upset after you read the texts." That sexy growl lowered further. "Is he harassing you? Has he put his hands on you?"

Reflexively my gaze shot to his fingers, and sweat popped out over my body. They looked capable and strong. I imagined them gripping my hips as inch by inch he slid inside me, stretching and filling me. He'd be huge and hard, and I'd feel him for days.

I'd like your hands on me.

Idiot. Stop it.

"No. I wouldn't put up with that shit."

"But he clearly upset you. Why?"

I scratched my head. "I don't know.…We were together for three years, after all."

He made an impatient gesture with his hand, and I thought I heard a snort. "So what? He cheated."

"I *know*. But we have history. It's hard to let go." Why was I defending Oscar? He'd broken my heart, and I threw him out. End of story.

"Fuck that. It all goes out the window when someone cheats."

"Is that how you dealt with it when it happened to you? Just walked away and erased all traces of her from your life? People and emotions aren't emails you can delete and forget."

His nostrils flared, and that hard jaw tightened even further. "I've—no. I didn't say that. It's never happened to me, not personally."

"If that's so, who are you to give me any advice?"

He glared, obviously expecting me to be intimidated and back down, but he didn't know me. I liked a challenge and returned it in spades, our gazes clashing. My breathing slowed. Those blue eyes widened, and a firecracker of desire exploded in my belly. God, this was such a turn-on. I imagined his mouth on mine, his tongue pushing past my lips. He'd rip my clothes off and fuck me until I screamed. Unfortunately, my fantasy would no doubt remain simply that. Then he shocked the hell out of me by speaking in a rapid, low whisper.

"Because I grew up with it. My father cheated on my mother and walked out on us."

"But I bet even you can understand that sometimes you might do something not so smart because you're lonely." Yeah, I was goading him, but I wanted to get a reaction.

"No. Whether it's one time or you're a serial cheater, you don't change." He stared off into space. "I don't care."

Who are you thinking about?

I desperately wanted to know.

"As long as you don't let him do anything foolish. You thought you knew him, and he cheated. He might do worse." He checked his watch, and I bristled.

So sorry. Am I boring you?

I enjoyed teasing him and decided to see if he'd take the bait a second time.

"I know, but no one gets to touch me." I gathered my wits and winked at him. "Not unless I want them to." His nod was curt and dismissive, but I wasn't ready to lose him to his newspaper once again. "By the way, I'm Ethan."

Grouch-face studied me carefully; then instead of introducing himself like any other person would, the bastard picked up his paper and began to read. Not that I needed to make friends or anything, but one minute he was giving me dating advice, and the next he was ignoring me? That didn't cut it with me.

"Aren't you going to tell me your name?"

He remained silent while the train sped onward, getting closer and closer to my destination. *Dammit, MTA. Why couldn't you be more predictable and have train traffic now like every other morning?* What happened to those inexplicable delays in the tunnels when you needed them most? As much as I couldn't afford to be late, I wanted more time with Grouch-face.

"Why?" he asked.

If I didn't believe that violence solved nothing, I'd have punched him.

I gritted my teeth. "Common courtesy. I told you my name. You tell me yours. That's how it goes."

"Only if I want it to."

He was entirely too casual for my liking. That calm, measured tone only pissed me off more. As such, I wanted to rile him up, so I leaned in closer, touching my shoulder to his. "Why don't you want to?" I murmured in my most seductive voice. "Are you afraid?"

He turned his face so we were almost nose to nose, and I could've swooned at the proximity of his mouth. His lips were so full. So luscious. I imagined biting on the bottom one, sucking it into my mouth. He smelled good, too. I caught a hint of cinnamon and vanilla that made my mouth water to taste and lick him. Those big baby blues, so fiery earlier, now narrowed to slits and shined cold with disdain. Then he jerked away.

"I'm not afraid of anything."

"That's a lie." I shifted in my seat, pretending the train moved me closer to him. "You're scared of me."

"You're delusional. Why would I be scared of you?"

"I don't know. Maybe you need to ask yourself that."

"There's nothing to think about," he forced out.

My smile was slow. "Oh, yeah? Then why do you get so…worked up whenever I get personal?" I licked my lips, deliberately egging him on, but I couldn't help it. If he wanted to move seats, he could. It was a free train. Okay, not really, but the point was, Grouch-face could sit wherever he wanted. He got on before me. He didn't have to pick the same two-seater as last time.

"I'm not worked up," he snapped.

I busted out laughing. "Now who's being delusional? If you were clenched any tighter, you'd need a tetanus shot for lockjaw." For good measure, I decided to lay it on thick. "And tight is only good in certain situations. Know what I mean?"

There was no mistaking the blaze of lust in those eyes, but he refused to back down. "No. And I don't want to." He picked up the paper again just as the train ground to a halt. "By the way, if you don't leave now, you'll miss your stop."

Damn him and his nonchalance. My surprisingly wobbly legs managed to carry me out of my seat and onto the platform. Needing a breather, I leaned against the filthy pillar, something I never did, but today it couldn't be helped. As the train pulled away, I peered into the car to see my seatmate staring at me through the grimy window, only to hastily retrieve his paper and stick his face between the pages.

Well, well. I'll figure you out yet, my pretty.

I left the station and joined the streaming masses on Seventh Avenue, running around the slow-walking tourists and early-morning commuters. I refused to be late two days in a row. My manager, Wesley, might appreciate me because I was one of the highest-selling sales associates in menswear, but I wasn't about to take our relationship for granted, and with two minutes to spare, I clocked in. A quick pee and a touch-up of my hair in the mirror, and I hustled out to my register.

A few years earlier, they'd reimagined the entire men's section, and I loved working in the brand-new space. I worked on the mezzanine in the Designer and Contemporary Collection, and my discount allowed me first access to sales, plus a chance to cozy up to buyers and sometimes get invited to soft openings, fashion shows, and boutiques. I happily accepted the clothes they sometimes gifted me, which I hoarded like a miser.

"Ethan, how are you? No train problems today?" Wesley greeted me with a pat on my shoulder. "Looking spiffy. Is that Hugo Boss?"

"Yes. Several years old, but it's holding up pretty well."

"But the tie is new, isn't it?"

I smoothed my hand over the thick, silk fabric. "Yes." I sighed with reverence. "It's Gucci. I got it a while ago. I took a trip to Woodbury Common and bought five—I couldn't resist. Saved for six months and ate peanut-butter sandwiches, but it was worth it."

"She's a beauty. Can't wait to see the others."

He might not be so anxious if he knew there was a method to my madness. I'd been with Wesley for four years, and though he was a great manager and taught me about the business, I was ready to move on, preferably to one of the designer collections. Gucci would be my first choice, but I would take any of the high-end designers—Vuitton,

Dior, Saint Laurent. There would be a pay increase as well as a higher commission rate. I had bigger plans than being a salesperson—not that there was anything wrong with it, but I wanted to do more than sell. I wanted to influence how men looked. Despite what Grouch-face thought, I had a business degree in fashion marketing from FIT, and my ultimate goal was to be a buyer for luxury menswear. I lived in the boutiques on the weekends and was a fast learner.

"I'm hoarding them. Can't afford to put all the goodies out for show at once." We were heading into a big sale, and it would be chaotic as hell once the doors opened. "What's today looking like?" Normally I enjoyed the rush and buzz of the customers, but today my mind was still on the Uptown 2 train as I straightened and poofed out a table of cotton sweaters. I restacked the bright colors in the front. Men didn't always have to dress in brown and beige—a nice, bright blue or green could do wonders. Take Grouch-face, for example. He wore a plain navy suit with a white shirt. Even the expensive tie couldn't save it from being…boring. If I could style his wardrobe, I'd liven him up.

Who are you kidding? You want to undress him.

How many stops past mine did he travel? Did he transfer cross-town at 42nd or work on the West Side? Why did he keep asking me about Oscar if he didn't want to talk?

"Ethan? Did you hear a word I said?"

"Huh? Oh, sorry. I was…thinking. What did you say?"

Wesley's smile was indulgent. "Late night? Did you and Oscar kiss and make up?"

I scowled. "What? No way. I told you we broke up."

"Oh. I thought maybe you'd reconsidered." Wesley sounded surprised by the strength of my denial. When I initially discovered Oscar had cheated, I'd poured my heart out to him about how devastated I was and how much I loved him. Wesley must have assumed I'd be willing to try again.

"Why would I?"

"You were together a long time. People make mistakes. And sometimes if you love someone hard enough, they can be forgiven."

Dismayed, I stared at him, my hands twisting a beautiful sweater. "Forgiven? *I* never cheated on him. It never crossed my mind. Oscar meant everything to me."

"Exactly why I don't think you should be making a rash decision. Maybe just listen to what he has to say before breaking it off completely."

I didn't believe I was wrong. As annoying as Grouch-face was, he was right about one thing: cheaters didn't change.

Security unlocked the doors, the customers trickled in, and I abandoned all thoughts of Oscar and put on a smiling face. Wesley took hold of my arm, and I faced him with a quizzical tilt of my brows.

"Just a second," he said. "I want to apologize. I'm sorry if I overstepped. I've known you all these years, and from what I've seen, you were never happier than when you were with Oscar."

"Maybe so, but it was a fool's happiness. And I'm anything but a fool."

CHAPTER ▶ 3

Who the hell was I?

It made no sense that I would look for a stranger on a train, but that didn't stop me from tensing with anticipation at the Bergen Street stop. More crowded than usual because of residual delays from an earlier train taken out of service, there were no seats, so I leaned on the door at the end of the subway car. There were people everywhere. The doors opened and I surreptitiously scanned the entering passengers, and when I didn't see him—*don't kid yourself, Nash; you remember his name is Ethan*—my already lousy mood deepened.

Then, through the window panels between the two train cars, I caught sight of a familiar mop of hair from the back. Ethan. He was squashed against the door and didn't see me, so I could observe him without notice.

As usual, he wore a well-fitting suit. He would certainly mesh with the beautifully dressed salespeople, but with his effusive personality and stunning face, Ethan could've been a model. Recalling the muscular thigh pressed to mine and his strong neck, I could only imagine him without a shirt—ridged abs, a tight ass…

Damn, it's hot in here. Too many people and not enough air.

I snapped to attention as a man, who looked a little younger than Ethan, started talking to him. Ethan smiled, and the two began to chat as if they were old friends. My lousy mood got even lousier, but like a voyeur, I spent my entire train ride spying on him and his new train friend. My gut swirled with dismay as I watched Ethan take out his phone and show the man something. It was too far away for me to see what was on the screen, but my imagination filled in the blanks. Maybe they were arranging a date or exchanging phone numbers.

The train stopped at Penn Station, and Ethan shouldered his way through the crowd and disappeared. My annoyance intensified at the hoard of humanity surging into the subway car, making it even more difficult for me to push my way out at my stop. And my morning deteriorated further once I entered my office and found Julia waiting.

"Did we have a meeting?" I asked her.

"No. I wanted to know if you were going tomorrow night."

Puzzled, I gazed at her. "Going where? What's happening?"

She looked skyward as if I were trying her patience. "The awards ceremony. How do you not know? It's all over the hospital."

I set my coffee on my desk. "I don't pay attention to that stuff."

"Your father is being given a huge award." She tapped a dark-red nail to her cheek. "Why aren't you going?"

"I never go to these things. So if that's all…"

"Come on, Nash. Everyone attends. This isn't the Christmas party or some silly Valentine's Day thing. It's a biggie."

"Still not interested."

"Your father—"

"Julia," I snapped, harsher than intended, but I was getting annoyed at her harping. "I'm not interested. I don't do parties." I sat behind my desk. "So if you'll excuse me."

I had to give her credit. She was relentless. "Oh, come on. I've heard all the bigwigs in the hospital will be there. You have to go."

"I don't have to do anything, Julia, except get to work."

"We can put in an appearance and go home and finish the night with a bang." Her smile was bright, and her eyes sparkled. "So to speak."

I was about to say no, but then I thought for a second. Would it look worse for me if I didn't show up? My father would likely assume I didn't want to face him, which was true—I couldn't stand to see his face. But he might think I was hiding from him and giving him too much space in my head.

"If we do go, I'll only stay for a little while, and certainly not for the awards ceremony. The last thing I want is to suffer through all the glad-handing and lousy rubbery chicken."

Julia planted a kiss on my cheek. "It's at The Pierre, so we can go together after work. Make sure you wear your nicest suit."

"Bye, Julia. I have work to do."

The door slammed behind her, and I shook my head in frustration. Why I'd let myself be sandbagged into this farce was beyond me, but I guessed it was better than sitting home alone again. Unfortunately, sex with Julia was becoming as solitary an endeavor as jerking off.

The day passed with me sitting in my office, answering phone calls from Roger, our CFO, figuring out how much to parcel out to each department, and working out the intricate details of our scholarship funding and how to manage all the different streams of money flowing to the hospital.

I loved numbers. They were black and white and never lied to you. What you saw was what was there. They weren't trying to hide from you. Numbers were real. Figuring out a budget and having all the dollar amounts reconcile at the end was often a thrill. Almost as good as sex.

Hmm. Maybe I did have an issue.

At six p.m., I slipped on my jacket and left. My secretary had already gone, as had most of the administrative staff. I was usually the last one out the door. I took the train, and despite myself, I looked around to see if Ethan came on the train at Penn Station, but he didn't. I went to the gym, ignored Mario's subtle hints that he was free for the evening, and went home. Mario was a trainer, and a few times a month if I found the time, I'd go exercise. If he was there, sometimes he'd come home with me for a quickie, take a shower and leave.

I was angry for allowing Julia to talk me into going to the dinner. Before my father joined the staff at Mercy Hospital, I'd been able to keep my connection to him a secret—no one had ever asked if we were related. My father had attempted to pull me into his orbit, assuming I'd want to give a joint interview when the hospital news did a piece on him, but I'd refused. I loathed having my personal life on display. Unlike my father, I did not enjoy the attention.

Tomorrow night, despite Julia's urging, I would only make a brief appearance in front of the big shots, then leave. With my father so in love with the camera, he most likely wouldn't even notice.

The sight of a train leaving the station while running

down the steps was one of the most frustrating things any New Yorker could experience. Thanks to a sleepless night over this damn dinner, I'd woken up late, something I never did. To compound the problem, one of the elevators in my building was out of service, which meant the remaining two were overcrowded, and I'd had to wait close to eight minutes before I could squeeze on. No matter that I'd hurried, I missed my usual train.

"Dammit." I paced the platform, my annoyance escalating as people entered the station shaking out umbrellas. I hadn't had time to check the weather. With a rueful glance at my feet, I hoped my dress shoes would withstand a soaking.

The train arrived, and my mood improved when the doors opened at Bergen Street and Ethan appeared. A slight smile tipped up the corner of his generous mouth as he strolled toward me and sat.

"Good morning." He placed his bag on his lap and leaned in. "Miss me yesterday?"

I tried not to react, but I could feel my damn face growing hot. "You weren't here? I don't remember."

"I was, just not in this car. It was too crowded, so I squeezed into the other one. It all worked out. I met a friend."

I know you did.

"Nice for you." I opened my paper, hoping he'd get the hint, but as I was learning about this man, he didn't pay attention to my subtle indicators that I had no desire to talk. Maybe he saw through my bullshit.

"Yeah. It's someone I knew from FIT."

"Mmhmm." I pretended to be interested in the price of gold skyrocketing. Of course, Ethan continued to babble on.

"Yeah. He's getting married, and when I told him I work at Macy's, he wanted to know if we sold tuxedos. Good thing we have Wi-Fi on trains because I was able to show him all the brands we carry."

That got my attention, as I recalled the two of them,

phones in hand, huddled together. I set my paper in my lap. "He's getting married?"

Ethan grinned. "Yeah, you know, that thing where two people pledge to spend the rest of their lives together. They exchange rings, have a big party, and smash cake in each other's faces."

I grimaced. "I'm aware of the practice."

"Not your thing, huh?"

I stared into space. "No."

Ethan sighed. "I think it's romantic. Ronnie met Steve in school, and they've been together forever. They'd finally saved enough money to have a wedding and a fabulous honeymoon in Hawaii. I'm happy to help. I told him I'd get all the groomsmen my discount and help him with the registry and stuff."

"That's very nice of you."

"I'm a nice guy." He leaned in close, and I could feel his breath in my ear. "I'd do anything for my friends. If you ever need anything, come by, and I'll make sure to take care of you. Personally."

Jesus, why did every little innuendo make me think dirty thoughts? "Thank you, but I'm good."

"I'll bet you are."

"Will you stop?"

"What am I doing?" Pretending innocence, he batted his outrageously long, thick lashes. "All I meant was, if you ever need clothes or accessories, I can get them for you with my discount. And I bet you're good because I can see your suits are very high quality. Italian, right?"

"Yes."

"That's a pretty fancy tie for a workday. Different than the ones I saw you wear earlier in the week."

I glanced down at my shirt. I'd worn one of my better suits, and yes, the tie was a new one, a little flashier than my normal subtle stripe or plain, dark silk. It was bright blue with a paisley design.

"It was a present."

"Old girlfriend?" he asked with a cocky grin.

"No. From my mother on my thirtieth birthday. She'd gone to France and went to all the stores—Hermès, Louis Vuitton, Chanel. She said I needed to spice up my wardrobe."

"She's right."

I didn't feel the need to correct him and mention that she passed away several years ago.

We entered 34th Street–Penn Station, and he gathered his bag and stood. "Have a good day."

I watched him leave and touched my tie, feeling the thick silk slide between my fingers. No one else would ever understand, but wearing this tie to a dinner honoring my father was like carrying a tiny piece of her with me.

Once outside, I noticed the rain had stopped, which I took as a good sign. My secretary greeted me with a stack of messages and an apologetic face. "Sorry, Nash, but your father's called at least three times."

"Did he say it was urgent?" I had a suspicion about his reason.

"No, just that he'd like you to return the call as soon as you can."

"Well, unfortunately, you can't always get what you want. Even the Rolling Stones knew that." I smiled at her. "I have reports to get out. If he calls again, please tell him I'm busy. In fact, just hold all my calls. I have to accomplish a ton before close of business."

"As you wish."

Madeline was a gem, and though I was sure she was as curious as anyone else about my relationship with the famous Dr. Martin Roman, she never pried.

I spent the day with my head down and ate lunch at my desk. It was my own fault that I spilled my fourth cup of coffee all over my pristine white shirt and tie.

"Goddammit," I shouted, and Madeline came flying in, to witness me standing with a brown stain spreading rapidly across my chest.

"Oh, no. I'm sorry, Nash. Can I do anything?"

Uncaring about the shirt, I whipped off the tie. "What do I do? I can't let this get ruined." Maybe I was overreacting.

"The dry cleaner around the corner can get the stain out. I know some of the board members use them. Would you like me to send it out? They can put a rush on it if you need it right away."

"Thank you, yes." The wet shirt and undershirt beneath it stuck to me, and I pulled them away from my skin. "I have to get a new shirt, I'm afraid. This one is beyond help."

"You've been working nonstop all day. Just run to the store and buy a new one. Macy's isn't that far away."

"Good idea."

I slipped on my suit jacket and put my wallet and phone into my pockets. "I should be back in an hour."

"Not a problem." She took the tie. "Everyone is so busy getting ready for the big dinner tonight. You're going?"

"For a little while."

"It's three thirty, so I'll make sure they have this to you by five. The dinner doesn't start until seven thirty."

"Thanks, Madeline."

It was a quick walk to the department store, and I was curiously light-hearted at the prospect of seeing Ethan.

Except I didn't see him. Another sales associate approached me.

"May I help you?"

My smile was wry. "I seem to have dumped a cup of coffee on myself and need a new white shirt."

The young man, who appeared to be in his mid-to-late twenties, laughed. "You'd be surprised how many busy executives we get with this problem. You get so caught up in what you're doing, you miss your mouth and it lands on your shirt."

I chuckled. "Glad to know I'm not the only klutz." I scanned the floor.

"Are you looking for something in particular?"

The last thing I wanted was for Ethan to discover I'd asked for him. I wouldn't want him to get the wrong idea. Like I was interested in him. I wasn't. It was just natural curiosity.

"No. These shirts are fine." I picked my way through the plain white shirts until I found my size. "I'll dispense with the undershirt for tonight. I'll be wearing my suit jacket and tie the whole time anyway."

"Is it a special event? And I can take that for you and hold it at the register." He held out his hand, and I gave him the shirt I'd picked.

I decided I might as well take a few extra shirts to keep at the office, and chose another white and a blue one.

"Yes. I have a dinner at The Pierre hotel, so I need to look presentable."

"How about a tie? We have a great selection, some forty percent off."

"Sure. Why not?"

Did I need any more ties? No. But I felt bad for only buying a few shirts, so I picked up a few ties as well, in case I made another mess like today and couldn't get to a dry cleaner in time.

"That's it," I told him.

"I can ring you up over this way."

I followed him to the register and took out my credit card. He continued to chat as he took off the security tags and placed the ties in tissue paper before bagging them.

"That's a nice hotel. A work function or pleasure?"

I couldn't consider being with my father a pleasurable experience.

"Definitely work-related."

I tapped my card, and he handed me a receipt.

"Enjoy your evening."

"Thank you."

I made it down the elevator and was near the doors leading to Seventh Avenue when I heard a familiar voice.

"Couldn't bear to be away from me? Is that why you came to visit?"

My gut tightened, but I checked my step and slowly turned around. "I'm sorry?"

Ethan's laughing face came into view, and I couldn't help noticing again how beautiful he was. His suit hit him in all the right places, showcasing his muscular arms, broad chest, and strong neck. A shockwave of desire ripped through me, and my mouth dried.

Get a grip.

Ethan said, "I was getting ready to leave when I saw you at the register. You didn't have to pretend to want to buy something just to see me."

"How do you manage that ego? I needed a new shirt, and this was the closest place." I held up the shopping bag as proof.

"What happened to the old one?" I opened my jacket, and he laughed at the coffee stain. "Oh. Well, better the shirt than in your lap. Don't want to damage the goods." He winked, and my face burned. I'd always prided myself on being able to control my emotions, but with this man, I'd lost that talent when I seemed to need it the most.

"Well…I'd better get going. I have lots of work waiting."

"Yes, I'm sure you do, being an über-busy executive." The heat in those big green eyes intensified. "Have a wonderful evening. Maybe I'll see you tomorrow on the 2."

I nodded and rushed out, feeling like a fool. Why did this man make me so tongue-tied and off-center? He was just a guy—good-looking for sure, but not the first gorgeous man I'd had flirt with me, and yet I couldn't for the life of me figure out why I wanted to flirt back. Ethan was a stranger I talked to on the subway. I barely said hello to work colleagues I'd known for years, yet I'd confided things to Ethan I hadn't told a soul.

Maybe it was the anonymity of the train and never knowing if I'd see him again that made it more comfortable. But now I'd broken through that wall by seeing him outside the safety of the subway. I should switch cars and stay away.

The more distance I put between the store and me, the more I could breathe, and by the time I returned to my office, I was back to normal. Whatever that was.

I finished my reports and emailed them to the CFO and the COO just as Madeline buzzed me.

"I have your tie, and Julia is outside."

"Thanks. Please bring it and send her in."

Before I had a chance to set the receiver down, the door opened and Julia strode in. Her black hair hung like a gleaming silk curtain over her shoulders, and she pirouetted in front of me.

"What do you think?"

Her gown was electric blue and clung to her slight frame. I knew she worked out almost every day, and the dress showcased her toned body.

"Very pretty."

"Don't sound so enthusiastic, Nash. I'm not sure I can handle all the praise."

Madeline came to hand me the tie, but before I could take it, Julia grabbed it. "Here, let me."

Her fingers swiftly tied the knot, and she tweaked it, then pressed a kiss to my lips. "You look gorgeous."

"Thanks."

Her perfume swirled between us, and she looped her arms around my neck. "We should get going."

"Julia." I held her elbow and made sure she looked me directly in the eyes. "You realize we're not a couple.

Nothing's changed between us."

She patted my cheek. "Silly. I'll get a car for us."

We entered the ballroom of The Pierre, and I immediately spotted my father with his wife, Diana, in a circle of admirers. Julia tugged at me.

"Let's go say hello."

"No. I said I'd come to show my face. That's all."

"Nash…" Her expression grew fierce, but I wasn't having it.

"Look. This isn't happening. I'm going to say hello to Roger and Barney, then leave. I have no desire to make small talk with people I barely know and in most cases don't care to." I yanked my arm free and made my way to the bar, where I was offered a glass of wine. I stood by a towering potted plant, surveying the crowded room full of hospital dignitaries, philanthropists, and doctors. Of course, my father's entire department was there to cheer him on.

"Hi, Nash." One of my father's associates, Dr. Alex Stern, bounded over to me. "I didn't expect to see you here." Alex was the type to never give up if he wanted something. And for some reason, he'd decided he wanted to be my friend and refused to take no for an answer, no matter how many times I'd tried. And despite myself, he and I had become friendly during the various cancer drives held at the hospital, where he'd confided that he dedicated every day of his job to his brother, Seth, who'd died of leukemia. The story of how he and his husband had adopted a dying woman's young son had become legend in the hospital.

"Hi, Alex. I was just leaving."

A good-natured grin spread over his face. "Why am

I not surprised?" He took a glass of white wine from the bartender. "Have you said hello to your father?"

I grimaced. "No. I've only been here a few minutes—"

"And you came straight to the bar. I don't blame you. I can't stay late either."

"I'm not staying at all. I'll see you soon."

I left him behind and found Julia talking with Diana. "Hello, Diana. Nice to see you. Julia, I have to leave."

Disappointment flashed across her face. "I was about to sit down. The ceremony is starting."

"I know, but I told you I wasn't staying."

Diana said, "I'm sorry to hear that, Nash. I know Martin would've loved to share this night with you. Are you sure you can't stay a little bit longer? He's just talking to the head of the hospital right now and should be back any minute."

My smile was halfhearted. "I'm sorry. I've had a brutal day, and I need to get home."

Julia chimed in, "Oh, come on, Nash. Sit and have something to eat. You'll feel better." She patted my shoulder like I was a child, and addressed Diana with a conspiratorial wink. "You know how men are. They get so grouchy when they're hungry."

"Actually, I'm not at all hungry. And since you seem to have found yourself in excellent company, I can leave now. Good night."

Annoyed beyond belief, I strode out of the ballroom. Julia treating me as if I were her partner and sharing cutesy confidences with my father's wife was the final straw.

I was done.

CHAPTER ▶ 4

After meeting my subway companion on my way out, I turned right around to go up the escalator and find out what he'd bought and why and for where. Ernesto was on the floor, and I snagged him by the men's designer jeans.

"Yo, Ethan, dude, what're you still here for? Spending your paycheck?"

"No way. I got too many clothes already. Listen, help a friend out. Did you ring up this guy—a little older but good-looking? He spilled coffee on himself?"

"Ooh, yeah. He had some fancy benefit at The Pierre tonight and needed a shirt. Ended up buying extra ones and some sale ties to keep at his office." Ernesto brushed his lapel with his fingers. "You know your boy has a way of making a good sale."

"A benefit, huh? At The Pierre. Fancy."

"Uh-huh. He's got the goods, though. I can tell when someone's faking it, but he wasn't. Used a Platinum Amex, and his wallet was the shit. Hermès."

"Yeah. He's real for sure."

"You know him? How?"

"Long story, but not really. Just seen him to talk to. You know his name or anything?"

"Nah, sorry. I didn't even look. I had a line. Wesley was watching me, and you know he don't like when we get too chatty and the customers have to wait."

I slapped him on the back. "No worries. I'll catch you tomorrow."

Now that I had a bit of information, I was ready to get home, become one with my futon, and dig deeper into the mystery that was my train-ride companion.

Suddenly hungry, I thought I wouldn't mind an egg roll and some lo mein to go along with my detective work. With that in mind, I stopped at the corner Chinese place, and then bag in hand, trudged home. Much as I liked Gladys, my landlady, I hoped she was busy. I had some sleuthing to do and didn't want to have to listen to who had the best price for chicken legs and how many pounds of tomatoes Pete had picked out of the backyard garden that afternoon.

Luck was on my side as their car wasn't in the small driveway, and I hustled up the two flights to my tiny apartment. I plopped down on the couch, opened my laptop, and went to The Pierre's website.

"Of course it wouldn't be listed there." I dug into the bag, found an egg roll, and chewed on it with one hand while clicking on Twitter. "Come on, baby. I know you're gonna tell me where my hunka-hunka is tonight."

Was it a wedding, or an anniversary party for a friend? Or was it strictly business? I scrolled past the uninteresting tweets about their history and found the evening events. One was a jazz club and the other a bar mitzvah. I kept looking, not feeling the vibe.

"Huh. Now this looks interesting." I clicked on the event for Mercy Hospital and began to eat my lo mein.

"An evening celebrating the achievements of Dr. Martin Roman, the new Chief of Oncology and Head of the Cancer Research Center."

That had to be it. I slurped up the rest of my noodles, then clicked over to Mercy Hospital and checked the images for the board of directors, but my subway seat sharer wasn't one of them. Discouraged, I tossed the empty container and bag into the trash and checked my emails to see if I'd had any responses to the résumés I'd sent out.

Nada. Disgusted, I slammed down the lid of the laptop and immediately reopened it, determined not to let my stalled attempts at moving up the corporate ladder prevent me from moving forward.

My phone rang, and I didn't recognize the number so I let it go to voice mail, figuring it was a scammer. It stopped ringing but started up again. Annoyed, I picked it up.

"Yeah?"

"Ethan?"

"Yes? Who's this?"

"This is Arlo Cheswick, from Paul Stuart."

I sat up straight, the remote falling to the floor. "Oh, hello." I'd applied to them for an assistant-manager position. Maybe this would be my big break.

"I'm sorry to be calling so late, but we've been slammed with a sale and there was no time for a break. I'd like to know if you could come in tomorrow for an interview."

"Yes, sure. When?" I rubbed my face. "I work from nine to three thirty tomorrow." I held my breath, hoping it wasn't too late, already preparing to tell Wesley I had to leave early. Did I feel guilty? Kind of, but this could be the break I'd been waiting for, and I had to do whatever was necessary.

"That works. Be here at the Madison Avenue store at four thirty."

"Sure, yes, I'll be there."

"Good night."

I danced on my toes around the apartment for a few minutes, then sped into the bathroom and took a shower, moisturized myself, and slathered serum all over my face. For the next hour, I tried on my best suits and decided on one of my Gucci ties with a sparkling white shirt. I went to bed with stars in my eyes, dreaming of the first day of the rest of my life.

With a spring in my step, I entered the subway car and found my mystery man standing at the far end. Grouchy-faced didn't begin to describe his demeanor, but I wasn't about to let him rain on my parade.

"Good morning," I said in my perkiest voice. "Did you have fun last night, wherever you were going?"

Instantly suspicious, he narrowed those glacial eyes. "What makes you think I had something planned?"

"Most men don't find it necessary to replace a shirt they spilled coffee on if they don't have someplace to be after work. They'll wait until they get home."

His troubled face cleared. "Oh. Well, you're right." His admission, begrudgingly given, still didn't give me the answers I was looking for.

"Was it a work thing? Where do you work?"

His jaw tensed. "It was. But I didn't stay. It wasn't necessary."

I instantly regretted asking two questions at once, but my mouth had gotten ahead of me. That gave him the out to only answer one, which of course he did, and it wasn't the one I'd wanted.

"Well, since you obviously hate talking about yourself, let's talk about me. I have a job interview today."

He gave me a sharp once-over but said nothing.

"It's with Paul Stuart—not the *haute-couture* luxury I'm looking for, but a good start. It's for an assistant-manager position at their flagship store on Madison Avenue."

"Good luck."

Damn him. I'd never seen anyone so tight-lipped. "Thanks. So if I get it, that'll cut our morning meetups. I'll have to change at Atlantic for the 4 train."

He said nothing. Frustrated, I refused to let this virtual stranger who'd somehow wormed his way into my days ruin my good mood. I practiced what I was going to say to Arlo Cheswick, building up my excellent eye for trends and how I was a true team player. By the time the train reached Penn Station, I'd almost forgotten Grouch-face was there. I prepared to leave the car, my mind already on four thirty that afternoon.

"Hey, Ethan."

At the sound of him calling my name, I froze and peered over my shoulder. I might be getting jostled from all sides by both incoming and outgoing commuters, but I'd wait. Hell, I'd miss my stop to hear what this man had to say to me.

"Yeah?"

"Good luck. I hope you get what you want."

"Uh, th-thanks." The bell dinged, signaling the doors were about to close, so head down, I rushed through them.

For a hot second I stood on the platform and watched as, with a huff of the engine, the train rolled out of the station. Only when it disappeared into the tunnel did I make my way to the staircase. His well-wishes had hit me hard.

As he did every morning, Wesley made the rounds of the floor, and as usual the dressing rooms were a mess.

"I swear, Devon is such a crap manager. I hate complaining, but…"

"He sucks. You've been saying it since I first started working here." I helped him carry the clothing left on the racks to the floor, and we began to hang them up.

"He always has an excuse. I'm just tired of hearing them." Wesley straightened the shirts, then faced me. "You're looking sharp. Hot date tonight?"

Here came the hard part. "Not exactly. I, uh, I have an interview. At Paul Stuart."

Wesley's elegant brows rose high. "I…see. Paul Stuart. That's not exactly your speed, is it?"

"My speed is whoever pays me a great salary," I said, trying to make a joke of it. "I mean, you're right. Paul Stuart isn't my style. But I can learn."

"I'm sure you can." Wesley pursed his lips. "When is the interview?"

"Four thirty."

"I appreciate you telling me." We crossed the floor to log in to the register and opened it to make sure the cash and coins coincided. "I hope it works out well."

"Thanks. I'm not gonna leave you in the lurch. If I get the job, I'll make sure to stay on until you get coverage."

It was coming up on opening time, and Wesley touched my arm. "Just make sure you're certain about what you want."

Between Wesley and my landlords, I had all the parental figures I needed. I was grateful for those who cared.

The day passed in a blur, and I was never more anxious to leave than that afternoon. Wesley caught my eye when I clocked out, and I gave him a brief but excited smile. For once the trains cooperated, and I walked into the Paul Stuart store thirteen minutes early and approached the salesperson.

"Hi. I'm here to see Arlo."

"Sure. Hold on a moment." He picked up a phone and

spoke softly. He set the phone in the cradle. "He'll be here in a minute. Applying for a position?"

"Uh, yes." I didn't want to say which one, as technically I might be his boss soon.

"Good. We really need the help. It's hard to keep track of everything."

"Ethan?"

A tall, thin man with dark-brown eyes and bad skin stood before me with a haughty air.

"Yes. Are you Arlo?"

"Come with me, please."

I waved good-bye to the salesperson and scrambled after Arlo, whose purposeful stride took him to the rear of the store to a door marked Employees Only. I assumed it was to his office, and I was eager to follow him to see how it looked behind the scenes, but instead we walked past closed doors to a huge receiving area filled with shelves and racks. People hustled to and fro, pushing carts of clothes being loaded out of trucks.

"This is where our stock comes in, and we check every piece against our inventory. We air it out, iron it, and price it."

"I…see." Not really, but I was trying to be polite. "Do the managers work with the employees here?"

Arlo's brow furrowed in puzzlement. "Manager? We need a supervisor for the loading area. You working in an atmosphere like Macy's would be perfect."

"Oh." All the excitement and goodwill I'd built up during the day vanished. "I thought I'd be with the sales associates. You know, working on the floor."

Arlo gave me a patronizing smile. "No, we wouldn't be able to use you for that. Your experience as a sales associate in a high-volume environment doesn't exactly qualify you for that type of position at this point in your career. Luxury brands require a different mindset and retail education. Perhaps you should think of a commission boutique first if that is your intention."

"I see." I held my head up. "Thanks for the interview. I appreciate it."

"You're welcome, Ethan. Good luck."

How different it was to walk out of the store with crushed hopes and dreams after entering it with a vision of the world at my feet.

I made it home and undressed, heated a frozen burrito, and curled up on my couch. I shouldn't complain, and I made a mental list of everything good in my life: I had a steady job and worked with great people. I could afford to buy myself little luxuries. Sure, my apartment was tiny and I didn't have a boyfriend, but plenty of people had it worse.

Still, it would've been nice to have someone to talk to, but the list was frighteningly short these days. In the three years I'd been with Oscar, I'd let most of my friendships slide because Oscar had always found something he didn't like about them, and we'd ended up hanging out with his group of friends.

I stared at the wall, then picked up my phone and texted Clay, a work buddy. We'd started at Macy's the same day and met at orientation. He worked in men's skincare and fragrances, and he'd give me free samples while I'd set aside the new markdown items I knew he'd like so he'd have first pick. I'd mentioned to him I was interviewing, since we'd often sit together at lunch and talk about future plans. He wanted to own his own skincare spa for men one day. Everyone had hopes and dreams.

Didn't get the job.

A few minutes passed before he answered.

Wasn't meant for you. Something better will come along. Talk tomorrow.

Maybe I was anxious to grab on to positivity, but simply knowing someone out there thought about me was enough.

There was a knock on the door, and for a wild moment

I hoped it was the man from the train, which made no sense because he didn't know where I lived.

I opened the door and frowned when I saw it was Oscar. "What're you doing here? How'd you get into the building?"

He winked. "I wanted to see you," he said, ignoring the second question. Bright teeth flashed white on his handsome face, and he took a step inside and tried to nuzzle close. I retreated.

"Why? I told you we're done."

"Yeah, but you didn't mean it."

"Says who?" I thwarted his attempt to advance farther inside my apartment, but with a lightning-fast move, he leaned in and tried to plant one on me. He missed, hitting the edge of my mouth.

"Don't you remember how good we were?"

My hand to his shoulder set him flush to the doorjamb, and I took some satisfaction in his shocked expression. "Yeah, but I also remember seeing you getting your dick sucked in a bathroom by some trash and who knows what else."

"Baby, I told you." He reached out, but I batted his hand away.

"You can tell me from today until the end of time, but you know what I've learned? Words mean nothing. Actions do. And all I see is you cheating. So get out." Oscar opened his mouth, and I folded my arms. "Now. Before I call the cops."

Without another word, he turned and left.

Monday morning I entered the train, still mulling over the prior week's misfires. It wasn't crowded, but all the seats were taken, which worsened my already sour mood.

But seeing my gorgeous mystery man at the opposite end of the car brightened my outlook.

I grabbed on to the pole near his hand. "Good morning."

He graced me with his now-familiar penetrating stare. "How did it go with your interview?"

Damn. I couldn't believe he remembered.

"No luck, but I'm not letting it get me down. It wasn't the right fit for me."

The train rattled on to the next stop before he answered. "I'm sorry it didn't work out, but that's the best attitude to have."

"They said my experience didn't match what they were looking for. But I could've done the job. I know I could."

"You certainly have the confidence."

"I've seen enough in the industry." I huffed. "So many of these people don't have a clue as to the history of a brand or anything about the designer. They just hop on trends, and because they have tons of followers, people think they know what they're talking about."

"But they don't. According to you, of course."

Did I sense sarcasm? I set my jaw. "Not just me. And you can laugh and make fun of me, but I know I'm right. Those people will say anything is *the best* if you pay them. I have standards. I can tell you who hand-stitches their buttonholes and who uses the highest quality leather for their coats. Plus, I know there's more to marketing than blasting out to Instagram followers. There's a certain mystique in luxury."

"Impressive."

I narrowed my eyes. "Are you making fun of me?"

"No. Why would I do that?"

The train sped on.

"It was a crappy week altogether. Not only didn't I get the job, but my ex showed up again."

Grouch-face's expression darkened, surprising me. "What the hell did he want?"

Why the hell do you care?

I lifted a shoulder. "It's not important."

"Then tell me."

I should've realized a brush-off wouldn't fly.

"Same old, same old," I said, trying to make light of it. "I don't want to get into it and rehash everything."

Troubled eyes met mine. "I hope you didn't fall for that bullcrap."

"As if."

"Good," he responded softly. "Some people will say and do anything to get what they want." He paused. "Or whom."

"Well, he can't have me. I'm too good for him. And I'm too good not to be taken seriously in an interview. I'll just keep on trying. I won't stop until I get what I want."

Did I see the hint of a smile curve those delicious lips?

"I have a feeling you always do."

Is that so? I want you, yet it doesn't seem to be working. Maybe I'm not trying hard enough.

"Guess I'll have to see."

CHAPTER ▶ 5

Why this guy?

The thought consumed me for the rest of the day, even as I sat in a three-hour-long meeting with our financial people. Where I was usually in full business mode the moment I passed through the front doors of the hospital, that wasn't the case now.

Instead of listening to how to deal with staffing shortages and potential union issues, I wondered if Ethan was still upset over the failed interview. On a conference call with the head of surgery who was hoping for money to magically appear in the budget for the newest robotic equipment he coveted, I should've been listening to his pitch, but all I could think of was how soft Ethan's lips looked and how amazing they'd feel wrapped around my dick.

"Okay, Harvey. I get it. Robotics would be amazing, but we need to come up with the initial purchase price and then the annual maintenance." I took a quick note so the next day I'd remember what the hell I'd promised.

"Thanks, Nash. I'll see what we can do and get back to you with some figures. We need a fairy godmother to sprinkle hundreds of millions of dollars upon us."

"That's the truth."

Damn. It was only three thirty in the afternoon, and I had a mountain of work to accomplish, but all I wanted was to go home. A vision of Ethan rose before me: him lying next to me, eyes drowsy, his body still twitching from the amazing orgasm I'd wrenched from him. My mouth watered, and I swallowed.

Jesus, get a fucking grip. I rubbed my hands over my suddenly perspiring face. *He's a guy on the train. You know nothing about him, and every day there's a chance you'll never see him again.*

That thought shouldn't have made my stomach twist in a painful knot. And yet it did. I stood at the window of my office, consumed by a pair of laughing green eyes in a face that should be gracing magazine covers. I could almost smell his aftershave and feel the stubble of his cheek on mine.

Why can't I get him out of my mind?

I had no issue finding willing partners for sex. Aside from Julia, there was Denise, an accountant I'd met at a conference a year or so ago, who came to the city—and to me—every few months. I also had a nice thing going with Mario. Never with any talk of staying over, dating, or commitment. Nothing stupid like that. Why screw up a good thing?

My phone rang, and I grimaced. Talk about screwing up a good thing. I debated ignoring it, then decided what the hell. I wasn't getting any work done. Might as well fuck my night up.

"Hello, Dad."

"I thought I'd see you at The Pierre last week for the dinner."

I raised my gaze to the ceiling and rubbed my eyes.

"Why would you think that?"

"Oh, I don't know, Nash." His long-suffering sigh filled my ears. "Maybe because it was one of the biggest nights of my career? A gala for a lifetime achievement award for my cancer research? I know you were there. Diana told me you spoke to her, albeit briefly. Why didn't you stay? I would've liked to talk, and we could've taken a picture together. You know how much that would've meant to me."

Maybe I should've felt guilty, but I was never good at faking it when it came to him. "Sorry."

"No, I don't think you are. Don't lie. You didn't even want to come, did you?"

"What do you want me to say?" I gritted my teeth, amazed I didn't crack a filling. No matter what the subject matter, my father and I always rubbed each other the wrong way. "You're mad because I didn't stay to take a picture for your photo op."

"No. I wanted you to stay because you're my son. It was a huge night for me, and I wanted to share it with you."

"Again, why?" A headache began to pound behind my eyes. "I don't understand why you would think I would be happy to come. You made it clear how disappointed you were that I didn't follow in your footsteps and refused to be the little *protégé* you could trot out and show off to your colleagues as the son you forgot to mention you had. Oh, and of course, who could forget walking out on Mom and me for your girlfriend?"

"I was wrong. I was young and dumb, and I let my success get to my head."

"I don't care. You hurt us when you left. How many women were there?"

"Only that first one. And she ended up cheating on me, so I suppose it was payback. I mean, since then I've had girlfriends, but…"

"Diana's the one who managed to put a ring on it."

"Diana is my wife. Show some respect," he growled.

"Deserve it," I snapped back. "And I'm not talking about Diana. She wasn't the one you cheated on Mom with. I have nothing against her. What I can't understand is why the hell you'd think I'd ever want to be like you."

"Because you're wasting yourself as a pencil pusher for the hospital, when you could be doing something important with your life. With my name and connections, who knows where you could have been by now?"

"Miserable as fuck, for sure. Because I never wanted to be a doctor, dammit. I despise that mightier-than-God opinion of yourself. Did you think you were my role model? I'm fine where I am, and what do you think I'd use your name for to get ahead? Cheating?" I was on a roll now and couldn't stop. "Abandoning your wife and son?"

"I'm not the first to divorce their wife. Your mother and I weren't happy." The unapologetic tone was what always pushed me over the edge.

"Mom loved you. I did too. Until you threw it in our faces. You cheated on her. And just because you're happy now doesn't make it right."

"You're not a child any longer. I'm sure you understand that sometimes you fall out of love with the person you're with. You've had girlfriends and broken up with them."

Was he kidding? "Girlfriends? This wasn't a date. She was your *wife*. There's no comparison. And I'm aware that people fall out of love and get divorced. But there's a right way to do that, which doesn't involve cheating and abandoning your kid. So thanks to you, no, I don't believe in any of this bullshit of marriage or commitment. Why bother?" My lip curled in a sneer. "People will only lie to your face about loving you, right, *Dad*?"

"I never said I didn't love you, Nash. You're my son."

Was he serious? The man who always put work first? The man who walked out on his family the day before

Thanksgiving? I might've only been six, but I could still hear myself begging him to stay and love me, love us, but he chose his girlfriend.

"Wow. So all those years when you made sure you sent child support and Christmas and birthday presents, that proves…what? You think it meant you cared? Is that your idea of love? News flash: blood doesn't mean family."

"I couldn't help it. I had to go where the jobs were."

"Please spare me," I drawled. "I know all about your very important positions as head of whatever department you were chairing in California, Texas, or Wisconsin. But there were phones. And planes. Like you said, you were hardly the first man to divorce his wife. But you were the only one I knew who forgot he had a son. Now, I'm busy, and I have to return to work. And while we're on that subject, I'm fucking sick and tired of telling you to back off."

"Back off what?"

Oh, I had to admit he was good, but I knew better. "I'm not interested in the CFO position. I'm happy where I am. Unlike you, I don't always have to be number one."

"I never thought my child would settle for mediocrity."

The snide, supercilious tone grated on my nerves. "I had you as a father figure, didn't I?" I spat out. "Doesn't get more mediocre than that. Now I really do have to get back to work. Congrats on the award. I know it means *everything* to you."

"You're making a mistake. I love you, Nash," he shouted.

I disconnected the call and stared at the wall. I'd gotten a job in healthcare administration out of school and worked my way up through several hospitals to land as Deputy Chief Financial Officer of New York's Mercy Hospital five years ago. Maybe the medical field was in my blood, but I had no desire to be a physician. I preferred the numbers aspect and had become adept at coordinating the wants of my CFO and the board to spend as little money as possible with the greatest results for patient care and the needs of the hospital.

Occasionally someone would ask if the famous oncologist, Dr. Martin Roman, was a relation, but I would always downplay it with a quick shrug and my standard answer: "A very distant one." Which wasn't far from the truth.

The day it was announced my father was hired as the new Chief of Oncology, my quiet and orderly life went to shit. From the moment he walked the halls, he made no secret of our familial connection and his expectation for me to be, if not Mercy's CEO, then at the minimum, their chief financial officer. Roger White, my boss, wasn't too thrilled to hear that, considering CFO was his position, and though I'd spent innumerable hours insisting I was happy where I was and had no desire to be the head honcho, I could tell Roger wasn't so sure. It annoyed and angered the hell out of me that my father was intruding on my life.

For the rest of the afternoon, I buried myself in budget proposals until a knock at the door sounded. It opened without giving me a chance to answer. Julia stuck her head inside.

"It's six. Feel like getting dinner and…" She arched a brow.

Losing myself in sex sounded pretty good, and my annoyance with her pushy behavior at the gala had faded. "Sure." I hopped up to my feet and grabbed my phone, eager to get out of the office where my father's last words continued to echo in my head like Janet Leigh's shower scream in *Psycho*. "Let's go."

We took the subway, and on the way to Julia's place downtown, for some ridiculous reason I couldn't fathom, at the 34th Street station I searched the onboarding passengers for his face. It made no sense—we weren't even on the right subway line, and I had no idea what time he got off work, yet disappointment settled in my chest when I didn't see him.

Ethan.

"What's wrong?" Julia nudged me.

"What? Nothing, why?"

She shrugged and returned to scrolling through her phone. "You had a funny look on your face. Did you forget you had another date and need to cancel with me? It's okay. We can do it tomorrow."

"No, not at all."

"Okay. Feel like sushi?"

"Yeah, sure."

We exited at Franklin Street and stopped off at a sushi place near her building, where we had *saké* and shared some rolls. At her place, Julia again took control and got on top, and as usual once she'd finished, she rolled off me and sighed.

"Mmm. That was good."

"Yeah."

Guess she didn't notice I hadn't gotten off. I left the bed and stripped off the condom. In the shower, the hot water pounded over me in an insistent rhythm. I grabbed my still rigid shaft. Luminous green eyes sprang to mind, and my lids slid shut.

Am I naked?

Wanna try me?

"Fuck," I groaned and shot into my hand, my trembling legs barely able to hold me upright. I braced a hand on the cool tile wall, watching my come swirl down the drain. Why did I even bother doing this with Julia? The sex was barely enjoyable, and we weren't pretending to be in love. But I knew the reason—at least for me. Because even with the sex so predictable, it was still better than being home. Alone. Staring at nothing and thinking too much.

I rinsed off and got dressed. Julia smiled at me and snuggled into the pillows, cocking her head at the sound of rain lashing against the windows.

"You can stay, you know."

She lived closer to work, and I'd get soaked if I left now. I could see how it made sense, and yet a chill settled over me. Once would lead to twice, and then she'd expect it every time.

"Thanks, but I'd better be getting home while it's still early enough." It was barely ten.

She yawned and shook out her hair. "Suit yourself."

By the time I'd slipped my shoes on, she'd fallen asleep. I made sure the door was set to self-lock and left. Under the awning, I bent my head into the wind and rain and headed for the subway. Normally I wouldn't mind the walk from Julia's place off Franklin to the Chambers Street Station so I could get the Number 2 directly, but not tonight, with the sky pouring rain and the streets flooded. I ran down the steps to the underground station and swiped my card. It was late, and the trains didn't run as quickly, especially the local. I watched, annoyed, as two express trains zipped past me.

I sat on a bench and wiped my wet hands on my soaked trousers. Sex usually washed away the day's problems and was a precursor to a good night's sleep, but not so much lately. And definitely not tonight. I was buzzing and antsy, and after waiting a while, rose to pace the platform until the Number 1 train finally appeared. As the doors opened on Chambers Street, another Number 2 rumbled to a stop, and three-quarters of the car raced toward it, all of us anxious to be on our way home.

The rain had let up by the time I walked out of the station in my Brooklyn neighborhood. Cars hissed by on the still-wet streets, and the last of the dog walkers were out for the night. The overhead clouds parted, allowing a view of a sliver of moonlight against the windblown trees. From somewhere on Flatbush, a truck horn blasted, bellowing long and low, competing with the wail of a firetruck in the distance. I should've gone straight home and gotten out of my damp clothes and still-wet socks, but instead I walked to the Soldiers and Sailors Arch and stood, watching cars swing around the traffic circle. After several minutes, I crossed the street, dodging the cars, and walked along the outside railing of the park. Above, in the dark sky, stars twinkled and beckoned with promises waiting to be broken. I didn't need to wish on one of those stars—I'd long since given up on what could never come to pass.

My father's call had upset me more than I'd thought or cared to admit. Was I being stubborn and unyielding because I was afraid to let go of decades' worth of betrayal and hurt? I'd spent my life angry, not only at my father for his cheating and absence, but also at my mother for her willingness to be treated like a doormat and never speak ill of him.

I was tired of being angry.

Maybe that was why I'd become distracted by the stranger on the train in the first place. But he was no stranger anymore.

Ethan.

I could easily change cars and never see him again if I chose, but I didn't. And wouldn't. I deliberately continued to place myself where he'd be, and had begun to look forward to the morning conversations and simply seeing him. Ethan added a little spark and fire into a day normally filled with dry numbers and balance sheets. I could pretend to ignore his chatter, but the truth was, I enjoyed hearing his stories. Except the ones about his ex.

Our morning conversation had wormed its way into my every free thought, and it concerned me. For someone who claimed to be happy and so willing to share intimate jokes on the subway with a stranger, he'd shut down quickly when I pushed slightly to delve deeper. He was hiding.

Ask me how I know.

"Tomorrow you'll have answers for me," I muttered and headed home.

CHAPTER ▶ 6

I'd had a long-ass day and couldn't wait to get home. Clearance days were the worst, and I'd worked extra shifts to make money, but on the flip side were my aching feet and throbbing head. Even worse, Grouch-face hadn't been on the train for the past few days. Guess he'd given up, and I wasn't sure why that bothered me so damn much. Now all I wanted was to snuggle on my couch with my Five Guys and binge-watch something until I fell asleep.

My only concern was Oscar. He'd texted me several times during the day, but I'd been too busy to answer him, and now, at eight thirty at night, I wasn't about to ask what he wanted. I already knew, and mentally smacked myself for again forgetting to change the lock on my front door. I'd have to get Pete, my landlord, to do it, which shouldn't be a problem. He and Gladys had never liked Oscar anyway.

I'd changed out of my work clothes, and when Oscar hadn't shown by nine, I figured he wasn't coming and breathed a sigh of relief. On a sale day, the last thing I wanted was to deal with drama. I finished my burger and fries, made some popcorn, and poured a beer. I wiggled my toes and turned up the volume on *Law and Order, SVU*.

"You go, Olivia. Don't let those men give you shit." I crammed a fistful of extra-buttery popcorn into my mouth and chewed noisily, then washed it down with the beer. As much as I had loved being with Oscar, he always frowned at the things I enjoyed the most—which was mainly hanging out at home, ordering takeout, and watching a TV series or a movie. Sure, we went out to dinner and clubs, but once you found that special someone, you wanted to spend time alone with them, didn't you? My perfect night would be lying on the couch with my guy, reading or snuggled up. Every once in a while we'd look up at each other and smile.

Maybe that should've been my first hint that something wasn't right.

At the commercial, I went to the kitchen to refill my glass, when the door opened and Oscar blew in. I could see right away he'd had a few, and a knot of anxiety formed in my stomach. Oscar loved to boast that tequila made him horny as hell, and I could vouch for that. There were so many times we'd come home from clubbing where he'd want to have sex three times in a night.

"Hey, baby."

"Oscar, why are you here? And you need to give me that key."

Dark eyes narrowed. "I texted you."

"But I didn't answer. And since I've already made it clear I've got nothing left to say, you need to get the hint."

"Maybe you don't, but I got plenty to say. You're still my man."

More secure with the counter between us, I set the glass aside. "No. I'm not. You decided you needed other guys. That's fine, but you can't have me."

"I swear to you, that was the first time it ever happened.

I had shots, and Sal wouldn't leave me alone. You know I love you. No one satisfies me like you." He tried the charming smile that had won me over in the first place, but now I knew what lay behind it, and I wasn't falling for the same trick again.

"Well, that's too bad, but hopefully Sal is still waiting for you, because I'm not. And don't lie. I know it wasn't your first time because I saw pictures of you on Instagram, dancing all up on a bunch of other guys." I shrugged. "Go party. You're free to have your dick sucked by all of them now."

He swayed. "But I don't want them. I want you."

"But I don't want you."

My words set him off, and he charged at me, stumbling around the corner of the counter. He grabbed on to the post and reached for me. "Ethan. Please." To my shock and dismay, he sank to the floor, shoulders heaving, and despite myself, I felt pity and knelt at his side. Call me a fool, but I didn't like seeing people suffer, even if they had done me wrong.

"Go home. Please. It's over."

He blinked away the tears. "One last hug? Please? I promise not to bother you again, but we were together a long time."

God, I was a schmuck, but we did have three years. "Only a quick one," I warned. "Then you gotta go."

"Baby." He pulled me close and leaned in, trying for a kiss, but I shoved him off, and his eyes widened with shock.

"Like I said, I don't want you. Now get out. If you don't, I'm gonna call the cops."

Muttering to himself, he got up and shuffled to the door. "It ain't over."

"Yes, it is." I shut it behind him, this time double-locking it and putting the security chain on. I grabbed my phone, looked up locksmiths, and found one around the corner. That would be my first thing to do in the morning before work.

I gulped down the entire glass of beer, opened another, and tried to finish my show, but the whole experience had me on edge. I'd always been such a good judge of character, and Oscar had acted like the perfect boyfriend.

"Perfect boyfriend. There is no such thing. They use you, then they lose you. It's the way of the world." I reached into the bowl for more popcorn and munched. "Maybe Grouch-face has it right. Why bother with a relationship? I should pay more attention to my career."

I stared at the TV screen, thinking not about the crime about to be solved, but about my sexy seat companion on the 2 train.

"I bet no one ever cheated on you. Who would want to lose out on all that?" I mumbled into my glass.

Lots of people liked the kind of arrogance he possessed. It made him unattainable and therefore even more desirable. A gorgeous guy like Grouch-face could pick and choose the women he wanted, discarding them when he got bored.

Funny how he held such strong views on cheating. Guess his father fucked him up. Parents had a habit of doing that to you. Case in point, my "loving" parents who had little desire to find out how their gay son was doing alone in the big bad city that they couldn't wait to get out of.

I drained my third beer and turned off the TV.

"Damn, you look like shit." I squinted at my reflection in the foggy bathroom mirror and rubbed my bristly jaw. Three beers on a weekday wasn't my norm, and I was paying the price this morning, even with the nighttime moisturizer I'd remembered to slap on my face before I fell asleep. The sun coming in through my blinds was bright, and I slid my shades over my eyes to keep from squinting and getting premature crow's feet. "Well, another day, another fifty cents. Inflation's a bitch."

I gathered what I'd need for the day, stuck it into my cross-body, and cursed at the time. "Shit. I'm late."

I didn't want to miss my train, so I hotfooted it out of my apartment and ran for the train, still on the steps into the station when I heard the squeal of brakes as it came to a halt.

"Fuck, no."

If I missed the train, I missed a chance to see him, and that sense of urgency pushed me to move even faster. I made it past the turnstile and slid inside the doors as the *ding-dong* announced they were closing. Not my usual spot, though, and I was in one of those new trains where you couldn't walk between cars, so I'd have to wait for the next stop to switch. I refused to think how silly I was being—all this rushing around for a man who, most likely, barely gave me a thought. He'd probably grown tired of me and decided to take a later train.

None of those thoughts stopped me from making a mad dash out the door to run for the second-to-last subway car. The grin on my face faded and my heart plummeted when I saw our usual two-seater was occupied by a couple. This morning *sucked*. A *zing* of disappointment hit me but hoping that maybe he'd been shut out of our seats as well, I scanned the car and spotted the familiar pink sheets of the *Financial Times* obscuring the reader's face on the other two-seater at the opposite end of the car. My heart pounding, I sauntered over.

"You're back. Can't hide from me," I murmured as I slid in beside him, and I heard the increasingly familiar huff of displeasure, which made my lips curve upward. He side-eyed me, and I wiggled my fingers at him. "Hi, there. Miss me? I thought you'd disappeared for good."

"I had early morning meetings." That intent blue-eyed gaze probed my face. "Why are you wearing sunglasses inside?" The hard lines of his face grew more granitelike. "Are you hiding something?"

"Are you insinuating I have a black eye?" I pulled down the shades and batted my eyes. "Or did you just want to see my face?"

That stony facade didn't crack. "I remember you were afraid of your ex showing up. I thought something might've happened."

I adjusted my cross-body bag because I didn't know what to do with my hands. Well, not quite. I wouldn't have minded throwing them around his neck and holding him tight for saying something so…caring. Grouch-face admitting he thought about me and was actually concerned took me by surprise.

"Don't tell me you have nothing to say." His eyes warmed, and was it my imagination, or did I see a slight uptick of his lips? "I thought you had an answer for everything."

"Uh…not when it shocks the hell out of me. Like you just did." He tilted his chin and waited. I fingered the buckle on my bag. "Anyway, last night my ex showed up and tried to convince me it would never happen again. That he wanted me back."

"This seems to be an ongoing thing. Maybe you should think about a restraining order. He could get violent. And why haven't you changed your locks?"

Shit. I'd forgotten.

"Thanks. I'm not stupid. I plan to call the locksmith today." Seeing the disbelief in his eyes, I decided to share even more. "He tried to kiss me, and I pushed him away. Then I got upset because it was three years of my life down the drain, you know? So I had two more beers."

The smile turned full-fledged. "You're hungover on a

couple of beers? I would've figured you could hold your liquor better than that."

"Three beers," I retorted, then got tired of him asking all the questions and decided to pose some of my own. "Why would you think I could hold my liquor?"

He shrugged. "You look like you enjoy partying."

Before I could stop, I poked him in the shoulder. And a very muscular shoulder at that. "Well, you're wrong. One of the reasons Oscar and I broke up was because he liked clubbing, while I preferred to stay at home. He was the partier."

I waited for him to come at me with some snarky retort, but he merely raised his brows. "*Hmm*," he grunted and returned to his newspaper.

We'd crossed into the city, and my stop was rapidly approaching. I desperately wanted to know his name, so I said, "Thank you for thinking of me. That's very nice of you, considering *I don't even know your name*."

"I can be nice," he responded, ignoring my not-too-subtle attempt to get the information I wanted.

I grimaced and folded my arms. "Are you famous? Is that why you won't tell me your name? Like, should I know who you are and because I don't, you're making me feel bad? Are you a movie star hiding from the public and going through a messy divorce? Are you incognito? In witness protection?" I let my imagination run wild, recalling all the books I'd read with outrageous plots. Anything to try and get a rise out of him. "A famous politician?" My eyes popped wide. "A paid assassin. That's it. Like The Coyote… or Wolf…what the fuck was that guy's nickname from that book I read last year?"

By this point he'd set the paper down and was openly laughing at me. "You've got quite an active imagination. Are you sure *you're* really a salesperson at Macy's? I could see you onstage."

Stern-faced, he was *GQ* handsome, but alive and laughing, with those sparkling, bright-blue eyes? The man was devastating, and I couldn't help staring at him. The laughter faded, and his gaze hooked into mine, the blaze of desire unmistakable.

"Carlos the Jackal."

"Huh?"

"The assassin you were thinking of. From the movie *The Assignment*. His nickname was The Jackal because when he was a fugitive and escaped capture, one of the newspaper correspondents found the book *Day of the Jackal* left behind. The nickname stuck."

I couldn't help grinning. "So are you?"

His eyes glittered. "If I were a paid assassin, do you think I'd tell anyone? Especially on the 2 train?" There went that sexy, slight twitch of his lips again. "Maybe you're a Mata Hari come to do me in."

I'd like to do you in. In the bed, in the shower…

The announcement blared: *"This is Thirty-fourth Street–Penn Station. Connection is available…"*

The train slowed. *Dammit.*

I rose to my feet and waved. "Bye."

His eyes narrowed, and he spoke softly. "Nash."

Midstride, I stopped in the doorway, earning curses from the entering passengers. "What?"

He picked up his paper. "My name is Nash."

A thrill shot through me, and my lips tugged up. "Cool name." I would've said more, but some big guy shouldered his way past me.

"Make up your mind, buddy. In or out. I ain't got all day."

With regret, I exited the train and waited until the doors closed before muttering, "Asshole." But at least I'd gotten something out of my mystery man, aside from an amazing smile and the knowledge that he wasn't made of stone and ice.

"Nash," I repeated to myself, over and over, my grin widening as I crossed Seventh Avenue. Even his name sounded exciting and unusual. Like a racecar driver or a cowboy. Neither one of whom would typically be found reading the *Financial Times* on the Uptown 2.

I passed through the employee entrance along with the hundreds of others working the morning shift. Even though I occasionally had to work some weekends, I didn't mind it. I always found opening much better than closing, and because more of the men's department employees wanted later hours, I almost always got the shifts I wanted.

I clocked in, put my stuff in my locker, and said hello to the security guards on my way to the mezzanine area. Wesley waved from behind the register. He'd taken several days off—something he rarely did—and had left me in charge.

"Morning, Ethan."

"Hey. Everything went smoothly. No problems." I joined him and logged in to the system, while Wesley leaned on the glass-topped counter, that inquisitive, sharp-eyed gaze trained on me.

"I didn't think there would be. Knowing you were here, I felt confident to take the time. We've been so busy lately and haven't had a chance to talk much. How's it going?" He'd given me a pep talk after my fiasco of an interview and held no hard feelings.

"Oscar came by. Again."

Of course Wesley wanted a recap, but I wasn't ready to start running my mouth the second I walked in. I finished on the computer and took a sip of my coffee first.

"He did? What happened?"

"Exactly as I predicted. He tried to be nice, but when I didn't give in, he pushed and pushed hard. I had to tell him to get out and not come back. *Again.*"

Meticulously groomed brows rose high. "And did he?"

"Eventually, but he needed persuading."

"You think he'll listen and stay away?"

I shrugged. "Probably. He'll get bored when he discovers I'm seriously not interested anymore. He's not one to go without, if you know what I mean." The preopening buzz of the other sales associates reverberated throughout the store, and Wesley and I, along with the other employees working on the opposite side of the department, took a quick walk around the floor, scanning the shelves and tables, making certain all the clothing was in perfect position.

Never one to let work interfere with his quest for knowledge about my dating life, Wesley continued the interrogation even as he straightened the display of Herno sport jackets.

"You don't seem upset."

"Because I'm not. I told you Oscar and I were through." A wrinkle puckered his smooth brow, and I laughed. "Don't do that. You're ruining your Botox treatments."

"There's someone else, isn't there? You've met a new man. Who?"

Damn. Wesley was as good as I was when it came to sniffing out personal info.

"You're wrong. I haven't, and there isn't." Much as I'd like there to be.

I mean, I wouldn't mind being able to claim Nash as mine, but it was only a silly flirtation on the train. I was surprised he didn't take a private car into the city. From his expensive clothes, he could afford it. Nash was caviar, champagne, and filet mignon, while I was more takeout pizza, six-pack of Heineken, and microwave popcorn on the couch. I was sure Nash wasn't checking out the dented cans and day-old bread at his local Key Food and eating peanut-butter sandwiches for weeks to afford those designer clothes he wore.

Sure, he had *that look* when he checked me out from head to toe. The one that let me know he wouldn't mind getting down and dirty, and I could only imagine how fierce he'd be in bed. I'd had a couple of deliciously naughty dreams about it. I might not know a glass of Dom Pérignon from the cheap-as-hell prosecco they poured in my Bellinis for brunch, but I was nobody's fool or jerk-off secret boy toy.

"Well," Wesley persisted, "something's got your eyes brighter when you come in every morning, and much as you love working with me, I don't think that's it."

"You have an overactive imagination. We're open, and I already see a return headed our way," I said, smoothly changing the subject, and waited for the man on the escalator, who was holding a shopping bag where I'd no doubt find some crumpled piece of clothing.

"I don't think so, but time will tell."

I ignored Wesley and helped the gentleman, then manned the register for the rest of the morning. Our weekly sale for VIP customers was on, and the never-ending stream of tourists and beginning of summer season bargain-hunters made it impossible for me to take a break aside from lunch. Which was probably a good thing as I didn't need to browse the concession departments and part with more of my salary.

I'd never been a clock-watcher, but I was damn glad when it was quitting time and the evening shift arrived. I got to use the bathroom for the first time since lunch, hefted my bag over my shoulder and said good-bye to my coworkers. On the corner of Seventh and 33rd, I met my friend Clay.

"Hey, Ethan. How was it today? Were you as swamped as we were in skincare?"

We walked to the train together.

"Busy as hell with that fifty percent off sale on designer shirts and an extra fifty off on already marked-down designer ties. Plus the usual clearance stuff."

"I'll bet you were working nonstop. We're running a promo, and it's a nice duffel bag, so you can imagine how crowded we were." His smile was filled with sympathy.

"I need a massage and a drink, and not necessarily in that order."

"Yeah, I'm half an hour behind because the area was a disaster." I didn't like to leave all the cleanup for the late-shift associates, so I always tried to tidy up the department as best I could, clearing the fitting rooms for the next wave of customers and returning everything to the shelves. Even though they rarely returned the favor, I refused to get into turf wars and throw blame on people.

Clay said, "I'm meeting Duncan at a place on Washington Avenue. Want to come? It's happy hour—five-dollar beers and half-price margaritas."

My feet hurt from standing all day, and I couldn't wait to get home and out of my work clothes, yet the thought of sitting alone again held little appeal. Especially if Oscar was going to make an appearance.

"Are you sure he wouldn't mind? I know you don't get to see each other much."

Duncan was a detective and always working odd shifts, so I didn't get to see him that often. He and Clay had been married for three years and were in that disgustingly-in-love phase where they held hands and called each other *baby*.

I couldn't admit I was jealous, but yeah, I wanted that. Duncan might be big and macho, but there was no doubt how much he loved Clay, and I wasn't sure I could spend an evening with them making goo-goo eyes at each other.

"He loves you. We're both happy you're not with that cheating bastard anymore. You deserve better."

"Thanks. Okay, I'll come, but I won't be mad if you want to leave early to be alone."

We entered the train, and though it was way too early and I'd never seen Nash on any of my return rides, I couldn't help but scan the car. It was typically crowded, filled with shoppers and tourists and people going about their busy lives. Ladies dressed in their designer clothes and tired office workers with their lunchtime purchases in shopping bags stood side by side with the tattooed hipster kids, and not a soul paid attention to the other. The trains were truly a microcosm of the city.

"Don't you worry about us. We get plenty of alone time." Clay winked. "Duncan's finishing his assignment. He's going to be off-duty for the next two days, which is why I put in for the time."

A pang hit my chest. Much as I was happier without Oscar in my life, I missed having a lover. It was more than simply sex. I liked the closeness and the knowledge that someone was thinking of me and cared where I was and what I was doing. I sighed and held on to the pole, moving into the sway of the train. "That'll be nice for you."

Clay's brow furrowed. "I'm sorry. I didn't mean to make you feel bad. Let's have fun tonight, and maybe you'll pick up a hottie. You deserve a fling." His face brightened, and I faked a smile.

"Yeah, sure."

Problem was, the only fling I wanted was with a man I didn't know and might never see again.

"Hey, Nash. Wanna catch some lunch?"

Alex popped his head into my office. I was having a shit morning of being on a deadline and welcomed the break.

"Damn, where did the day go?" I reached up and stretched. "I thought it was only eleven."

"Dude, it's past one. I just finished rounds with my patients and wrote up all my notes. I'm starving." Pouting, Alex rubbed his stomach. "Rafe had an emergency at the vet hospital this morning and didn't get to make me lunch."

I couldn't help laughing. "You get him to make you lunch? Damn, he must be crazy about your annoying ass."

Alex plopped himself in the chair in front of my desk and winked. "He loves my ass, thank you very much. And yes, it's a great trade-off—he gives me lunch, and I give him whatever he wants." Cackling, he pulled the cap decorated with watermelons off his head, releasing his mop of wavy, golden hair. Alex might look and act like a surfer boy without a care in the world, but he was a brilliant oncologist and an incredibly dedicated doctor to his patients.

"He's a good guy." The first time I met Rafe Hazelton, I'd been shocked by his quiet demeanor, but it made sense after I observed the two men together. Alex was such a huge personality, he needed someone steady and calm to keep his feet on the ground. I'd enjoyed Rafe's dry wit and how he never let Alex take total control of the conversation. He was the balance in the relationship, and it was obvious to everyone how much Alex adored him.

"The best. Once we got close, I knew I couldn't let him go."

With nothing to add, I remained silent.

"I, uh, had a meeting with your father this morning."

"Yeah? What did he want?"

With a rueful smile, Alex shook his head at me. "You do realize he's my boss? I might be Chief Oncology Resident, but I still report to him. I know you two are somewhat estranged—not that you've ever said why, and you don't have to, of course—but I can't simply dismiss him because you and I are friends. Besides, he's an incredible diagnostician, and I'm lucky to learn what I can from him. My contract ends next year, and I'm hoping to get a permanent spot on his team."

"I understand," I replied begrudgingly, flipping a pen between my fingers as I contemplated Alex. This would take our slight friendship to a different level. One of personal insights into the screwed-up dynamics of the Roman family, something I'd never shared with anyone. Then again, I'd been doing many things differently lately, starting with speaking to a stranger on my morning train ride.

"I'm glad," Alex said. "I know I can be a pushy bastard, but I've enjoyed getting to know you. I don't want my job to be a problem between us."

"You deserve the job. I know how hard you work, and I've heard about your research and how it's on the edge of a breakthrough. As for my father…*somewhat estranged* is one way of putting it."

Surprising me, Alex held up a hand. "Before you go any further, I can tell you with all certainty that I do understand where you're coming from. I don't get along with my father, and I haven't spoken to him in years."

"Why's that?"

A grimace tightened Alex's jaw. "We don't have all day, do we? In short, he loved my twin brother more than me and doesn't approve of me being gay. And married. He wanted me to be a doctor, but I quit med school to become a surgical nurse."

Shocked yet equally fascinated, I leaned forward. "But you *are* a doctor."

A quick uptick of his lips showed his lightened mood. "After I met Rafe, I decided I wanted to eradicate the disease that killed my brother, so I went back to med school. But by then my relationship with my father was irrevocably damaged. Things were said and actions taken that I could never forgive." He checked his watch. "Listen, I'm starving. How about we order sandwiches from the deli on the corner? We can eat here while we talk."

Aside from his charm, Alex was also persuasive, and I nodded. "Yeah, sure. Turkey and Swiss on rye with mustard and tomato for me."

Alex called them and ordered our food. "They'll be here in ten." Expectation was written all over his face, and I knew he was waiting for me to unburden myself. Funny how I had no problem spilling my guts to a stranger on the train, but here with Alex, I hesitated.

"To say my father and I aren't close is an understatement."

When I didn't continue right away, Alex, more intent than I'd ever seen him, said, "Whatever you tell me won't be repeated. It might surprise you, but I am remarkably discreet."

I decided to keep it as short and sweet as Alex had. No need to get into the messy, ugly details. "My father cheated on my mother and wasn't much of a father to me. When I was six, he left, taking jobs all over the country. He paid support, sent birthday and Christmas cards, but nothing else. Then later, he was—is—extremely disappointed I never became a doctor."

At a knock on the door, Alex left his seat and opened it, received our lunch, and closed it behind him. I took the time to ease my dry throat and get a drink of water from the cooler.

Alex said, "Is that why you didn't stay for the awards ceremony at his dinner?"

My face heated. "Yeah. I'm not one for pretending."

"I can tell. I'm the same way. Rafe says I'd make the world's worst liar since my face can't hide my emotions."

How did you explain you had zero feelings for the man who was supposed to be your hero? I took a bite of my sandwich instead of answering. Alex finished his and tossed the wrappers into the trash.

"Listen. My mom is babysitting tonight, and Rafe and I were going to go hang out at this new place in Park Slope. You don't live too far from there. Why don't you join us?"

"Me? Why would you want someone intruding on your date night? I know the late hours you keep between your research and your patients." A curious pang of longing hit my chest, and for a crazy moment I considered saying yes. My apartment might be beautiful, but at times it felt akin to a prison—the loneliness like bars of steel, trapping me inside.

"Oh, don't worry about that. It's a sleepover. We'll have the whole night to ourselves, and I intend to take full advantage once we're home. I'd like to get to know you better, and so would Rafe." Alex's pager went off, and he grimaced. "Shit. I'm running tests in the lab; I gotta go. Listen, here's the address of the place. Please text me and let me know you're coming. It'll be fun. Just the three of us."

He scribbled on the notepad on my desk and took off. I picked up the paper and stared at it. My phone rang, and I set the paper aside to take the call from my boss.

"Roger?"

"Can you come to my office?"

A warning bell rang in my head. "Yeah, sure. Everything okay?"

"See you in a few minutes." Then he hung up. Roger wasn't a man of many words on a good day, but we'd always had a decent relationship. We worked well together, and he appreciated that I wasn't always harping on about a raise. I did my job and enjoyed finding ways to bring all the moving parts together to keep the hospital running smoothly.

On my way upstairs, I wondered what it could be. We'd finished a huge fund-raising project and now had to figure out where and how to divide the money. That had to be it, and in the elevator, I began to put ideas together in my head. His secretary nodded me in.

"He's waiting for you."

At my knock, he called out, "Come."

I entered with an easy smile. "Hi."

"Sit, please." He gestured to the conference table. Roger was a veteran of the hospital—his tenure began in the late 1970s, and there wasn't anyone who knew the ins and outs of hospital administration as well. I was happy to learn at his side.

"Everything okay?" I watched him take a seat across from me. Something was wrong, and my skin prickled with nerves.

"Well…let me ask you. Are you satisfied with your job here?"

And immediately I knew. "We've had this conversation before. I'm very happy to be exactly where I am."

His eyes were troubled. "That's what you said, but your

father says otherwise."

Son of a...

"My *father* doesn't know shit. Excuse my language, but I don't understand why we need to revisit this."

His gray brows drew together, his dark eyes fixed on mine. "We're revisiting it because I'm hearing something different."

My anger rose. "My father has no right to speak on my behalf." Roger dipped his head in acknowledgment, and my hands balled into fists. "He's wrong."

"You say so, yet this morning he had a meeting with Barney."

Barney Holmes was CEO of the hospital and a no-nonsense guy. I'd heard he'd given my father everything he'd asked for to get him to come to Mercy, hoping for the prestige of having world-famous cancer research done at the hospital.

"And?" I prompted.

"And he made several statements—very insistently—that he wanted you moved into the CFO position. That having his son in the job would make him more amenable to staying here for the remainder of his career."

I had no recollection of standing up or kicking away the chair I'd been sitting in, and it was only when Roger put a hand on my shoulder that the red haze of fury vanished from my vision. I found myself staring into his worried eyes. My heart galloped, and it took me several moments to catch my breath.

"No, no, *no*. I refuse to allow him to do this—to you or me." I grabbed Roger's arm and watched his brows fly up, but I didn't care. "For the last time: I do *not* want your job, and I have no qualms about marching into Barney's office and telling him to his face. Right now."

Roger's gaze latched on to mine. "I believe you. I'm just not sure Barney cares."

Knowing the two men had been friends for decades, I was rocked to the core. I said, "Maybe I should resign. I can find a job at another hospital."

Now it was Roger's turn to grow angry. "I will not let you do that. One day I *will* retire, and I'd want you to take over." A fleeting smile passed over his lips. "I'd just like it to be my decision. Now sit."

I picked up my chair and straddled it. "I apologize for losing my temper. But my father is not going to bully people or use his influence to get what he wants. He's trying to control me the only way he knows how. And I won't allow it to happen."

"We've never discussed your father's hire. Am I correct in assuming you two don't have a close relationship?"

"We have no relationship *at all*. Which means I don't want to waste any more time talking about him. When you called, I was almost finished with the appropriations from the last fund-raiser. Do you want to set up a meeting to discuss?"

Roger's expression was hard and grim, but his eyes reflected a fleeting glint of sorrow. I winced, hating the sympathy. He said nothing and simply nodded. "Yes. Tell Sharon on the way out."

Still shaking, I left him, made the appointment, and once I sat behind my desk, I took the scrap of paper Alex left me and tossed it into the trash. I wasn't going to be fit to sit at a table with pleasant, normal people and make small talk. But the thought of going home to look at the walls held even less appeal.

I could get together with Julia, but doing that too often might give her the idea I wanted more, especially after the offer to sleep at her place. So that was a no. Mario was on vacation in the Bahamas, and Denise wasn't in town. I rarely went out alone after work to a bar, but the more I thought about it, the more it sounded like a plan.

I texted Alex with an excuse that I needed to prepare

for a meeting the next day—lame and barely plausible, but the best I could do—and finished the rest of my work. I left around six, and along with the rest of the swarming crowd, took the train home. With little desire to stare out my living-room window or watch TV, when I exited my usual station, I wandered the opposite way, down Washington Avenue until I came to a place that seemed crowded enough for me to sit and blend in but wasn't sports-bar rowdy.

I slid into a seat at the bar and ordered a Scotch. The bartender, a man with cobweb tattoos encircling his neck and wrists, held up two bottles—J&B and Laphroaig. "High or low?" I pointed to the Laphroaig, and he chuckled. "I figured, but I wanted to make sure."

He poured a generous two fingers, and I took a healthy swallow, grunting with satisfaction. "Thanks. And why did you figure?" I finished and slid the glass toward him. He poured another, this time to the top.

"The suit. And the swagger."

"Swagger?" My lips twitched. "I don't think anyone's ever said that about me."

"No?" He raised a pierced brow. "I'm sure they were thinking it. You look like someone who knows what he wants and goes after it." He grinned. "Or them."

Was that an invitation? I had no time to respond, as he received a flurry of customers at the opposite end of the bar. Not wanting to get plastered in the first half hour, I sipped the drink more judiciously and took in my surroundings. It was an airy space, the bar a dark lacquer, and behind it, instead of a wall of bottles as a backdrop, an interesting shelf arrangement showcased various hard liquor and wines.

Spiderman returned, and I handed him my credit card. "Start a tab, please. And can I order food at the bar?"

"Sure can. What do you want?" He pushed over a small laminate menu.

I scanned it quickly. "The steak *frites*, please. And save

my seat? Just hitting the john."

He checked my card. "Sure thing, Nash." Laughing brown eyes met mine, and I wondered if I would, in fact, be going home alone. Thick muscles bulged under his T-shirt, and I already knew how good he'd feel.

Threading my way through the crowd, I did experience a twinge of regret at blowing off Alex and Rafe, but I wasn't in the mood for small talk with people who'd likely become a constant presence in my life. This was a night to blow off steam, to let go with someone new and different who didn't know I was the famous Dr. Roman's son. I could simply be Nash, who wanted to forget and get laid.

I used the urinal, glad it was empty, and after washing my hands, I splashed water on my face, then undid my collar and loosened my tie. The Scotch had hit me a little harder than expected, and I needed a minute to get my bearings. The door opened, a man walked in, and when our eyes met in the mirror, my heart slammed. I found it hard to catch my breath, my head spun, and a buzzing noise invaded my brain.

"Well, hello there." Ethan sauntered over, a dimple-popping smile curving his lips. "Fancy meeting you here."

CHAPTER ▶ 8

Holy fucking hell.

There he stood in his all-too-gorgeous flesh.

Nash.

My dream guy from the train. And from the looks of him, he'd already brought the happy in happy hour. He swayed and caught the edge of the sink, and I rushed to his side.

"You okay? You seem a little out of it."

My chest hit his back as I propped him up, and I grew still at the enormous amount of heat radiating from his bulk. I leaned in close to smell his hair and drag in the scent of his skin.

"I-I'm fine. Thanks."

Yes, you are. Fine with a capital F that means fuck me.

"I know that," I joked, trying to keep the mood light, but when he met my eyes in the mirror again, the white-hot fire of lust hit like a lightning bolt, sizzling through me from chest to toes. Without thinking, I pressed my lips to his ear, and he trembled but didn't pull away. Our gazes still pinned to each other in the reflection, I kissed his sharp jawline, licking the sweat, sucking his skin to taste all that bitter sweetness.

He whipped around. "What are you doing?"

I caged him between my arms. "What do you want me to do?" I drew close and ran my nose down his cheek, resting my lips on the hard line of his mouth.

Next thing I knew, I was slammed against the door, his lips over mine, and I held on to his broad shoulders to keep from falling into a heart-pounding swoon. His tongue sought entrance to my mouth, and I opened willingly, teasing and playing with it until he sucked mine and I thought I'd died and gone to heaven.

"Nash," I whimpered. "Oh God, Nash." I knew he could feel my erection through my pants, and his bulge thrust out hard and huge. Like a cat, I rubbed all over him, drawing out a deep growl I'd be jerking off to for months. His kisses hadn't stopped, and he bit and sucked on my lips until I tangled my fingers in his hair and kissed him back, wanting that hot, honeyed tongue in my mouth.

My legs trembled and began to give way as the throb of my impending orgasm drummed deep in my belly. My toes curled, and I was reaching…reaching…

The door opened halfway, and the movement shocked me into reality. I was unceremoniously shoved across the small space, my side bumping painfully into the sink. Nash, red-faced and gasping, stared at me as if I were the devil incarnate. Without another word, he wrenched open the door, ran past the man standing there, and disappeared.

"Did I interrupt?" the stranger asked with a quirk of his brow. He unzipped his fly and turned away to use the urinal. "If you want, I can finish what he started."

"No, thanks. It wasn't…never mind. Why am I talking to a stranger in the bathroom while he's pissing?" I muttered.

"Listen, I'm no fool." He zipped up and came to the

second sink to wash his hands. I moved over, not wanting to give him any ideas I was up for a comparison between him and Nash. As good-looking as this man was, I wouldn't be ridding my senses of the taste and smell of Nash for days. I planned on savoring it.

"Never said you were. Bye."

One quick glance in the mirror reassured me that although I did have a bit of beard burn, it would be hidden in the dim lighting of the bar. I wound my way through the room to our table, where Clay gave me a wave. Our meals had come, and I grabbed a few fries from my plate and stuffed them in my mouth.

"I thought you met someone and blew me off." Clay gestured to our plates. "They just brought the food over, so it's still hot."

"Hey, I'd never do that to a friend. It just took a little longer than I thought. How is it?" I picked up my chicken sandwich and took a big bite, while casually scanning the restaurant to see if I could get a glimpse of Nash. He wasn't at any of the tables with a date. My lips tingled, and I ran my tongue over them.

"Pretty good burger," Clay commented, "and the fries are awesome."

"Where's Duncan? Isn't he coming?"

"No, stuck at work."

"Ah, that sucks."

"Happens. Sometimes reports take longer because he has to brief his commanding officer and then make sure every form is signed and filed." Clay waved a fry as he spoke.

"Another time, then." I took a few fries of my own, dipped them in ketchup, and chomped on them. "So how's it going in skincare? Thanks for the Chanel samples, by the way. I know those are hard as fuck to come by."

"I know what you like." He set his burger on the plate and picked up his beer. "And, I dunno. I'm getting tired of the huge-retail-store experience. I'm thinking of putting out feelers to boutiques to see if they need skincare consultants and salespeople. I'd rather be in a smaller, more intimate setting."

"Are you an aesthetician? I didn't know you took classes."

"Mmhmm." He nodded as he drank. "Graduated and have worked at some big spas in the city on my days off. One day I'd like to own a spa, as you know."

I could appreciate the hustle. "Cool. You should definitely look around. I'm not letting that one bad interview discourage me either. I want to get with a luxury brand and work with them. But I know there are a thousand people like me. It's pretty competitive."

"Nah. There's only one of you, Ethan. You're different because you're not stuck up like so many high-end designer associates. They all think they're better than the customers and look down on them. You'd never do that."

"Thanks. I appreciate that. I remember once I was shopping at Saks and a salesperson came to me and asked if I was only interested in sale items since I was looking at the clearance rack. I thought that was so freaking rude, I walked out. So what if a person wants to shop sales? Maybe that's all they can afford, but they want a little taste of luxury when they've been saving for months. People shouldn't be made to feel less than."

"See?" Clay chewed and swallowed the bite of his burger. "You're so passionate about what you care for. That's what makes a good salesperson. And boyfriend. Anything new on that front? You know Duncan has friends he can hook you up with."

We'd double-dated a few times, but Oscar didn't like Detective Duncan Rivera. He used to make snarky comments about how Duncan probably cheated because he got to see all the action, but I suspected it was more because Duncan saw Oscar for who he was—a controlling narcissist.

Instead of answering, I took another bite of my sandwich and chewed, all the while searching the bar for a sign of Nash. A thrill ran through me as I spotted those broad shoulders and waves of golden-brown hair at the bar. He was eating while listening to the bartender play him with bullshit lines.

"Ethan?" I dragged my attention over to Clay, whose eyes brimmed with amusement. "Who's that?"

"Busted, huh?" My grin was sheepish. "He's…a guy."

"Wow. Your powers of observation are incredible. I can see that. All guy too." I stared at him in surprise, and he shrugged. "I'm in love, not dead. I can appreciate a gorgeous man, even if I have one of my own. Is he the one you kissed in the bathroom? And when were you going to tell me about it?"

"Damn." I laughed weakly, shaking my head. "Nothing gets past you."

"Listen, when you went to the bathroom your skin was smooth and clear. You came back with swollen lips and beard burn. I know my skin…so?" His brown eyes twinkled. "What's the deal?"

I darted a glance to Nash, who was busy eating, and decided to tell Clay the story from the beginning, admitting the kiss, but leaving out the ferocious, greedy hunger he brought out in me. When I finished, I gulped the rest of my beer and flagged down the server.

"Another round please. Silly story, right?"

Meanwhile, Clay was busy craning his neck to get a good glimpse of Nash and nodded. "No. People meet in stranger situations. Let me ask you something."

The server approached with our beers, and Clay waited for her to set the glasses in front of us and leave, before continuing.

"Do you want him? Besides sexually? Do you want to

get to know him better?"

I shrugged. "I'm not sure it matters. I mean, you heard what I said. And look at him—we have nothing in common."

Clay snorted and drank some of his beer. "From what I'm seeing, the guy practically ate your face off. I think you have a good jumping-off point. And who's to say it can't all start with sex?" He lifted a shoulder and ate the last bite of his burger. "Obviously, you're compatible there. See where the rest of it takes you."

I didn't answer as I cleaned off my plate and finished my second beer, subtly keeping tabs on Nash. He rose from the bar and tossed a few bills to the bartender. They had a brief conversation, and I held my breath—was Nash asking him to get together? How could he do that after kissing me? Relief flooded through me when Nash turned to leave…and he caught me staring.

I lifted my chin and gave him a brilliant smile, figuring he'd turn away and ignore me like he did in the bathroom. Instead, he tipped his head and graced me with a ghost of a smile before walking out the door.

"Oh yeah," Clay said. "You're definitely on his radar."

The next morning, I made sure to be on time for the train and strode into the subway car with an eager step. And stopped dead. Our usual two-seater was unoccupied. I looked around the car, which was only half-full, and my heart sank. So much for Clay's prediction. Nash had gotten his taste and was through. I sat lost in thought, watching through the window the swiftly passing dirty walls of the tunnel as we sped along the tracks. But after speaking with Clay, I'd made a decision. After work today, instead of going home and watching Bravo or *Forensic Files*, I was going to take that first step toward making a change.

I'd worn my best suit today—a Goodwill charcoal-gray Zegna find—with a plain white shirt, a purple-and-navy Fendi tie, and I'd buffed up my Coach shoes, which I'd gotten at the outlet up in Woodbury Common. At lunchtime I would run out and get a manicure, and I would get some serum from Clay to brighten my skin.

Of course, part of it had been in hopes of showing off to Nash, and I couldn't help the rush of disappointment that he'd blown me off. Sure, the kiss was amazing, but a guy liked to be wined and dined a little. What if I'd done that to him? I slumped in my seat.

Damn, I was a lousy liar. When Nash had shoved me against the door and kissed me, I would've dropped to my knees on that dirty floor and done whatever he wanted. His kiss was the accelerant to my flame, and the resulting explosion reduced me to cinders from a single touch.

My preparations didn't go unnoticed, and Wesley's gaze traveled over me top to bottom. "You either have a hot date or an interview." He cocked his head, and my cheeks burned.

"Neither, but I do want to talk about my future."

We were at the fitting rooms, and I groaned, seeing the mess the late-night crew had again left for us—sweaters tossed in a heap, not folded and reshelved, suits not reracked, hangers and tags all over the floor. I lifted up a pile of clothes and marched over to the table where they belonged and began to fold. Wesley trailed behind, watching me.

"Your future here? You know you're my top-selling associate. I plan to tell Holbrook you deserve to be assistant manager."

While I appreciated it, that wasn't good enough when I didn't want to be on this side of retail. "Thanks, but I'm really looking to move toward high-end boutiques. I want to be a buyer, you know that. I've never made it a secret."

I made sure the sweaters lay neat.

"I do, but four years working retail isn't so long." He sounded about as convincing as a man denying murder, standing over his wife's dead body with a bloody knife in his hand.

Hey, I said I watched a lot of murder shows.

"Wesley, come on. That's an eternity. I'm ready to take the next step, but that doesn't mean I don't love working with you and appreciate everything you've done for me. Besides, it's not like I'm leaving so soon. You know these things take time."

"I'm not angry. I knew you were here on borrowed time. Just give me enough time to find someone else."

"I will. And you don't have to look far. Ernesto is great and knows his designers. We talk all the time. And Barry? The floater? He's a good worker too, and I know he'd love a permanent position."

"*Hmm.* Good to know."

The customers trickled in, and the workday began. As the hours passed, I couldn't help growing angrier at Nash, but there was little I could do about it. I lost myself in the monotony of ringing up people at the register, doing my best automaton imitation, and didn't realize until too late that Oscar stood in front of me.

"Hi, baby."

I glared. "I'm not your baby, and I'm at work. And busy." I always took the last hour of my shift at the register, and I couldn't wait to leave and put my plan into action. "Leave me alone, or I'm going to get a restraining order."

"But—"

"No buts. Unless you're buying or returning, please step aside and let me take care of the next customer."

He held up a handful of merchandise—a tie, boxer shorts, and a few sale shirts—and placed them on the counter. "I'm buying."

With a tip of my head, I took the clothes to remove the sensor tags and scan them. Oscar, of course, used that as an opportunity to chat me up.

"I'll stop as soon as you listen to me." I remained silent, and Oscar continued to run his mouth. "Come on. Are you really willing to throw away three years because I made a stupid mistake when I was drunk? I swear it was the first and only time, and I haven't been with anyone else. Those pictures were all fake."

I handed him the receipt and his bag. "Yeah, sure. Not interested. Next in line, please."

"You're making a mistake. You'll never find someone as good as me."

"I already have. Better, in fact. Me. I'm better than you. I'd rather be alone. Now leave before I call security."

Oscar's handsome face darkened, and he grabbed the bag off the counter. "You think you're better than me? You're still ringing up underwear at your age while I'm gonna buy my own franchise soon. Who's really the loser?"

He stormed away, and the hot embarrassment of my humiliation burned through me at the long line of customers witnessing my personal life. "Sorry, everyone. I never bring my drama to work, but I guess it followed me."

An older man with a bow tie and vested suit handed me a pair of socks and several button-downs on sale. "Don't worry, young man. Stand firm. That one looks like trouble."

I offered up a faint smile and continued to ring up his merchandise. Wesley joined me and nudged my shoulder. "Time to go. You can take off now. And I'm sorry I pushed. I agree with you. Oscar isn't good enough for you."

I logged out of the register. "Thanks, Wesley."

Oscar's barb had hit harder than I'd believed possible, and I vowed that I was going to prove them all wrong. Oscar, Nash, no one was going to use me again. I was nobody's fool.

CHAPTER ▶ 9

Okay, so I was a coward.

And I'd be the first to admit it.

I deliberately let the train I normally took to work pass me by rather than face Ethan.

Because of that kiss.

Jesus.

That kiss.

Days later, I was still thinking about it.

In the morning while shaving.

In the office when I was supposed to be concentrating on balancing departmental budgets.

And even worse, late at night, when I should have been sleeping, I couldn't because I was too busy fucking my fist, wishing it was his wet, hot mouth surrounding my dick instead of my fingers. And hating myself for what I'd done.

When Ethan had touched me in that tiny bathroom, I'd lost it.

Me.

The man who never lost his self-control, had lost his mind from that smallest gesture.

His breath on my cheek.

His scent.

The taste of his tongue in my mouth.

Groaning, I buried my head in my hands.

What the hell was going on?

The phone rang.

"Roman," I croaked out and heard an answering laugh.

"Are you dying?" Alex laughed, and I took the opportunity to drink from my water bottle and get my shit together.

"No. What do you want?"

"Damn, you're grouchy. Listen. Since you blew me off the other day for dinner, I need a favor. You have good taste. I need to buy Rafe a present, and I want input."

"What the hell do I know?" I growled. "I'm not married."

"No, but you dress well, and very similarly to Rafe, in fact. Understated but classy. It's for our anniversary, and I want to get him something special."

"Again. I wouldn't know."

"God, you're frustrating. Come with me to SoHo, please? I hate shopping by myself. I'm off at six today, and Rafe has a late night at the clinic. My mom said she could watch the kids, so it's the only chance I'm going to get."

"I barely know your husband."

"My best friend, Micah, he usually goes with me, but he's got some school thing with his kids. Come on, Nash. Don't make me beg. I'll even treat you to dinner."

"You're not going to take no for an answer, are you?"

He snickered. "I've been told I can be persistent when I want something."

"Annoying as shit is more like it."

"Great. See you at six."

Despite myself, I had to laugh. Alex was like a puppy tugging on my pant leg. "I don't recall saying yes." I heard a beeping sound.

"Gotta go," Alex popped off cheerfully, and the line went dead.

I could simply leave the hospital early and not show up, but I wasn't a total bastard. Alex was a nice guy, and I knew he was trying, however unsuccessfully, to get friendlier. I should tell him not to bother. I didn't have much to bring to the table. Pretty soon even Julia would get sick of my moodiness and find another playmate. Not that she was so satisfying, but there was comfort in the familiar.

Speaking of the devil, a text popped up from her: *Feel like catching a movie and then back to my place?*

Something seemed different with her lately. Normally we'd meet once a week, twice tops, and always spontaneously, but recently, she'd been stopping by my office every day and acting, for want of a better word, *flirty*. Massaging my shoulders and offering to bring us lunch. Suggesting weekend plans. I'd ignored it for the most part because my mind wasn't on her.

Ethan.

Again.

I didn't want to see Julia and have sex with her, pretending she was someone else.

Ethan.

It wasn't right to use her that way when she wasn't the person I really wanted. I wanted Ethan, and since I couldn't have him, it was either spend another night jacking off to my dirty thoughts, or shopping and dinner with someone who would fill the empty spaces with conversation so I wouldn't have to dwell on how much I wanted to see Ethan.

I huffed out a sigh, knowing I was a fool. A gorgeous man, who looked to be ten years younger than me, wouldn't be wasting his evening thinking about a reckless kiss from a virtual stranger.

Ethan had said it himself—he liked the thrill of sex out

in the open. The sexual tension and danger of being caught outweighed the risk. For him, a public kiss wouldn't mean much, while here I was, agonizing over being so wild and free.

He'd probably forgotten all about it.

Unlike me.

The phone rang, and it was Roger.

"Nash, do you have those reports? You were supposed to send them to me half an hour ago."

Cursing my stupidity for wasting time on something that could never be, I pulled up the operating budget on my screen and my work papers. "Yep. Sending now. Sorry about that."

"I'll be waiting for you to get here so we can go over them."

"On my way."

I didn't mind Roger's brusque manner—he wasn't about to ask me to come out with him after work and go shopping and have dinner.

I considered calling Alex to cancel, but then didn't simply because I knew if it wasn't tonight, he'd hound me until I did agree. I'd go with him and get it over with. I sent Julia a quick text saying I was busy.

Meeting Alex wasn't that important in the scheme of things. A few hours of my night wouldn't be a big deal.

At exactly one minute past six there was a knock on my door, and it opened without me giving the okay. I scowled at Alex's blond head poking inside.

"Don't you wait for an invitation to come in? What if I was busy with something private?"

"Oh, please. Like what?" He waggled his brows. "You have someone under the desk, maybe?"

My face heated, and I rolled my eyes. "Don't be ridiculous. This is an office." I shut down the computer and pocketed my cell phone and wallet. "I'm ready if we're still doing this."

"I'm not arresting you and taking you to Rikers, you know." Alex frowned. "If you really hate the idea, forget about it."

An unaccustomed emotion I recognized as shame rolled through me. "No. I didn't mean it that way. I don't go out much, so I guess I'm out of practice socializing." I shut the lights off and locked the door behind us.

Shoulder to shoulder, we walked to the elevator. "How is that possible?" Alex asked. "I've heard you and Julia from Legal have a thing going. You're a good-looking guy even if you're wrapped as tight as a roll of adhesive tape."

I stiffened but said nothing until the elevator doors closed on us. "You heard that from whom?"

Alex's brows drew together. "From whom what—oh. About you and Julia? I overheard her chatting with one of the doctors, and she mentioned you two have been seeing each other for almost six months."

"If by seeing each other, she meant occasionally we get together and have sex, then yeah, she's right, but we aren't dating. I thought we had an understanding that it was casual, but I guess not."

Slack-jawed, Alex stared at me. "Well, damn, you don't hold back, do you? So you're basically each other's booty calls?"

I pursed my lips. "I don't use that term myself, but I guess that's appropriate. I'm not interested in relationships, and she told me she felt the same." It hit me with a devastating sense of clarity. "And now it all makes sense. Since my father came on board, she's been pursuing me more aggressively.

Once she connected that we're related, she must've thought or hoped that by hooking up with me, it'll help her career here. She knows how much power my father wields. What she doesn't know is that power means nothing to me."

Alex nudged my shoulder as we walked to the train. "Let's not think negative thoughts about you. Let's talk about me and my problem. Like I said, you and Rafe have a similar style. What would you like more—a nice wallet, a cashmere sweater, or a leather jacket?" Alex scratched his head. "I know it's not that inventive, but Rafe is very modest. He's not into overspending or lavish, overdone things."

"Except you?"

"Damn right. I chased him until I wore him down." Alex fluttered his lashes. "I wouldn't let the best thing that ever happened to me go. He had no choice."

I couldn't help but laugh. It was impossible not to respond to Alex's lightheartedness, and I was surprised to find myself enjoying his company.

"So where are you dragging me off to? SoHo? I prefer large department stores, so I'm not followed by overanxious sales associates hoping for a commission."

"Don't worry. I'll protect you. Besides, there's always a place for the grouchy and uninterested to sit. I'll bring you over what I pick out, and you give me a yeah or nay."

"Sounds okay to me."

We entered the train and passed 34th Street. I couldn't help wondering about Ethan. After I left the bar the other night, I hung out in front for a few minutes, watching him and his date. They laughed and joked enough for me to see they got along perfectly, but that didn't stop the painful fist twisting my guts into knots. Especially now that I knew what he tasted like.

Once above ground again, we strolled along Spring Street among the crowds. After the third time someone bumped into me, I appealed to Alex.

"Where are we going to first? I'm not fond of hordes, and the Bridge and Tunnel crowd especially."

Alex cackled. "Come on, Mr. Sunshine. Gucci's on Wooster. It's iconic. Like you."

I followed him around the corner to the boutique, and my eyes lit up when I spotted a section with books and a large sofa. "I'll be over there." I pointed, then grabbed a mystery and settled in with a sigh.

"I'll be back." Alex made a beeline for the men's section, and of course immediately engaged the help of an overly friendly salesperson who was only too happy to help him spend his money.

I opened the book but made only a feeble attempt to read, preferring instead to think about Ethan. Kissing him had been the height of foolishness on my part, and I regretted it.

Liar. No, I didn't. What I regretted was losing control.

"What do you think?" Bright-eyed, Alex bounded over with a blue cashmere sweater and a black leather jacket.

"They're nice."

His face fell. "Nice? That's it?" His shoulders slumped.

"Come on, Nash," Ethan's husky voice cut in, and I froze. "That's a gorgeous jacket. It's lambskin."

Alex's wide-eyed gaze shifted from me to Ethan and back to me. "You two know each other?"

"No," I answered at the same time as Ethan's, "Yes."

"Well, okay. That clears it up." Alex was enjoying this a little too much.

Ethan's dark brows pulled together, and his eyes narrowed. "Are you two dating?"

Alex whooped with laughter, drawing stares from both customers and salespeople. "Nash and me? Dating? As if. He'd probably strangle me within the first two minutes. No. I'm married and I wanted his opinion on an anniversary present for my husband." Alex held up the sweater and jacket. "What do you think? I can see you've got great taste too. A bit more stylish than Nash, but my husband would like it."

Ethan ran a critical eye over the items Alex showed him. "I mean, I love clothes, and if my boyfriend wanted to buy that for me, I'd be so grateful." He winked, and Alex snickered and shot me a look. I scowled. "But for my husband? Eh. Kind of boring. What about something like this? Come with me."

Alex followed, and I watched as Ethan picked out an assortment of candles, men's toiletries, a pair of silk pajamas, and a bathrobe. I could hear Ethan's chatter.

"Set up a nice bubble bath, get a big bouquet of flowers and something decadent, like chocolate-dipped strawberries. Those are my favorites, but you know what he likes, I'm sure."

"Yeah…that sounds great. Rafe loves them, but with two kids, we never get the chance."

"And"—Ethan grinned, eyes sparkling—"for the *pièce de résistance*, bring in a massage table and give him a nice rubdown."

"I like you, Ethan. Can I ask you something?"

"Yeah, sure."

"How the hell do you know Nash?"

Ethan met my eyes. "We don't really know each other. We ride the same train in the morning. Sometimes."

"What do you do?" Alex handed the items Ethan had picked up for him to a sales associate and gave him his credit card but stayed put to gossip.

"I work at Macy's in the men's department, but I'm hoping to move up. I'd like to be a buyer for a luxury brand."

"Like Gucci?" When Ethan nodded, Alex seemed impressed. "Not too shabby."

"Yeah…but when I approached them, they told me to send in a résumé. Even if I wanted to be a salesperson, there's a huge wait. I'll likely get lost among everyone else doing the same thing. I figured if I showed up and let them see me, I'd make a good impression and maybe get an edge."

His initiative was admirable, but I could've told him the corporate world didn't work that way. Plus, I was sure he wasn't the only one to come up with that plan of action. None of which would help him, but I couldn't figure out why I cared so much about this man's job search.

"But that was silly of me, right?" Ethan mused. "Just another idea in a whole slew of ones I've had. I thought having a degree in business from FIT would give me a leg up, but looks like I'm gonna stay where I am and forget about it for now. Guess I'm lucky I have a job."

It wasn't easy watching someone's dreams shatter in front of your eyes. I didn't enjoy seeing Ethan hurting, and an unexpected desire to comfort him welled up inside me, but I remained frozen in place. I was the last person anyone should turn to for consolation.

"Don't get discouraged," Alex said with much more kindness in his voice than I could ever muster. "You're young, and these things take time. I changed careers in my thirties—I was a surgical nurse, and then I decided to go to medical school." The salesperson approached Alex and handed him his bag and credit card. Alex thanked him and raised his brows at me. He scowled and gave me a pointed stare. When I failed to respond—I had no idea what he wanted—he rolled his eyes. "Listen, Ethan, we were going to have dinner after this. Why don't you come with us?"

I blinked. Was he fucking crazy?

Since this was Alex, I shouldn't even bother to ask. I knew the answer to that question. Apparently, my face must've reflected my inner thoughts, as Ethan shook his head. "N-no. That's nice of you, but I'm not about to butt into your evening plans."

"Nah. Don't worry. You aren't. We were just going to sit around and have a couple of drinks and shoot the shit.

Nothing more. Right, Nash?"

I could hardly say anything different without looking like a complete asshole, which normally I wouldn't give a damn about. But Ethan seemed particularly fragile, and considering the shitty way I'd treated him after ravaging him in that bathroom, I owed him one.

"Sure. It's no big deal."

But I'd lied.

Knowing I'd have to sit across from him when I couldn't stop thinking about that kiss? That made it a very big deal.

CHAPTER ▶ 10

The three of us walked out together, and I held the door and murmured to Nash as he passed, "I know you didn't want to be stuck with me a whole evening."

He met my eyes with that penetrating, icy-blue stare. "Don't be ridiculous. I don't do things I don't want."

Like kissing me?

Oh, how I wanted to ask about that, but it would have to wait. Right now, the prospect of spending an entire evening with Nash was more than I could've ever imagined. And exactly what I needed to lift me out of the doldrums of my failed job search.

We stopped in front of Balthazar. "Who's up for fries?" Alex's eyes twinkled, and I could hardly believe this funny, vivacious man was friends with the cool and distant Nash.

"I'll get us a table." Nash left us to speak to the hostess, returning only a minute later. "Come on." He waved. "They've got one ready now."

Once seated, we were offered menus, and my stomach

took a dive to my knees at the prices. A thirty-dollar burger…
this was not a place the average salesperson on a budget
could afford to frequent. Five Guys was more my speed.
I mentally ticked off what I'd have to give up that month
to afford a dinner where I knew I'd never be able to spend
less than a hundred dollars.

"Would you gentlemen care for a drink?"

I couldn't do it. Not when I knew it would be a twenty-
dollar cocktail on top of the food.

"In case you didn't know, I promised Nash to treat him
to dinner, and that offer stands for you as well." Alex met
my eyes with understanding. "It was the only way I could
get him to come shopping with me."

"Not true," Nash grumbled. "If you'd told me Balthazar
was one of the choices, I would've said yes right away."

Alex put a hand to his ear. "Excuse me? Was that the
sound of ice cracking? Because I know hell would freeze
over before Nash Roman ever made a joke."

Okay, I was officially having fun, and even Nash
laughed, which set my stomach to doing not only dives
again, but flips, and for an entirely different reason. A smile
from him brightened the whole world, and you were lucky
to be bathed in his golden sunlight.

"I'll have a Scotch on the rocks," Nash answered first.

"Chardonnay for me, please." Alex answered next.

"Uh, do you have Heineken?" I felt like a slug ordering
beer, but tequila was out of the question if I wanted to stay
sober, and drinking other hard liquor or wine with a burger
seemed out of place.

"Of course."

The server withdrew, and we were left staring at each
other. Or rather, Alex stared at Nash, who kept his eyes fixed
on his water glass. I'd never been inside the restaurant and
enjoyed being part of a scene I'd only read about but had
never been privy to. Wesley and his partner had been, so

now I could finally have something to talk about with him other than Oscar.

"Do you live in the city, Ethan?"

"No. In Brooklyn, on Pacific near Atlantic and the Barclays Center. I have a small studio. It's so tiny, I bump into myself when I turn around, but I don't mind. I help my landlords out with stuff, and they give me a break on the rent, so I'm lucky."

"Oh, that's not too far from me," Alex said with a smile. "We're in Windsor Terrace."

"Pretty over there."

"It is. And you're not that far from Nash, either. He lives off the park. We're all Brooklynites."

I hadn't known that, but a quick glance over to him found his eyes on me. "I hadn't said, but yes. I live on Prospect Park West."

Naturally. Those old, prewar apartment buildings had been redone and cost a fortune.

Our drinks arrived, and the server took our order. Nash had the trout, and Alex had salmon. I couldn't bear to order anything but the cheeseburger.

"And two sides of fries," Alex said firmly. "We'll share." He picked up his glass. "To new beginnings. Ethan, I think you'll go back to work with a renewed sense of how to go about moving up the ladder."

I sipped my beer. "I guess I wanted too much, too soon. Climbing the ladder can take years rung by rung. Maybe it's better to stay with a huge company like Macy's and get a job in-house there and make contacts."

"Sometimes that's for the best. Macy's is a well-respected name. Plus, you'll meet hundreds of vendors." Nash kept that intent, focused gaze on me. "It'll give you a better idea of what you really want."

I know what I want. And whom.

During dinner, Alex told us how he met his husband and

why he'd left nursing to become a doctor. The bill came, and though Alex had said he was treating, I still wanted to make the effort.

"Please let me pay for something."

"Absolutely not." Alex swiped the folio off the table and gave it, with his credit card, to the server. "Next time."

"It was really nice of you to invite a stranger to tag along."

"Strangers are just friends we haven't met yet. Didn't you ever hear that quote?"

"No, but thank you."

I figured we'd all take the train together since it was late and we were going in the same direction. Alex held up his phone. "I have to go to the hospital. I forgot something."

Before either Nash or I could answer, he hopped in the car that had pulled up in front of the restaurant. The two of us stood on the sidewalk, staring after it as it drove away.

"Are you taking a car home too?" I figured it was late and he wouldn't want to be on the subway.

"No. Come on. The train is this way."

"I know, bossy."

His dark brows pinched together. "I wasn't—I didn't mean to be rude. It's just that the sidewalk is narrow, and I don't like being banged into."

"I was only teasing."

Funny how before he kissed me, we could tease each other on the train without a second thought, but now we were each as wary as a stray cat.

We walked the busy streets until we found our station, and when a train arrived, automatically chose the two-seater in the corner. It was several minutes before Nash clasped his hands together and huffed out a sigh.

"Look, Ethan. I'm sorry."

I raised a brow. "For?"

Cheeks red, he bent his head. "You know." He lowered

his raspy voice to an even sexier growl. "Kissing you."

"Why?" I could see my question flustered him, and it made me happy to know something could knock the unflappable Nash Roman on his ass.

Especially me.

That steely gaze captured mine. "It wasn't right of me to do it in a public place. A bathroom. And not ask you first."

Well, damn.

"I appreciate the apology. Thank you." A thought popped into my head as the train hurtled along on the tracks, passing the stations. "Is that why you weren't on the train the past couple of days? You were embarrassed to see me?"

His cheeks reddened. "Maybe, yeah."

The doors opened, and a group of men and women, who looked in their twenties, walked in and sprawled on the bench seats at the opposite end of the car from us. An older woman sitting there stood up and walked to the two-seater near us.

"Whassamatta lady? You don't like us?" one of them called out. "We ain't good enough for you?"

The tallest of the bunch jumped to his feet and came to stand in front of her seat, towering over her. "You afraid?"

Nash rose and stood beside him, and even over the noise of the train, I heard his harsh words. "The lady doesn't want to be disturbed. Leave her alone."

The young man turned with a smirk. "Yeah? Whatchu gonna do about it?"

"I don't argue with children. Leave her alone. Would you want someone harassing your mother like this?"

The train stopped, and when the doors opened, two MTA cops walked in. I might not be a fan of the police, but I'd never been happier to see them than at that moment. Nash, who'd barely flicked an eye, turned around and sat next to me, while the pack leader waved to his crew, and they exited the train with much mumbling and glares.

"You've got balls," I whispered to Nash as the train started again, and that drew a heated stare from him. My dick stiffened.

The train slowed as we approached the station.

"This is Bergen Street. Next stop: Grand Army Plaza."

"My stop." I got to my feet, heart pounding when I realized Nash was following me. We walked up the stairs into the cool night air, the traffic whizzing past us. "You're a long way from Grand Army Plaza."

He said nothing.

I chewed the inside of my lip and took a step closer to him. "You can ask me. I won't say no."

Those intense blue eyes blazed. "Not here."

This time I was the one who remained silent. I crossed the street, Nash at my heels. It was four blocks from the train to my apartment, and every step we took, I was certain it would be the last before he turned around and walked away. By the time I unlocked the door, my nerves were on edge, and I was vibrating with an unfamiliar combination of fear and the hungry need to feel Nash's hands on me.

I closed the door and locked it. Nash stood there, at my shoulder, his breath hot on my cheek. I opened my mouth to say yes, but he covered it with his, and I melted into his arms. His lips were everywhere, and I moaned, sucking his tongue so greedily, he grunted.

"Don't swallow it. I'm going to need it for other things." He kissed me and played havoc with my lips, his hands moving over my body, brushing my neck, undoing my tie, sucking at the base of my throat. When he licked the rim of my ear and teased the tip of his tongue inside, I dug my hands into his shoulders.

"Yeah, please. Oh, God. Do it. Everything. Fuck me."

Nash took my chin in a firm grip. "Not yet."

"Why?" I heard my whine and didn't care. I was out of control, out of my mind with lust for this man.

"Because you deserve better."

And then the bastard left me, aching, hard, and so damn confused, I wanted to bang my fists against the wooden floor and cry with rage and frustration. The door closed, and I sank to the floor and hugged my knees to my chest. My head swam, and I closed my eyes, but like a neon-bright sign, Nash's words played in my mind.

You deserve better.

What did he mean? Better than him? Impossible, in my eyes. Nash had that enviable quality most people only hoped to achieve—when he entered a room, he owned it, and though he spoke quietly, everyone heard him. Not to mention, whatever he wore sat perfectly on his sculpted frame.

I grasped for anything and remembered he'd said *not yet*, after I'd shamelessly begged him to fuck me. Did he mean there would be a next time? Did I want that? My face grew hot as I remembered how I would've gotten naked for him without a second thought.

I might not know much about Nash Roman, but I could damn well guess he wasn't about to start dating me—someone over ten years younger who worked behind the register at a department store. He was used to evenings like tonight, to shopping in luxury stores, then dropping a few hundred dollars on a casual dinner. I couldn't imagine him ordering cheap takeout.

I scrambled to my feet and got my laptop. I searched his name and found a treasure trove of history. Private school, Ivy League college, all of it what I'd expected. His father was a famous cancer researcher, and his stepmother was young, maybe even younger than Nash.

"I deserve better. Well, Nash, you're pretty much the definition of better, considering what I've been through." I closed the computer. "But it's time for you to admit more than you have." I yawned and rubbed my face. "I gotta get some sleep."

I went to bed, wondering if I'd see Nash in the morning.

I made the usual train and was surprised to find Nash in our seats. At my approach, he tipped his head, his face inscrutable. "Please sit." I complied and expected him to speak, but he remained silent. Unable to stand the quiet between us, I broke first.

"If you're going to say you're sorry again, don't. Because I'll leave and not come back."

He blinked and finally met my eyes. "I'm not sorry I kissed you," he murmured. "But I didn't want you to think I was taking advantage of you. That's why I left."

Weird flutters played around in my stomach. "Th-that was nice of you. But you wouldn't have been. I wanted it."

A devilish light danced in his eyes. "Yes. I know. You almost swallowed my tongue."

"Rude," I responded with a smile. "But I'm serious. On both accounts. I-I appreciate you taking it slow. You might think I'm a flirt and that I'm easy, but I'm not." It wasn't pleasant to recount my lousy dating history, but knowing Nash better now, I didn't believe he'd judge me. At least I hoped not. "I've only had two serious boyfriends my whole life. I've hooked up occasionally because it gets too fucking lonely sometimes, you know?"

Nash never took his eyes off me. "What happened with the boyfriends?"

"I met Calvin at a diner where we would both pick up our lunches. It was when I was in college and worked at a small clothing store for men. He asked me out and took me to a club. We danced, and he called me the next day. We started seeing each other almost every night. After a few weeks, we got together." God, remembering it all made me feel like a fool. "He'd never spend the night, and we couldn't get together on the weekends because he said that's when he was busiest—he was a used-car salesman."

"What happened?" Nash asked softly, leaning in close.

"I was young and dumb. I fell for him so fast." I forced out a laugh. "Turned out he had a long-term girlfriend who tracked him to my apartment. When she appeared at my door, he tried to get her to believe he was only having fun and it was no big deal." My voice caught. "I was only fun to him," I spat out bitterly. "That's why when I saw Oscar with his pants down, I wasn't interested in hearing excuses. I won't let anyone use me. Not again."

"Exactly why I wanted to take things slow." Nash's face was troubled. "I don't ever do this sort of thing. I don't want you to think I'm being cavalier."

"I'm not sure what you mean by cavalier. And by this sort of thing, you mean…" I raised a brow. "Pick up a man on the subway? Kiss a man in public?" I lowered my voice as more people crowded around us. "Or is it the man part you're freaking out about?"

Nash's smile was wry. "If it matters, I'm bisexual. You're not the first man I've kissed."

I'd like to be the last.

The thought startled me. Damn, where had that come from?

He folded the paper on his lap in half. "But no, I don't date, nor do I pick up people on the subway or anywhere else. This is totally out of character for me."

I'll bet it is. I'm sure they usually come to you.

I kept quiet, as it seemed he was working something out in his head. The train rocketed out of the Union Square stop, and I knew I didn't have much time, but it wasn't my decision.

Nash said, "Yet I don't like thinking one day you'll walk out of the train and I'll never see you again." He met my eyes, and joy leaped inside me.

"You don't?"

"Yeah." He rubbed his face. "I don't know how it happened or why, but I want to see you again." He peered at me. "If you want to, that is. It's up to you."

CHAPTER ▶ 11

Up to him?

Was I seriously leaving the decision to Ethan? And with less than thirty seconds before he had to leave the train? A man I barely knew…but for whatever reason, I itched to learn more about. God, I was ten times a fool—no, actually, make that a hundred times and counting. I'd never been led around by my dick. But even as I thought that, my mind rebelled. It was way more than that.

He…intrigued me. I knew that by taking this step I was willingly walking into a fire, likely to get burned, but craving the heat. His heat. Ethan had rocked my steady world, and even knowing the danger, instead of getting off that roller coaster, I buckled up and held on, anxious for the ride.

"I get off work at three thirty, but I can hang at the store until you're finished."

The train stopped, and the doors opened. "Don't be silly. I'll come to your place. Later."

Those big green eyes flashed a combination of hesitancy

and happiness, but he nodded and dashed off, slipping through the doors as they began to close.

What the hell had I done?

The rest of my train ride passed quickly, as I was lost in thought about my impetuous decision. On autopilot, I walked the few blocks to the hospital, stopping for a coffee and bagel, then made it to my office. I sat behind my desk, ate my breakfast without tasting it, and powered through my morning meetings. I ordered a sandwich for lunch and listlessly chewed it while staring at the computer screen without seeing whatever the hell was on it.

I started at the brisk rapping at my door.

"Come in."

Why was I not surprised to see Alex's grinning face? "Did we have a meeting?"

He flung himself into the chair. "No. But I wanted to do a recap of last night. I finished rounds and my lunch and don't have much time."

"Recap?" I shuffled some files on my desk.

"God, you're a horrible faker. Don't pretend you don't know what I'm talking about. Or whom. Ethan. I deliberately left you two alone after dinner to see if you'd make a move." His grin broadened. "He's adorable. And very nice."

"I'm glad you like him. Too bad you're married."

Alex snorted. "You're such a dick."

"Tell me something I don't know." I clicked into my calendar and frowned. Budget meetings the rest of the day meant I'd need to be at the top of my game, and after what happened with Ethan, my mind seemed unable to focus on numbers. I rubbed my face and saw Alex sitting across from me.

"You're still here."

"Your powers of observation are stellar." He hitched his chair closer. "What're you afraid of?"

"Afraid? Me? Nothing." I scoffed and pulled up the

first spreadsheet I'd need. "You're talking out of your ass."

"You like him. So what's the problem?"

Like might not exactly be the right word. I wanted to ravage him. Become one with him. Crawl inside his skin and live there. It fucking scared me how bad I wanted Ethan.

"I never said there was a problem, and I never said I liked him. Now can I please get back to work?" My gaze was steady even as my heart pounded.

With a huge sigh, Alex bounced out of the chair. "You can deny, deny, deny, but I know better. My best friend Micah was like you—a loner, thinking he didn't need anyone, or need love. Until he met Josh." A sweet smile curved his lips, and despite myself, I wanted to hear the story. "Now he's married with two children and is so fucking happy, it's almost nauseating."

After Alex left, I didn't review the numbers for my meeting. Instead, I thought about a pair of laughing green eyes and a hot, clinging mouth. I rubbed my eyes and scooped up the files from my desk, then picked up the phone.

"Madeline? I-I'm not feeling well. I'm going home."

"I'm sorry, Nash."

My secretary must've been shocked. I hadn't taken a day off or a sick day in years.

"I'm sending the information to Roger now, and I'll let him know."

"I can do that for you, if you'd like."

"No. I will. Thanks anyway."

My next call to Roger didn't go as well.

"You're leaving me in the lurch. I haven't had a chance to go over those figures. I was counting on you."

The snappish response was so out of character for him, I almost changed my mind.

"I'm sorry, Roger, but I'm not feeling like myself and… uh…"

Roger sighed. "Sorry, Nash. I didn't mean to take out

my bad mood on you. Of course. Go home and rest."

"Anything wrong?" I was curious what had set Roger off, since he was usually mild-mannered. "Can I help?"

"Not unless you want to adopt an overactive Australian shepherd puppy? My wife just called and said she caught him in my closet, chewing up my shoes. Four pairs of Prada loafers."

"Ouch."

"And that's only today. Last week it was my computer charger, my wife's phone, and her new Chanel bag."

"Damn. Expensive little bastard."

"Tell me about it. But I love the demon. We've hired a trainer, so hopefully that'll work."

"I hope so. I've emailed you all the reports, but it's not much different than what we discussed the other day."

"*Hmm.*"

His tone set off an alarm bell. "What's not sitting right?"

"I see you haven't increased the funding for the cancer center."

My antennae went up. "No. But they still garner the bulk of the money after hospital salaries."

"And you're not doing it because of the animus between you and your father?"

My stomach took a nose-dive, and at the moment my pretend illness wasn't so fake. "What're you insinuating? That I'm allowing my personal feelings to cloud what's best for the hospital?"

"Are you?"

I slapped my desk. "I resent that. These numbers are valid and you know it. And me. I don't let personal feelings interfere with my work. I'm a professional."

"I know you are. I hope you feel better. I'll see you tomorrow."

I powered down the computer, slipped my suit jacket on, and left.

Before Ethan, it had been years since I'd stepped foot in Macy's, Herald Square, and now it was twice in a month. As someone who wasn't particularly fond of crowds or people in general, the vastness of the store was way outside my comfort zone.

But the prospect of seeing Ethan again held all the appeal in the world.

At two forty-five, I took the escalator up to the men's department on the mezzanine and scanned the floor. Ethan was standing by a row of suits, talking to an older man and his wife. Even at this distance, his charm and charisma were evident, and I could see he excelled at his job.

"May I help you, sir?" An immaculately dressed older man approached me. "Are you looking for something special? I'm Wesley, the manager. We're running a twenty-five percent sale on sweaters today, and buy-one-get-one fifty percent off on suits, although"—he ran a critical eye over me—"I'm guessing you don't buy your suits off the rack?"

Chatty Wesley seemed nice, but I needed him to leave me the hell alone. I allowed a faint smile. "I'm not a shopper by nature. I have a tailor who makes them for me or I go to Zegna or Armani."

A slow nod. "Yes, I thought so. The cut and fabric are Italian. And unique."

"Nash?" Ethan joined us, unable to hide his shocked expression. "What're you doing here? I thought you worked until six."

"You two know each other?" Silvery brows arched high, Wesley looked from me to Ethan.

"Uh, yeah," Ethan said. "We take the same train in the morning and, uh—"

"Ethan suggested I take advantage of the sale on shirts," I cut in smoothly, hoping Wesley, nice as he was, would take the hint and go away. "I can never have enough."

Ethan remained uncharacteristically silent, and Wesley nodded. "Okay, then. I'll leave you in Ethan's very capable hands." He withdrew, and we stood staring at each other.

"Are you really here for shirts?"

I chuckled. "Are you really asking me that question?" I lowered my voice. "I left work early. So I could come home with you."

Ethan gulped, his throat working, and I wanted to press my mouth to it and mark all that smooth skin. "O-oh. I still have about half an hour left."

"I'll wait." I could see I'd thrown him off-kilter. "Do you want me to go?"

"No. Of course not. I'm just surprised. You didn't have to leave work early. I don't want you to get in trouble."

It was sweet of him to worry. "I won't. I figured it would give us more time to get to know each other."

Who was I? The words of reassurance coming out of my mouth…that wasn't me. I didn't get to know my bed partners. We knew what we wanted from each other, and there wasn't any need to delve deeper. Yet from Ethan's bright face, it had been the right thing to say. I liked seeing him smile.

"I'll find you when I'm ready. I have to finish up with my customers."

"Go ahead. I'll be here."

I wandered a bit and decided to buy a few shirts. I waited in line, and Wesley rang me up.

"I'm glad you found something, sir."

I said nothing and handed him my credit card.

"Would you like to open a Macy's account? You get an extra fifteen percent off."

"No, thank you."

He rang up the sale and continued to chat, even though I tried to keep my answers brief.

"How funny that you and Ethan met on the train. That's a real New York story for sure. How long have you known each other?"

"Not very long."

God help me.

"Ethan is a wonderful person and a terrific worker."

"I'm sure he is."

"Do you work around here?"

"Not far."

What next? My birthday? Home address? Blood type? I could've kissed the group of people who lined up behind me to pay, as Wesley no longer had the luxury of time to try and ferret out any more information. He handed me my receipt and the bag with my shirts.

"Thank you very much."

I made a quick exit, noting Ethan approaching with the husband and wife in tow. He held two suits, and the wife had several other items in her hands.

"I just need to ring them up."

"Don't worry," I soothed, as he seemed frazzled. "I'm in no rush."

His smile was grateful, and I wanted to kiss his mouth and taste the sweetness of his breath mixed with mine.

Hold up. You don't even know if you're going to have sex with him.

I wanted to. Desperately, in fact. But what would that mean? Would he expect us to be a couple? To start dating and be exclusive? I'd never done that. Could I? Did I want to?

I was getting ahead of myself. We might find out we weren't even compatible. A few hot kisses, no matter how explosive, meant little.

"Hi."

Ethan waited in front of me.

"Hi. Are you ready?"

"Yeah. I'm logged out, so we can go." He glanced at my shopping bag. "You didn't have to buy anything."

"I didn't want your manager to feel like I was some creepy stalker."

We stepped onto the escalator. "He already had a thousand questions about you as I was leaving. He's just being a little overprotective."

Outside, it was bright, and I squinted at Ethan. "That's nice of him, I guess."

Without saying, we instinctively walked to the downtown train station and headed below ground.

"He's a self-appointed father figure, since my parents aren't in the picture."

"Where do they live?"

"Texas. My father was in construction, and when the housing market slowed here, he lost his job. It worked for them, but as a gay man, I didn't feel like following, so I stayed."

The train arrived, and we took our usual seats. This time I didn't mind his thigh pressing against mine or our shoulders touching. I was hoping that by the time the night ended, we'd be touching in other places. He must've noticed, as I caught him smiling when the train speed shifted us closer. I made no attempt to move away.

"No brothers or sisters?"

"I had a sister, Cassandra, but she died when she was a child. I think that's another reason they moved. They wanted to get away from sad memories."

"Do you get along?"

Ethan shrugged. "I mean, we were never one of those super-duper close and lovey-dovey families. I told them I was gay, and while they never said anything negative, they weren't exactly supportive either. They ended up moving to Texas, a state where they felt more at home." His body language revealed there was more behind his words than he was willing to share. "Which, when I look back on it all, maybe told me everything I needed to know." He released a sigh. "What about you and your parents? Did they care that you've had boyfriends?"

My lips twitched at the thought. "First of all, I don't have boyfriends, nor girlfriends. Who I choose to sleep with is my decision alone. I'm forty-three. I gave up caring long ago what my father might think, since he never gave a damn about my opinion on how he lived." I studied the floor. "And I have no idea if he knows I've been with men or if he'd care."

"And your mother?" Ethan asked softly, leaning slightly against me.

"I have no idea if she knew, but I'd like to think it wouldn't have mattered." I blinked, my gaze still fixed to the floor. "She died. Six years ago from a heart attack. She was only sixty-six. Her whole self-worth was being my father's wife, and when he left her, she became severely depressed." I rubbed my burning eyes. "I know her death was a direct result of her broken heart."

Ethan touched my shoulder. "I'm sorry. That's rough."

I didn't talk about it with anyone. I never mentioned it or my mother because I was so damn angry she'd wasted her life on a man who wasn't worth her time. I tried not to think about it at all.

"Thanks. She deserved so much better."

"At least she had you. I'm sure she appreciated how close you two were."

Funny how the pain in your chest didn't fade. "We weren't close. I was hurt and felt abandoned myself, but at six it was hard to be brave, and I cried all the time, thinking it was my fault. Lost in her own grief, she didn't have much left to help me with mine. By the time I'd reached my teens, she and I had become strangers, and it was only after I graduated from college that we reconciled…but there were so many lost years." I hung my head. "I was a terrible son. I called her names…a doormat, a fool…" There went that burning in my eyes again, and I swallowed hard. "I was just so…so mad at him, I took it out on her."

"I'm sure she understood."

"No, you're saying that to be kind and make me feel better, but the truth is I meant it. I just shouldn't have said it."

Before I realized it, we were in Brooklyn and closing in on Ethan's stop, but I didn't want to go home with him. I had a need for the familiar tonight, and so I cleared my throat.

"Can we…would you mind if we went to my place? We can have dinner in or go out if you want."

A pucker appeared between Ethan's well-manicured brows. "I—we don't have to do this at all if you've changed your mind. I can just go home and—"

"No," I exclaimed, sharper than intended, but the thought of spending the evening alone filled me with dread. "Please? I'd really appreciate it if you'd be with me."

The announcement broke the silence: *"This is Bergen Street. Next stop: Grand Army Plaza."*

The train ground to a halt, and Ethan tensed beside me. "Please?"

CHAPTER ▶ 12

Going to a stranger's apartment? Totally against my rules. I never *ever* went home with someone I didn't know well. I'd heard too many stories and watched too many crime shows. Plus, I could hear the commentator on *Dateline*: *"Ethan was the kind of person who lit up a room. A bright light. Everyone loved him."*

I couldn't help being a bright light, but I could damn well make sure I didn't put myself into a foolish situation. But this was Nash. We weren't strangers. Not that I knew him—I had a feeling no one really knew Nash Roman well—but it wasn't as if we'd met in a bar as a casual hookup. We'd talked plenty, I'd had dinner with him and his friend and he'd kissed me in my apartment.

"Okay. I'll come to you."

Grand Army Plaza was one of my favorite places in the city. As congested as Brooklyn was, it evoked a sense of space. The soaring Soldiers and Sailors Arch stood in the center, anchoring the traffic circle, with the leafy greenness of Prospect Park on one side of Flatbush Avenue and the sweeping, curved facade of the Brooklyn Public Library on the other.

"Have you ever been to the West Indian Day Parade on Labor Day?" I asked Nash, who stared out at the traffic whizzing past. "It's so much fun, and the food the street vendors serve is to die for. Give me some meat patties any day and a Ting? Mmm." I rubbed my stomach.

"No. As someone who hates crowds to begin with, any parade would be a nightmare."

"Too bad."

We crossed the street and walked down Prospect Park West, passing huge old apartment buildings with ornate limestone facades and doormen in fancy uniforms. I knew Nash came from wealth, but as we entered his building and I gazed around at the vaulted ceilings and marble walls and floors…this type of money went way beyond my pay grade. These were the people who casually shopped for those labels I so desperately wanted to work for.

Nash tipped his head, seeming unaffected by my silence. "Follow me."

The elevator took us to the tenth floor, where we exited onto a hushed hallway. I doubted you'd hear any screaming arguments or shrieking children behind the heavy doors, and unlike my building—where I knew as soon as I opened the front door whether Gladys was making her lasagna or Mrs. O'Reilly her famous gas-inducing corned beef and cabbage—here a gentle, high-class fragrance wafted through the air, like a stroll through the finest hotel.

He opened the door to the corner apartment, and I walked inside.

Nash's apartment smelled of solitude and wasn't much different than his personality—quiet and understated. He'd had it decorated in muted navy, gray, and cream, and without any personal touches. Not a family picture or travel photo in sight. A large bookcase held volumes of classical literature I recalled attempting to read and understand in high school but failing miserably, sitting alongside books on accounting and finance.

"No fun reads? Trashy thrillers or horror stories?" I pulled out a thick book. "Oh, this looks like a joy to read—*The Upside of a Down Economic Cycle* by Wentworth Ford. Why do all boring books have authors with obnoxiously preppy names?"

Nash plucked the book out of my hand. "Are you nervous?"

My mouth dried at his intent stare. I didn't know if I should turn and run, or throw my arms around him and plant one on his mouth.

I huffed out a laugh. "Who, me? Why would you say that?"

He slid the book into its place. "Because you're chattering a mile a minute about nonsense."

"I doubt Wentworth Ford's mother would think it's nonsense." My heart pounded at his nearness.

"I don't see her here." He peered over his shoulder, then faced me and grinned. "It's only you and me."

"So it is. Unlike in the train, where we have an audience for our conversations. Do you think people listen in?"

"Of course. People are naturally gossips who love to eavesdrop."

"Not you," I scoffed. "You aren't interested in someone else's business."

"I'm interested in your business." He put a hand on my waist and drew me in close. "Did you think about your next move in your job search?"

"I thought we were going to come here and have wild, uninhibited sex, not a résumé-building workshop."

"Is that what you want?" he murmured in my ear, his breath warm and ticklish. A shiver ran through me, and he tightened his hold. "Cold?"

"No. Just the opposite." I turned my face so our lips touched as I spoke. "I'm burning up."

When his mouth crushed mine, I whimpered and sucked his tongue. A powerful surge of lust slammed into me, and I grew bolder than I'd ever imagined. My hands pulled at his belt and unzipped his slacks. His hard cock bulged through his briefs, and when I cupped him, he moaned. Knowing I was giving him pleasure was a heady cocktail, and I was drunk on lust as I sank to my knees, taking his pants and briefs with me.

Nash's fingers tangled in my hair. "You don't have to do this if it's too soon."

"Shut up." I teased the rim of his cockhead with my tongue, then played in his slit, tasting his silky juices. "I want to. I want you."

His cock jerked, and I held his hips and took his hot length in my mouth, licking and sucking as I swallowed him down. I gazed up at him and saw him watching me with hooded eyes, the only indication of his excitement in the rapid rise and fall of his chest.

Oh, fuck no. When I suck your dick I'm gonna make you fall apart and scream.

I gripped him tighter and scraped my teeth over the shaft on the way up, then swirled my tongue over the wide head. I sucked his dick like it was a soft-serve cone on a hundred-degree day. The muscles of his thighs grew rock-hard with tension, and his quiet breathing turned to heavy panting and audible in the otherwise silent room.

I hummed along the thick vein as I went deep, and he shivered, so I took him deeper still. My lack of a gag reflex worked well for me, as Nash was huge. My jaw ached and my lips were stretched to the limit, but I wouldn't release him. His hips thrust gently, and his fingers tightened in my hair.

"Mmm," I hummed, letting him feel the vibration at the back of my throat for a brief second before sucking him hard and fast.

"Ethan," he gasped, and a thrill shot through me at my victory. I bobbed in quick, short bursts and saved the best for last—I reached behind the pumping globes of his tight ass to stick my finger into his crease and play along his rim.

"Fuck. Oh, God. Fuck, Ethan."

He shot a steady hot stream down my throat, and I gulped it, knowing no Dom Pérignon could ever taste as sweet, loving his salty-bitter taste. I let him go, and though he'd emptied himself into my mouth, he was still half-hard. I licked my lips, watching him watch me. A slight smile tipped his lips, and he lowered himself to meet me face-to-face.

I didn't know what to expect—with Nash, he could be angry he'd given in to emotion. He leaned in close and kissed me.

"Your mouth is swollen." He ran his fingertips over where he'd kissed me. "Does it hurt?"

"No," I whispered.

"Good. So I can do this." He cupped my jaw and covered my mouth, his tongue seeking entry. We played tease-tag, and I wanted him so bad, I physically ached. I slanted my mouth across his, and he grunted, pulled me close…closer…

His phone rang, the sound loud and shrill in the silence. We broke apart, and he looked wrecked—eyes dark with passion, mouth reddened, cheeks flushed. I knew I looked the same, only add in a hard-as-a-rock dick.

"I have to see who this is." He pulled up his briefs and pants, then shoved his hand into the pocket to retrieve his phone. He rolled his eyes. "Julia, what is it?"

I rubbed my crotch. Who the fuck was Julia? I could hear her voice but not what she was saying. Nash ran a hand through his sweaty hair.

"No, I'm okay. I just left early.…No, I don't need you

to come over....I'm fine. I'll be in tomorrow. Good-bye." I heard her still speaking but he ended the call midsentence and tossed the phone onto the couch. "Sorry. A work colleague."

"She was worried about you?"

His smile was wry as he held out his hand to me. I took it and let him pull me to my feet. "Guess that's what happens when you never take a day off. People think you must be dying if you leave early." He drew me in closer. "Although I have to admit you made me see God there for a moment." His breath teased my cheek, and his finger trailed the line of my jaw. "I need to return the favor. It's not fair."

Before I could answer, he undid my button tab and zipper and slid a hand inside my briefs. I swayed at the first touch of his strong fingers grasping my dick. "Oh…this is fine, yeah. I forgive you for leaving me in my time of need." My head fell to his shoulder as he pumped me, slow at first, picking up the sticky precome dripping from my slit, then faster and harder. "I need…Nash. I need…oh, God."

"I know what you need," he growled in that rough, sexy voice. "You're so perfect…your face, your mouth," Nash mumbled and kissed me, messy and wet, his tongue sliding and swallowing my gasps. He bit my ear, and I flung my arms around his neck, wishing I could crawl under his skin and become part of the hot blood beating in his veins.

I wanted to speak, but I'd lost the ability to form words, and when my orgasm swept through me, I collapsed against him, my vision graying. Nash held on to me, and I shuddered through my climax and came all over his hand. When I returned to a passable level of awareness, his lips were buried in my hair.

"I'm sorry I made a mess." I tipped my head up.

Blue eyes locked on mine, Nash took a step back and raised his fingers to his lips and licked them, one by one. "Now I know what you taste like. I've been wondering since that first time on the train."

Oh. My. God. Could he be any sexier?

"You thought about me?"

His head dipped. "From the first time you sat next to me, I wondered what you'd be like."

I touched his face. "Be like where? How?" Damn, I was bold, but I wanted to hear him say it out loud.

"Naked," he said hoarsely and kissed me. "Over me. Under me."

His words vibrated over my skin, and I soaked them in. The blatant desire heating his normally chilly gaze left me wondering what was on his mind. Was I ready for the next step?

Then my stomach growled. Loudly. Laughter replaced lust as his eyes crinkled shut, and I could only stare in wonder at the beautiful sight I knew was a rarity.

"Come on. Let's get cleaned up. After all, I did promise you dinner."

He tucked me in and zipped me up, then took me by the hand and led me to a spotless bathroom. "Feel free to use whatever you want, including the shower. I'll just be a minute." He disappeared, leaving me a little disappointed that he didn't want me in his bedroom, but maybe he was exercising the same level of caution as me.

I washed my hands and face, a bit in my own head. *You're not here to be his boyfriend. You're here for sex and fun, both of which you already had. This is how the big boys play.*

I dried my face and hands and made my way back to the living room to wait for Nash. When he reappeared, he'd changed into athletic pants and a T-shirt, and I gaped at him, having never seen him in casual clothes before.

"I had to get out of the suit and tie."

"I-I see." And I liked what I saw. A black shirt clung to a broad, muscular chest and flat belly, and the thin fabric of the pants cupped his beautiful ass. It was hard to reconcile the stone-faced man from the subway with this relaxed, almost smiling man in front of me, and while I enjoyed poking and teasing him in the morning, I preferred this softer, less rigid Nash.

"What do you want?"

I blinked, seeing him standing in front of me, the screen on his phone open to a delivery app, and realizing he meant food-wise. "Oh, uh, I don't care. Sushi?" I didn't want him to spend lots of money.

"That's always my go-to. Take a look and let me know what you'd like."

Did he really think I cared what I ate? I'd had him in my mouth—perfection achieved. Nothing else would ever taste as good. But of course I couldn't say that. He'd think me cuckoo for Cocoa Puffs, and maybe I was, because all I wanted was to kiss him again.

"I'm fine with anything—Alaska roll, or a spicy tuna. Nothing fancy."

Nash frowned but said nothing and concentrated on the screen. "They'll be here in twenty minutes. Do you want a drink?"

"Sure."

"I have Scotch and wine. I don't have any beer, sorry."

"I'll have Scotch," I said firmly. I wanted to show Nash we could have things in common.

"How do you take it?"

I thought fast. I didn't want it straight, like he drank it. "Club soda and ice?"

His gaze was steady, and then he nodded. "Okay."

I watched as he made the drinks, and when he handed me mine, I raised the glass. "*Salute.*"

Nash didn't respond but tipped the tumbler and took a sip. I tasted mine and fought not to grimace.

"You don't have to pretend with me. I don't care what you like to drink." Nash's smile was gentle, and I felt it to my toes.

"Thank God, because this stuff is awful." I pushed it away, wishing I could scrub my tongue. "I'll have some wine."

He frowned but poured me a cold glass of *rosé*. "Let's sit." He pointed to the couch, and I followed him, taking a seat close but not on top of him. "I was serious when I said I was interested in your job situation. Any news on that front?"

I stared into my glass. "Well…I guess I needed that kick in the ass to show me I wasn't all that and a bag of chips. I'm not sure about my next step." The cool wine tasted delicious. This I could get used to. "It's not that I don't like my job now, but I want more."

"Want some advice?"

"Sure."

"You have a great rapport with people. I could see that from the few minutes I watched you with Alex, and then again today with your customers. I think the key to success in your industry is probably knowing every facet of the business. Can I ask you something?"

"Yeah." Over the rim of my glass, I met his frank gaze.

"How old are you?"

"Thirty-one." His brows rose. "Surprised? You think I should be further along in my career, more than just a salesperson?"

"Don't be foolish. That's not what I meant. I thought you were in your twenties. You're so carefree…lively. Not weighed down with the bullshit life throws at you."

"I've had plenty of bullshit. I had to put off college because I couldn't afford it. I worked two jobs to save up and be able to pay rent and eat. You know, minor things like that. My parents believed once you turned eighteen, it was out of the house and being responsible for yourself. And it's not like I had much choice, since they moved so far away. I didn't get to go to college until I turned twenty-one, and even when I went to FIT, I worked nights." My hands tightened on the glass. "It took me six fucking years to graduate, but I did it."

"And you should be damned proud."

My eyes burned. I didn't understand why I cared what Nash thought of me, but I did.

"It doesn't matter how long it takes you to accomplish your dream, as long as you keep pushing forward. If you reach a roadblock, find another path to take you to where you need to go." He shifted closer. "You can still become a luxury buyer. But maybe begin in a place where you can network and make the most contacts."

"That makes sense. I'm going to talk to my manager and see what he thinks and if there would be a place for me in the store where I am. He said he was considering me for assistant manager, so that's a start, I think. It's another way to meet all the stylists."

The buzzer sounded. Nash squeezed my knee before getting up to answer. He returned with a bag and set it on the table in front of us.

"One thing I've learned: half of making your way up the corporate ladder is knowing how to play the game." He rummaged in the bag and handed me my tray. "I'm sure hospital politics are no different than fashion, and I've seen a lot in my time. Have some soy sauce."

Did Nash's business advice hold true for him personally? Was this all a game?

CHAPTER ▶ 13

"This was very nice. Thank you."

We lounged on the couch after finishing the sushi, sipping the cappuccinos I'd made. It was after nine, and I was loath to let Ethan go, but tomorrow was a workday. Still, I wanted to draw out our time together.

"My pleasure."

"I think it was both of ours," he said with that cheeky grin.

"You never heard from your ex again, did you?"

Ethan hadn't mentioned him, but knowing how persistent he'd been, I was curious if he'd finally given up. I wouldn't need to go out to a random club and have my dick sucked if I had a man like Ethan in my bed. I wouldn't need to go anywhere at all.

Ethan made a face. "He showed up at my job, bought things I knew he didn't need just so he could make his case—*again*. Why I should forgive him and take him back."

"Didn't convince you, I gather?"

"I'm here, aren't I?"

My hands clenched into fists, and I was shocked at the hot rush of anger spilling through my blood. "Yes, but maybe you're still thinking about him."

A rude noise escaped him. "Fat chance. Like I told Wesley, I'm worth more than that. You have one chance to get all this." He made a sweeping gesture with his hand over his hard, muscled body. "Fuck up and you're out."

"I agree."

He shot me a thoughtful glance from under those incredibly thick lashes. "That was about your father, right?" I froze, but he continued. "You told me he was a cheater. You never gave him a second chance, did you?"

"No. He destroyed my family—my mother. Why the hell would I?"

As usual, talking about my father left me an emotional wreck, and I barely felt Ethan's hands on my shoulders until his face was in mine. "I'm not saying you should. But there are levels. Your father's cheating was a whole different kind of wrong. He was married and had a family. Oscar was my boyfriend. We'd been together three years. Do I hate him? No, because I'm not sure I ever loved him. But your father was a married man. With a child. I don't blame you for being so angry, you can't forgive him."

The constant rage boiling my skin settled to a simmer at Ethan's touch and calm voice. "I don't give a damn about him."

But I knew that wasn't true. I wished I could hurt him the way he'd hurt us. I wanted to cause him the same pain he'd brought to my life.

Ethan rested his forehead to mine. "I'm sorry."

"It's not your fault." I couldn't convey how much his being here meant to me, so I just stayed quiet, soaking in his nearness. A few seconds passed, and I dragged in a deep breath and disengaged from him. "I'm okay."

Those green eyes narrowed. "I doubt that." He sighed and set his cup on the coffee table. "Did I ever tell you about the customer who tried to return underwear?"

I didn't think I'd enjoy Ethan's chatter, but his stories of outrageous customer experiences brought a smile to my face. I appreciated that he cared enough not to dwell on the painful subject of my father and me.

"And then she had the nerve to try and return a package of briefs—open, mind you." His expressive eyes danced. "Now you tell me—who in their right mind is gonna buy an opened package of underwear? *Eww*, no one, of course." He wrinkled that perfect nose, and I couldn't help but laugh.

"What if she genuinely bought the wrong size? Maybe her husband lost or gained weight?"

"The measurements are on every package." He ran an assessing gaze over me. "You're a large."

"Is that so?" I caught him around the neck. I couldn't help it. Something about this man made me not only step outside my comfort zone, but run through the glass wall and shatter it into a million pieces.

"For obvious reasons," he murmured, his lips in a sweet curve against my cheek. "And getting larger, if I'm not mistaken."

"Wise-ass."

We hadn't kissed since the desperate groping where he'd blown my brains with that delicious mouth of his. Knowing he was on the verge of leaving, I wanted to touch him one more time.

"My ass is brilliant, thank you." He pulled away. "I'd better be getting home. I have some thinking to do about the next step forward." Without asking, Ethan picked up his cup and mine and brought them to the kitchen, in direct contrast to Julia, who, the few times she'd had a glass of wine or a meal here, left her dirty glasses and plates on the table and her wet towels on the bathroom floor after she'd taken a shower.

"Speaking with your manager, I thought."

"Yes, but I've already started laying the foundation for me leaving." He frowned. "I even suggested replacements."

"*Hmm*. Well, why not tell him the truth? That you did make inquiries but decided you'd be better off pursuing the career moves you want where you are now because Macy's gives you much greater opportunity for advancement. And how much you enjoy the people you work with. I highly doubt he started running around immediately to find a replacement when you haven't given notice."

I could see the relief in Ethan's face as he slipped his feet into the loafers he'd left by the door. "You're right. I'm just panicking because I can't afford to lose this job." His green eyes twinkled. "I know you might find this hard to believe, but sometimes I speak without thinking."

"Do tell," I responded dryly as I stuck my feet into my shoes. "Come. I'll call a car for you."

"I can take the train."

I held his arm. "I know you can, but I'd feel better if you didn't. Do you mind?"

"N-no. That's nice of you."

I tugged him close and kissed him. "Contrary to what you might think, I can be nice."

"Mmm." He hummed against my lips. "This certainly is. And thank you. I appreciate the concern."

We waited in front of my building, and he stood before me, his face in shadows. "I could've gotten my own car. I don't want you to think I'm mooching off you."

"I don't. It's not a big deal."

The car pulled up, and Ethan opened the door but stopped before sliding in. "Maybe not to you, but it is to me. Bye, Nash."

He closed the car door behind him, and I watched until the taillights disappeared from view. Once upstairs, I put the cups in the dishwasher and wandered around, seeing Ethan everywhere. I turned on the television for some much-needed background noise to drown out the emptiness echoing in the silent apartment. I tried to sit and watch, but it couldn't keep my attention, and I finally gave up and decided to go to bed.

"I should've had him text me when he got home," I muttered to myself, then realized I didn't have his phone number. "What is going on here? He's not a kid." Feeling foolish, I took a shower and got into bed. Ethan was a grown man and capable of taking care of himself.

Still, I couldn't help looking forward to seeing him in the morning.

At the Bergen Street stop, I waited for Ethan to enter the subway car, but he didn't appear. I half rose from my seat to see if he was running down the platform to catch the train, but the doors closed. It didn't matter, as I could see no one waiting as the train picked up speed.

Maybe he was running late. Maybe he overslept. Maybe…

God, you're being an idiot.

There could be a million reasons why Ethan wasn't on the train.

Too bad I couldn't think of one.

All of which put me in a piss-poor mood at work. Madeline nodded at me when I strode past her desk.

"Feeling better, Nash?"

Rarely inclined to make small talk, I was even less so this morning. "Yes, thanks. Any calls?"

"Roger."

I grunted. To be expected. I closed the door to my office and placed a call to him.

"Feeling better?"

"Yes. I'm fine."

"Good. My office, please."

"On my way."

I left my bagel and coffee on my desk and retraced my steps from minutes before to Roger's office. Once seated, Roger slid a cup of coffee to me across the desk.

"You must've really not felt well. I can't remember the last time you took an afternoon off."

"Never." I sipped the strong brew. "And yeah, but I'm okay now. How did the meetings go?"

He drank some of his tea before answering. "The funding numbers are up. Some very big donors have come through with trusts to the hospital that will enable us to expand our research and development. One in particular can change the future of this whole hospital. You've heard of the Ahmed family? From Dubai?"

"Yeah, of course. They're one of the wealthiest families in the world—oil, diamond mines, real estate…they have their fingers in everything that makes unlimited money." I thought for a moment. "Didn't a New York woman years ago cause a scandal by running off to marry an Ahmed? Someone twenty-five years older than her?" I didn't pay attention to gossip, but I remembered that story. It was all over the news, since the girl had barely graduated from high school.

"Right. Elizabeth Porter. She married Ali Ahmed and had four children. The family made their money in hedge funds—the usual billionaires. Ali Ahmed took part in the first trial of the procedure your father developed for treating rare blood cancers. I'm sure you're aware of his research?"

"No. Not at all."

Roger's brows rose high, but he dipped his head in acknowledgment. "Well, as I said, Elizabeth's husband suffered from one of the types of cancers your father was researching, and though he passed away earlier this year, he lived four years longer than his original prognosis. That enabled him to walk his daughter down the aisle and see his first grandchild born. For that"—Roger smiled—"Elizabeth has bequeathed Mercy, and Dr. Roman's research in particular, three-quarters of a billion dollars." He paused for effect. "Annually."

I let out a low whistle of appreciation. "Damn. That's…a lot of money."

Roger's face shined bright with excitement. "We can do so much with that kind of funding, the education and research that can come from it. It's indescribable how many people we could potentially help."

"Well, congratulations. I'm sure once all the paperwork is in place with the trust, we'll be meeting to make sure the wishes of the family are carried through to the letter."

"We sure will. Naturally, your father and his team are extremely excited and have already begun making plans—more staffing, equipment, and many more clinical trials here and worldwide. We're ready to reach out to universities and academics to fund scholarships and chairs," Roger prattled on. "It's truly a gift. We're going to name the center after the Ahmed family for their generosity."

"Of course." Standard procedure in the industry: give tons of money, and you get a building named after you. "I'd better be getting to work. I have to go through all my emails from yesterday."

"Yes, yes. I just wanted to give you the happy news myself." He walked me to the door. "I know you've said you and your father aren't close, but I'm sure you're thrilled for the hospital."

"I appreciate you letting me know. And I can assure you I'm just as happy as you are that the hospital will reap such an incredible benefit." I wasn't lying. I could separate the lousy father and human being from the brilliant oncologist and researcher.

Once in my office, I spent the morning powering through the emails and messages that had piled up yesterday. But in the back of my mind, I couldn't stop thinking about Ethan.

Why hadn't he been on the train?

The computer on the credenza behind my desk held all the network information I needed to upload my files to the various servers, so I wasn't facing the door when it opened. I didn't even turn, figuring it was either Alex or Julia.

"I'm busy. Can't talk."

"Too busy to see me?" My hands faltered on the keyboard, and I swiveled around to see not only my father, but his wife, Diana. Was she even thirty-five? I doubted it. I'd meant what I'd said—I didn't blame her, as she wasn't the woman he'd cheated with when he was married. That woman ending up cheating on him was poetic justice. But, Diana had lasted longer than I'd expected. I recalled the invitation to their wedding and the handwritten note inside the envelope, urging me to set aside our differences. I'd tossed it into the trash.

"Yes, actually. I have reports to get out and—"

"And we have news," Diana bubbled. "We wanted to tell you first."

I remained silent. Waited.

"Yes, well"—my father looked directly into my eyes—"Diana and I are expecting a child."

My gaze immediately switched to Diana. Where she usually wore form-fitting dresses accentuating her very toned body, now that she'd moved her large Hermès purse, I could see the slight bump. It hadn't been noticeable in the long, flowing gown she'd worn the night of the gala.

"I see."

When I was young, all I'd wanted was a little brother or sister, but that dream had died when my father left. Nausea bubbled in my stomach.

"Isn't that wonderful? You're going to have a little brother or sister," she gushed. "We're going to lunch and hoped you could come with us. We could go to La Scala. Maybe you could invite Julia. We'd love to get to know her better."

That makes one of us.

"I'm sorry, but I have to go to a meeting."

A lie, but I was damned if I was going to spend an hour with them, talking about their oh-so-cute upcoming bundle of joy. I'd rather eat dirt.

"Oh." Diana's smile faded. "We-we can make it another day."

My silence must've gotten through to my father, as he leaned down to kiss Diana's cheek. "Why don't you call and get the two of us a table? I'll just be a minute."

"Sure. Bye, Nash."

"Bye."

She hurried out, leaving my father, who closed the door and stood in front of it, as if he feared I'd be the next to leave.

"There's no need to take out your bad feelings on Diana. She's my wife."

"I'm aware."

"You can't even pretend to be happy, can you?" His voice rose, his frustration clear. "Are you that cold and unfeeling? This baby will be your sibling."

"Half-sibling," I corrected. "And not the better half, either." Eyes narrowed, he worked his jaw, but I continued. "It's not Diana I have a problem with. Matter of fact, I feel bad for her. She's young, and you probably dazzled her with your bullshit. I hope you don't cheat on her."

"Don't you dare talk like that. I love her," he blustered.

"Love. Well, you're the expert, aren't you?" I almost choked on my bitterness. "Of course you love her. She's young and beautiful and it makes you feel good to have someone pretty like that at your side and in your bed always puffing you up. I'm just trying to figure out what she sees in you." I picked up my jacket and pushed him aside to leave.

"Stop it."

"Or what?" I snarled. "You'll never speak to me again? What a shame."

I left my office and the hospital, the curious need to see Ethan growing by leaps and bounds with each passing minute. I rarely escaped during the day, and now it was twice in a row, but I didn't care. I put my hand out to hail a cab, and one pulled up not ten seconds later.

"Macy's Herald Square."

Lunchtime traffic was heavy, and what should've been a short ride took forever. I strode through the Seventh Avenue entrance and up the escalator to the mezzanine, where I searched for Ethan but didn't see him, only a lone salesperson ringing up a customer. I waited for him to finish, my foot tapping impatiently.

"May I help you, sir?"

It wasn't Ethan's overly nosy manager. This was a young Hispanic man with a neatly trimmed beard, wearing a sharp navy suit.

"Did Ethan come in today?"

"No, he's not here."

"Do you know when he will be?"

"I'm sorry. I'm just filling in."

Disappointment slammed into me, and without another word, I walked away. Where the hell was he? Did something happen? Was he sick? I burst through the glass doors onto busy Seventh Avenue, wanting to take the train to Brooklyn and Ethan's apartment and bang on the door. Instead, I decided to walk the blocks uptown and clear my head from the news I'd received. My father was about to have a child. I'd have a sibling forty-three years my junior.

I tramped on, feet hurting in shoes not meant for long distances, but I didn't care. I'd sneered at my father for marrying a woman young enough to be his daughter, and meanwhile, I was lusting over a man twelve years younger, whom I barely knew. A man I met on the subway, for Christ's sake.

A month ago, I'd been content and worry free.

What the hell was going on with me?

CHAPTER ▶ 14

I probably should've told Nash I had a day off, but I'd only remembered when the car drove off, and I had no way to get in touch with him. I used the day to take my dry cleaning to the store and do my laundry and some grocery shopping. Thank God my apartment was so small, there wasn't much to clean. I put a bandanna around my hair to keep it from falling in my face and tackled the tub. At five, I'd finished the bathroom and was about to pop open a beer and put my feet up when the doorbell rang.

At the sight of Gladys, my landlady, I smiled and opened the door. As usual, she didn't wait for me to ask her inside but hustled past me, the familiar scent of her Charlie perfume clogging my nostrils.

I sneezed several times, and she fixed me with her dark eyes. "You got a cold? I can make you chicken soup."

"No!" I exclaimed, maybe a bit too loudly. "I'm fine."

Gladys was a wonderful cook, but she put enough garlic in her chicken soup to kill a cemetery full of vampires. The one time I'd had it, Oscar complained the smell was coming out of my pores for days.

"I'll bring it anyway."

I didn't bother to respond. Once she got something in her head, not even the Pope could change her mind.

"What's new? I ain't seen you much lately."

Gladys and Pete's only child had gotten herself mixed up with the wrong crowd in high school and was killed in a drive-by shooting ten years earlier. Gladys had appointed herself my surrogate-mother-slash-buttinski, but I didn't mind. I understood her pain.

With Pete getting older, I often helped him around the place, like wrestling the garbage pails to the curb, changing light bulbs, or lugging their heavy grocery bags up the stoop and into their apartment. I also got them my Macy's employee discount for anything they needed. It was a far cry from Nash's luxury building, where I was sure no one had to lift a finger.

Perks of being a bazillionaire.

"Been busy, you know how it is. Gotta keep hustling."

"That no-good jerk ain't been by again, right?" She plopped herself down on the sofa, and I had to bite my lip as her feet barely touched the ground. I went to make her a cup of tea.

"Oscar? Nah. I think he finally got the message. But could Pete change the lock? I keep forgetting to call, and Oscar made a copy of the keys before he gave me his back."

"I'll make sure he does." She jabbed a finger at me. "That no-good bum cheating on you." Now that Oscar and I were no longer together, she was free to indulge in her bashing. "He don't deserve a nice boy like you." She sniffed.

My heart squeezed. My own parents hadn't shown a smidgen of the care and concern Gladys and Pete did. After that one trip early on after they'd moved to Texas, I spent the holidays with the Russos since I'd moved in.

"I'm not worried. I have to concentrate on my job now."

"You got a new one?" She smacked her leg. "Darn it. I haven't had a chance to go through the sales yet to pick out stuff for you to order and use your employee discount. Once you move over to all that fancy stuff, I can't afford nothing like that."

The kettle whistled, and I poured the hot water over the tea bag and added the milk. "Here you go. And no, I'm not leaving. Change of plans." I set the mug on the table. "I've decided to stay where I am and try to move up there. I think I have a better chance at meeting people and getting the contacts I need for the future from a huge store."

"Good. Smart. You're thinking." She tapped her head. "A place like that can only help you. Now you gotta find someone who's gonna treat you right. I got my eyes open, don't you worry."

Gladys also moonlighted as my matchmaker and was forever coming home from shopping expeditions with sightings of men she'd determined were boyfriend material. One time she'd even gotten a phone number. Relentlessness, thy name is Gladys.

"I'm fine. I'd rather concentrate on my career and not get into anything serious. I was with Oscar for three years, and I think I need a breather. You know, have some fun."

Could uptight Nash Roman be considered fun? I was pretty serious about wanting him inside me.

"You gotta be careful these days. Too many weirdos out there. I watch those shows. They'll say anything to get you alone, and then *bam*!" She smacked the couch. "They got you naked and tied up and—"

"Okay, okay, I get the picture. Trust me, I'm careful."

The buzzer sounded.

"You expecting company?" She took another sip of her tea.

"No." I hit the buzzer. "Who is it?"

"Nash."

A thrill ran from my toes to my chest, and I hit the button to open the door. Why was he here?

"Who is it?" Gladys asked.

Oh, God. The thought of Gladys interrogating Nash wasn't on my bingo card, and a wave of terror rolled through me. "A friend."

Her eyes narrowed. "*Hmm.* Ain't never heard you mention his name before."

I heard Nash's heavy tread on the stairs and took Gladys's cup to the sink. "Thanks for stopping by."

"I see what you're doing. Don't rush me out. I'll just make sure I get a good look at him. You know, in case I need to identify him later."

"I need to tell Pete he's got to cut you off from those serial-killer shows," I muttered and wrenched open the door. Nash gazed at me from the top step.

"You're okay?"

I screwed up my face. "Uh, yeah. Why?"

"You weren't at work. I thought something happened."

"Oh…sorry."

"Ahem." At my elbow, Gladys cleared her throat.

"This is my landlady, Gladys Russo. She was just leaving." I pushed open the door wider, but who was I kidding? Gladys would leave when she was damn well ready.

"After I say hello." She made no secret of checking out Nash, her inquisitive eyes sweeping over him. "You and Ethan are friends?"

Nash graced her with a slight smile. "Yes. I think we are."

"You think?" She crossed her arms and cocked her head. "You're older."

"I am," he acknowledged with a dip of his head.

To my surprise, she grinned. "I like that. You don't look like you're one of them party boys."

"Furthest thing from it." Nash caught my eye and raised his brows. "May I come in?"

"Sure," Gladys answered for me. "I'm leaving anyway. I gotta go downstairs and make dinner. Nice to meetcha."

"Same, Gladys." He stepped aside to let her pass. When her footsteps faded, he came inside, and I closed the door. "Sorry for barging in on you."

"I forgot to tell you I wasn't working today, and since I don't have your number, I couldn't. Want to sit? I can offer you a beer or water…" He didn't sit and moved closer to me.

"I didn't come here for refreshments."

My heart slammed. "Then what did you come here for?"

He blinked, and the vision of him ripping my clothes off vanished at the flash of pain and confusion in those normally cool blue eyes.

"Come on." I pointed him to the couch, where he dropped down and rested his head in his hands. I sat next to him. "What happened?"

"I was feeling pretty good after last night. No, not good. Great. So when you didn't show up this morning, I thought maybe you were upset…or that you regretted what happened."

"No," I blurted out. "No way. I enjoyed being with you. The whole evening, not just what happened between us."

A faint flush rose to his cheeks. "Yeah. Me too." He ducked his head. "That's why I was surprised not to see you. I even went to your job, but they said you weren't in."

"Is everything okay? I get the feeling it's more than just me not being on the 2 train this morning."

Nash clasped his hands together. "I had a surprise visit from my father and his wife." He huffed out a humorless laugh. "She's only a few years older than you."

"What did they want?"

His hands balled into fists, and his face turned cold. "I'm going to have a baby brother or sister. Isn't that great?"

"Apparently you don't think so."

Nash rose. "I shouldn't have come."

"I disagree." I jumped up and caught his arm. "And you did, so talk to me." I held on to him. "You're not happy with the announcement."

"He's my father and seventy years old. I'm forty-three. He seems to think I should be thrilled. As thrilled as him."

"I understand."

"Do you?" He faced me. "Explain it to me, then. Am I wrong for feeling like this?"

"Like what?"

"Like I'm not good enough, like I'm being replaced. Like I'm six and he's walking away from us…from me…all over again. It's silly, I know, because I'm an adult and I don't want him in my life. And I don't dislike his wife. She's trying her hardest to be nice, but I'm letting my anger toward my father color everything around me. I don't know…*should* I be happy about this baby? I know I should. I'm rambling…" He trailed off. "I told you. Silly."

I placed my hands on his shoulders, and his troubled gaze met mine. "Not silly. Human. It's natural to be knocked off your feet by news like this. I can't imagine how you feel."

His hot breath hit my cheek. "You knocked me off my feet."

"I did?"

The sadness in his face retreated, and tenderness took its place. "You do." Sparks fired in his eyes. "Like now."

His mouth met mine, and I clung to his broad shoulders, moaning with relief as he sucked my tongue. I worked his belt off and unzipped his slacks while he yanked at my pants, sending them to my ankles.

"Thank God for elastic waistbands." I sighed. He cupped my ass and gave a squeeze, then ran a finger up and down the crease. I shivered when he touched the rim of my hole.

"Thank God for this," he whispered.

"Come on." I kicked off my pants, and he did the same, removing his shoes and socks. I led him to the rear of the apartment where behind a screen, I had the futon I used as a bed. "Sorry it's not like what you're used to."

He caught my face between his hands. "I'm not used to wanting someone as much as I want you. When I didn't see you this morning, I couldn't stop thinking…what if something happened to him? What if I don't see him again?"

My eager hands undid his tie, flicked open the buttons to his shirt, and pushed it off his shoulders. I pulled off my T-shirt and kissed him. "I'm here now. And I want you."

Kissing frantically, we sank to the bed in a warm tangle of arms and legs. Nash's eyes blazed as he rolled me under him, and he sucked the tender skin at the base of my neck. "I don't care about anything now except being inside you. I need that."

"I need it too."

He parted my legs and slid between my thighs, his mouth trailing a wet path down my belly and skipping my aching cock. When his lips touched my rim, I writhed and gasped.

"Fuck, Nash."

"Shh." He licked over the hole before slipping his tongue inside, and I moaned from the excruciatingly sweet lust shooting through me. He left me way too soon, and I cried out, the craving for his touch as necessary as the air I breathed.

"Please, Nash. Please."

"Where's your lube? And condoms?" He stroked himself, and I couldn't take my eyes off his big, beautiful dick.

I tipped my head to the low table next to the futon, and he opened the drawer and pulled them out. "Come close first." He slid onto me, and I wrapped my arms around his shoulders, lining up our shafts, and rocked against him. The beautiful friction created an almost painful pleasure, and I could've kept up that motion forever.

His fingers, slick with lube, entered me, and I shivered in anticipation as he stretched me to fit him. When the head of his cock inched into me, I gripped him tight and pushed up to meet his thrust, taking him fully. The fierce intensity captured me, sucking me into a desire I'd never known existed before Nash.

This wasn't sex—it was ownership. Nash took me apart and put me together, piece by piece, into a man made solely for him. He drove in deep…deeper, and I hooked my leg over his hip, locking him in.

"I'm not letting you go, Nash."

He kissed me until I couldn't breathe and whispered, "Who said I want to leave?"

When his fingers grasped my cock and rubbed me from throbbing root to sticky tip, I lost control and came so hard, I saw stars.

"Oh, God." I sighed, and Nash hissed as I clamped hard on his dick, still pumping hard and fast.

"Fuck. Me. God. Damn." He slammed me into the mattress and came, collapsing on top of me with a noisy sigh.

I could've lain with him in my arms forever, his lips pressed to my hair, listening to the thunder of his heartbeat. I kissed the pulsing vein at the base of his neck and licked the warm skin, tasting the salty tang of his sweat.

"That was very nice," I murmured, not wanting to break the magic.

"It was." He slipped out of me and rolled over to get rid of the condom. I watched him, unsure whether he'd be staying, but then he pulled the sheet over him and scooted in closer to me. "Very."

"Do you—no, forget it." I couldn't believe I'd almost said what was on my mind.

He propped himself up on his elbow. "Do I what?"

Instead of answering, I gazed around my tiny apartment, taking in the old-fashioned, tiny white stove and fridge and dingy Formica countertops. No gleaming wooden floors and quartz countertops for me. I tried to paint the apartment every three or four years and got some bright cushions from Target, but that was about as much redecorating as I could afford.

He cupped my cheek, forcing me to meet his eyes. "What is it?"

"I was wondering if you wanted to, uh, stay…you know…the night. But then I realized that was ridiculous, since you have a big, gorgeous apartment with a king-sized bed. Why would you want to stay here, on an old, lumpy futon?"

His thumb played over my cheek. "You're right. Why would I? It's bad for my back."

My heart dropped to my knees. I knew I wasn't part of his world, but damn, I'd never felt the divide as big and wide until that moment. "Yeah, well, whatever. It's fine."

"Come home with me instead. We'll stay at my place."

Unable to believe what I was hearing, I gaped at him. "Your place?"

"Yeah." A light danced in his eyes, and he leaned in and kissed me. "Bring your stuff. We'll take the train together in the morning. I have a king-sized bed, after all. It's waiting."

CHAPTER ▶ 15

I woke up first, but instead of getting out of bed, I watched Ethan sleeping in my bed. A first, because I never had anyone stay over, but after what happened between us, I wasn't about to leave him alone.

He needed to be here. With me.

Well-muscled shoulders led to the strong curve of his back, dark hair curled at his nape, and I longed to kiss him from the top of his spine to his tight ass. Already full, my cock swelled further, and I squeezed the base to hold in the ache.

"I can feel you staring at me." Ethan chuckled, his husky morning voice the stuff dreams were made of.

"I like looking at you in my bed. You're gorgeous lying there naked and waiting."

"Oh, yeah? What am I waiting for?" He rolled over, his heavy dick standing straight up, and I forgot everything except the greedy hunger to taste him.

"Not what, but whom." I closed my lips over the fat

head of his cock and sucked, enjoying the sounds of his groans and whimpers rising in the quiet. I moved faster and teased his shaft with my tongue. His hips bucked hard, and he came, shooting hot cream I couldn't wait to swallow.

"Mmm. Good morning to me." I licked my lips, and Ethan waved his hand. "Get over here. You're not the only one who gets a breakfast treat." Surprising me with his quick movement, he pushed me down and nuzzled my groin.

He licked my balls before sliding his mouth over the throbbing length of my shaft. I tried to prolong the pleasure of his wicked, teasing tongue, but without warning, my orgasm ripped through me, and I came, clutching the sheets between my fingers. Ethan kept up the pressure on my cock, sucking me dry.

I fell back on the bed, my heart threatening to burst through my chest. A smirk rested on Ethan's lips as he sat on his heels and surveyed me, lying wrecked and breathless.

"Just making sure you won't forget me while you're at work."

With a wink and a cocky grin, he swung off the bed. "I'm gonna take a shower." He grabbed the duffel bag he'd dropped on the floor and entered the bathroom.

Forget him? That was becoming a frightening impossibility. I rubbed my face and picked up my phone from the nightstand. A slew of texts and calendar notifications awaited, and it was only six thirty in the morning. I passed over the meeting alerts as I had them all covered, and opened the text from my father.

Don't you think it's time to act like an adult? You're going to have a sibling, and I want you to be in the child's life.

I closed my eyes. Goddammit, it was way too early to be bombarded. It wasn't the child or even Diana who caused me pain. But he had no regrets for what he'd done, and I couldn't forgive him.

I read the next text, which was from Julia: *Where have*

you been hiding yourself? Dinner tonight. I won't take no for an answer.

"I'm afraid you'll have to, Julia." I typed back: *Sorry. I have plans.*

I set the phone on the bed and went to surprise Ethan in the shower.

The train pulled into 34th Street, and Ethan nudged me. "I'll talk to you later? At least this time we remembered to exchange numbers. I should be out of work by four at the latest."

"I get home around seven. Meet me at my place." It didn't make sense to stay at Ethan's when my apartment was so big. So empty.

I didn't know if Ethan expected a kiss good-bye, but I didn't believe in public displays of affection. Maybe he sensed it because he gave my arm a squeeze and took off. Of course someone immediately sat their ass in the vacated seat, their elbows overlapping into my personal space.

"Thank God. I gotta ride all the way to Gun Hill Road, and my feet are killing me." The woman set her large tote bag on her lap and pulled out a smelly tuna sandwich.

My stomach turned over. It was eight in the morning. Who the hell ate that shit so early? I mouth-breathed.

"Hope you don't mind, but I'm starving and worked all night. First chance I got to sit."

Giving a shake of my head, I stuck my face in my paper. I wasn't about to say no. Who knew what else she had in that giant bag of hers? I was grateful for her lack of table manners—if that was even a possibility when you ate on the subway—as she chomped that puppy down in less than six bites.

The train stopped, and I folded the paper, rose to my feet, and left. Even the crush of humanity on the platform was preferable to sitting next to Tuna Lady. Above ground, I walked and took deep breaths of semi-clean air, picked up my coffee from the cart outside the hospital, and made it to my office, where I could finally sit in peace.

But that state of mind eluded me—all I could think about was Ethan. In my bed. I'd never woken up with anyone before. Staring into his heavy-lidded eyes under all that messy hair wasn't anything I'd planned but now dreaded losing.

Stop being an idiot. He's had boyfriends. He's already said he gets lonely. This is another way to pass the time.

My door opened, and Alex's blond head popped in. "Hey. How's it going?" Without asking because, well, it was Alex, he plopped himself in the chair in front of my desk and stretched out his long legs.

"Good morning to you too." I sipped my coffee. "Did you need something?"

He snorted and drank from his travel mug. "You know, in this friendship thing, this is how people act. They say hello, occasionally meet for lunch or dinner, and check in on each other to see how they're doing."

"Thanks. Hello, I'm fine, how are you? I can't do lunch, and I've got dinner plans." I smirked. "How's that?"

"You're a natural." Alex rolled his eyes. "Seriously. Whatever happened with that guy we had dinner with… Ethan?" Alex waggled his brows. "He's a cutie."

I could only imagine what Alex would say if he found out I'd slept with Ethan and was seeing him again tonight. The teasing would never end.

"I don't know."

Alex's grin vanished. "So you never asked him out? Dammit, Nash. What's wrong with you?"

"Oh, cut it out. I'm too old for this stuff. I'm busy, I

have meetings."

"You always have meetings. That's your damn job. But you know what? I have important work too. Labs to run and patients to see. I'm still taking the time to try to be a friend here. You're forty-three, not ninety. And I bet there are ninety-year-olds getting more action than you."

Before last night, I might've agreed with him. I'd always thought sex was predictable, and while pleasurable, slightly overrated. Then Ethan blew my mind, and I wanted more of him.

"What're you afraid of?" He rolled the chair closer. "Is it because he's a man? Do you not want people to know you're bisexual?"

"I don't give a damn what people think."

Alex held my unblinking gaze and gave a sharp nod. "All right. Well, if it's an age thing, you're being ridiculous. He's not that young. And if not that…what the hell is the problem?"

"There is no problem," I snapped. "I have work to do. I'm sure you're aware of the huge donation to the cancer center. That's supposed to take up all my time, not sitting here gabbing with you about whom I'm dating."

"You're right." Alex rose to his feet. "But when you go home at night, you can't talk about your hopes and dreams to a spreadsheet. And budget allocations won't keep you warm. See you, Nash."

The door closed behind him, and I hated how guilty I felt. I should've called out and told him to stop, except my phone buzzed.

"Roman," I clipped out.

"Nash. I want to talk to you. Please don't hang up."

Guess it wasn't true that Mondays were the worst day of the week. Here it was a Thursday, and I'd already had an argument with Alex, the closest thing I had to a friend, and now my father wanted to talk. Again.

"I'm here."

"The hospital is planning an event around the Ahmeds' philanthropy. I'm the guest of honor. I'd like it if you'd come."

A headache throbbed behind my eyes. "You don't need me there."

"Please, Nash? Hasn't enough time passed that you can forgive me for what I did?"

Surprised, I stared at the phone. "Are you asking for forgiveness?" He'd never admitted making a mistake, so this was new territory.

"I'd like to talk about it. In person, not over the phone. Can we have dinner tonight?"

"I have plans."

I heard beeping on his side, and he huffed out a sigh. "I have to go. You decide when. Just know I'm here." The phone went dead.

The rest of the morning passed without incident, and I managed to make it through half of my to-do list. My stomach growled, and I was about to order a sandwich when Julia called.

"I haven't seen you in a while. Let's have lunch."

"I was just going to order a sandwich," I said, hoping she'd get the hint.

"That's fine. Get me a Cobb salad, dressing on the side. I'll be by in fifteen."

She ended the call, and I shook my head. Maybe it was time to tell her to move on to someone else. She wouldn't care. It's wasn't as if we were a couple or even dating.

She showed up as the delivery person was leaving and sat at the table. "Isn't it wonderful about the Ahmeds' gift to the hospital?"

I unwrapped my turkey sandwich and took a bite, chewed, and swallowed. "It is. I'm neck-deep in funding allocation and making sure it all gets directed properly, as the family wants."

She picked at the lettuce. "As I see it, she'll approve anything your father wants." Her fork jabbed into the salad. "And as to that little golden nugget of info…how come you never mentioned Martin Roman was your father?"

I shrugged and took another bite. "It has nothing to do with me."

Well-groomed brows shot up high. "He's one of the foremost cancer researchers in the world, and you say it's nothing? Do you know how influential he is in this hospital? Even before the money the Ahmed family gave, he could ask for and get whatever he wanted."

Except me.

"Like I told you, it has no bearing on me."

Her pink tongue swept across her lips. "I'm reviewing the legal papers of the trust. Maybe we should all get together and talk about it."

"No need. I have a copy of the documents. If I have a question, I can ask you."

"Okay." Her eyes flashed for a second. "I heard he and Diana are having a baby."

"Oh?" I wasn't aware they'd made the news public. "Are you that friendly?"

"We go to the same gym and take Pilates together. We didn't realize it until we saw each other the night of the event. She's very nice."

I said nothing, and we ate in silence. When we finished, she took a small mirror from her purse and reapplied her lipstick. I wished I knew how to gently ask her to leave without seeming like a huge asshole.

"How about tonight? I'm not busy." Finished with her makeup refresh, she rolled her chair closer and walked her fingers up my thigh. "I miss you."

"Me? You miss me?"

"Mmm, yeah. We always have a good time together."

Before I knew what she was doing, she was sitting on my lap and pressing her lips to mine. Then she whispered, "We can have a quickie right now to get in the mood for later. I'll lock the door."

"No. Julia. Please stop." I set her on her feet and stood. "We need to stop seeing each other."

"What? Why?" She gazed up at me wide-eyed.

"I'm sure you'll have no problem replacing me."

"Just like that?" She laughed. "I don't think so. You're just tired from all the work surrounding the Ahmed funding." Dark hair tumbling around her shoulders, she picked up her purse and kissed me, her tongue flickering against my lips, but I didn't open for her. "I'll call you later."

I had a feeling no one had ever said no to Julia Nickerson, but I forgot about her when I got a text from Ethan.

Do you want me to pick up dinner before coming to you?

I smiled, knowing his independence was important to him.

Sure. Whatever you want. I'm easy.

His reply was immediate.

That's what I'm hoping.

A winky emoji followed, making me laugh.

Which reminded me. I knew I had something important to set straight. My conversation that morning with Alex gnawed at me, and I sat for a few minutes before making a decision. An apology warranted a face-to-face, not me acting like a coward, hiding behind the phone.

The fifth floor of Mercy Hospital was dedicated entirely to cancer research. In all my years at the hospital, I'd never been there, and when I stepped off the elevator, I had no idea where to go. I flagged down a passing individual with an ID tag around her neck.

"Excuse me. I'm looking for Dr. Stern? Alex Stern?"

"He's in the lab, but you can't go in there now. They're running tests." She checked her watch. "They should be done in about ten minutes. Would you like me to tell him you'd like to speak with him?"

"Yes, I'd appreciate it. Tell him it's Nash."

She threw me a quick smile and hurried off through the swinging doors marked CENTER FOR Research and Development. I knew other hospitals in the city, much bigger and with worldwide recognition, had entire buildings dedicated to finding a cure for cancer, and I was certain the incredibly generous donation Mercy had received from the Ahmed family alone would benefit many critically ill people. I'd already begun gathering grant proposals from scientists and researchers eager to be part of this tremendous opportunity. I had meetings set up for the next several months with various universities to provide scholarships for graduate students, all with the ultimate goal of eradicating this disease.

My father had been in California when he'd treated Mr. Ahmed, and they'd followed him to New York. Regardless of what I thought of him as a parent, I knew he was an exceptional doctor.

I paced the hallway, practicing in my head how to best start off the conversation. Alex didn't deserve my bad mood.

"Nash?"

I turned to see Alex standing in his white lab jacket over his button-down and Daffy Duck tie. I'd been so in my own head this morning, I hadn't paid attention to him.

"Nice outfit."

Alex picked up his tie and flipped the end at me. "Thanks. My son helped pick it out." He leaned against the wall. "I was told you were waiting to talk to me?"

"Yeah." I glanced around, unwilling to get too personal in such a public space.

Perhaps sensing that, Alex tipped his head. "Come with me. I know a spot." I followed him to an empty room. Alex pointed to a couch tucked in the corner. "Let's sit."

In business I had no issues with confrontation, but facing

off with someone I liked, put me at a disadvantage. Maybe because it was a rarity. I didn't like most people.

"I…I'm…sorry for being an asshole."

"When?" Alex's smile widened, lighting up his bright-blue eyes. "There are so many instances. Narrow it down for me."

"This morning. In my office. You know, when you asked me about Ethan. I shouldn't have snapped at you."

"No, you shouldn't have. I was trying to be a friend."

Chastened, I hung my head. "I know. I don't really have many of those. I tend to keep to myself."

"Look. I don't know why you're afraid, but I think you and Ethan could be great together."

"I'm not afraid." I looked everywhere but at Alex's face.

"Lie to me all you want, but if you're lying to yourself and you push him away, it's your loss."

"I-I know. It's just…he and I…together…it doesn't make sense."

"Love doesn't have to make sense. It only has to make you happy."

I stared at him. Love? I wasn't in love with Ethan. I barely knew him.

"Because he's younger. And so…so…" I faltered, and Alex jumped.

"So what? Come on, Nash. Say it."

"Alive. He's so alive, and I'm not."

"But you *are* with him, right? You've been together since that time we had dinner, haven't you?"

"Yes." A sharp jerk of my head.

"And?" Alex pressed me. "You have feelings for him."

I met his eyes and couldn't lie. "He makes me want to take the risk."

Alex grabbed my arm. "Do it. Take that step."

"We're so different. I don't know if it can work. Or how."

"Forget about age and money. That's all bullshit. Rafe

and I are complete opposites. He's the yin to my yang, the calm to my storm. I didn't know how much I needed him until I had him. When you find the person who completes you, you grab on to that missing piece of yourself and never let go." His phone beeped, and he made a face. "Shit. I gotta go."

"Thank you for this. I really appreciate it."

"I hope it helped." He winked, and of course, because he was Alex, had to get one last zinger in. "Go home tonight and make sure you get lucky." Laughing to himself, he walked away.

Taking advantage of the quiet, I sat for a moment. I had Ethan as a lover and Alex as a friend. I was already the lucky one.

CHAPTER ▶ 16

"You got a date?"

I'd come home from work, showered and dressed again, in casual but nicer clothes than if I'd been bumming around my apartment. I didn't think Nash would care, but I didn't want to stand out in his high-end condo. I brushed back my wet hair while Gladys sat on my couch.

"Yeah. I have to pick up dinner first."

"I got something for you. Wait a sec." Before I could say no, she hopped up from her seat and dashed out of my place. I hadn't seen her move so fast since she found out Key Food had a 99-cent-a-pound special on ground beef.

Laughing to myself, I pocketed my wallet and slipped bare feet into soft loafers—not the Tod's I coveted, but my outlet Coach pair. They'd have to do. My phone buzzed, and I rolled my eyes when I saw it was Oscar. He wouldn't give up, and I finally blocked his number.

I heard Gladys stomping up the steps and huffing.

"Here. I made lasagna, and there was so much, I got an

extra tray. Take it." She held it out to me.

"Thanks, but…are you sure? I don't want Pete to go hungry."

She snorted. "He can live off the fat of the land—his doctors told him to lose some weight. So, is this the same guy I met the other day? The one in the fancy suit? What does he do?"

"Yeah. He's got something to do with finances for Mercy Hospital. I'm not sure what, but I know it's a big deal." Feeling a little self-conscious, I stared at the floor. "We're having dinner at his place. It's one of those expensive condos by Prospect Park."

"Hey."

I glanced up to find her dark eyes on me. "What?"

"Don't think you ain't good enough. You deserve the best. And don't let him talk you into anything you don't like."

The thought of Nash whispering sweet nothings made me smile.

"You got your overnight bag packed?"

My brows rose, and I burst into laughter. "Gladys, you little devil." I picked up the tray of lasagna. "And yes, I do."

"Good. He seems better than that no-good cheater."

"Gee, Gladys, I thought you liked me."

Oscar stood at my door, and Gladys glared at him. "What're you doing here?"

"I came to talk to Ethan in person since he blocked me on his phone."

"Well, he don't wanna talk to you."

Oscar leaned against the doorframe and smirked. "You let little old ladies talk for you now, Ethan?"

"Who're you calling old?" Her face a thundercloud, she placed her hands on her hips.

"Don't you speak to her like that. And why are you here after I've told you, *repeatedly*, to leave me alone?"

"Because I missed you, baby."

Gladys snorted, and I put a hand on her shoulder. "Thanks for the lasagna. I'll talk to you tomorrow." I kissed her cheek.

"You and your boyfriend enjoy it." She shot Oscar a triumphant look as she walked past. "He's such a busy, important man, he don't have time for home cooking. I know he'll appreciate it."

While I loved Gladys, I didn't need her fighting my battles for me, so I waited until she disappeared down the stairs. Oscar took a step, and I put out a hand. "Stop. I didn't invite you in. Give me that key."

The smirk grew broader. He held it up, and I grabbed it from his hand. Ignoring my warning, he moved past me and came inside. The small apartment closed further in around me. "You got a boyfriend already? And here you bitched about me cheating when I bet you were letting someone in all the time."

"Shut up, and get out."

He pushed my duffel off the couch. "Going somewhere?"

"None of your business."

"I think it is." He leaned in for a kiss, and this time I decided he needed to be taught a lesson and kneed him in the groin. He shrieked with pain, his face growing red.

Pete stood at the door with a baseball bat in hand. "Feel like hitting some balls, Ethan?"

My pounding heart subsided, and I'd never been more grateful to see his face. "Thanks, but I think I took care of that."

Pete glanced at Oscar clutching his crotch but remained where he stood. "Gladys said to pick up some garlic bread too before you leave." He rested the bat on his shoulder. "You want me to take out the trash?"

Oscar limped away, muttering, "You're gonna be sorry."

Pete grabbed him by the arm. "You threatening me? Or Ethan? Either way, that ain't smart. Now get the fuck outta here and throw away any other copies of that key I know you have 'cause I'm changing all the locks." He tossed Oscar out and slammed the door.

Maybe Oscar had forgotten that Pete was a retired cop who'd spent twenty-four years walking a beat in Brownsville and had seen it all. Handling a punk like Oscar was child's play to him.

"Thanks, Pete."

"Don't worry about it. You need a good deadbolt, and I'm gonna call my buddies at the precinct and have them do a few drives around to make sure that weasel leaves you alone." He leaned on the bat. "Maybe you should file a report, for like…stalking? They got laws for that, you know."

"I don't want it to get to that point. I'm sure he's got the hint this time."

Pete scratched his chin. "I dunno. Guy like that…he's got that vibe. Like if he can't have you, no one can."

I picked up my duffel bag from the floor and hefted it to my shoulder. "I'm pretty unforgettable, but he'll stop once he can't get into the building anymore." Maybe I was naïve, but I didn't want to ruin Oscar's life by getting him arrested. I just wanted him to leave me alone.

Pete laughed. "Okay, Romeo. Let's go get your garlic bread so you won't be late for Prince Charming."

I grabbed the lasagna and followed Pete.

Nash greeted me at the door. He'd changed out of his suit and wore jeans and a long-sleeved T-shirt. Damn, how'd a guy ever get this lucky? Who thought my flirting on the 2 would lead to this? Although I couldn't exactly put a word to what *this* was.

"You're staring at me. Do you want to come in, or stay out in the hall?"

Making certain to keep it nonchalant, I breezed past him and kicked off my shoes, leaving them in the foyer. "Look at you, being all cute and funny."

Nash shut the door behind me. "You must be rubbing off on me."

I handed him the lasagna. "That comes later, after dinner. Which I brought. My landlady made it."

"Here I thought you slaved all day over a hot stove in a little apron." He set the tray on the kitchen counter.

"I'd look cute. And while I have many talents, cooking isn't one of them."

He kissed me and nuzzled my ear. "Yeah? Like the aforementioned rubbing off?"

"I love it when you use big words like that," I whispered.

"What? Rubbing?" His eyes danced, and my heart stuttered.

Oh, God. I'm going to fall in love with him.

"Are you hungry?"

"Mmm," he murmured against my cheek. "Famished. Starving." Hot lips touching my ear made it impossible for me to think. Or breathe.

"G-good. There's garlic bread too. I hope you like Italian."

"I like you. Are you Italian?"

I smiled. "I'm many things. A mix."

"My favorite thing."

He settled his mouth over mine, and I held him tight. It wasn't a simple kiss. Nothing Nash did was. He owned me, and when he was done, we stood apart, blinking and staring at each other like the world had shifted and we needed to find our footing again.

"I-I'll take your bag into the bedroom."

He retreated, and I unwrapped the tray and put it and

the garlic bread in the oven to warm. When he returned, I watched as he opened a bottle of red wine and poured himself a glass.

"I have beer for you."

"Would you mind?"

"Of course not. Whatever you want." He opened the fridge and handed me a bottle.

"I grew up in a beer-and-potato-chip house. We didn't see much wine. I don't know a Chablis from a Chardonnay."

"I said it before, I don't care what you drink, Ethan. And I love potato chips. Jalapeño flavor."

"Ahh, you like it hot and spicy?"

Ignoring my attempt at humor, he fixed me with that penetrating icy gaze of his. "Tell me about your life growing up. You rarely speak about your parents."

My gut tightened. "Not much to tell. We were middle-class, able to put food on the table and take a yearly vacation to the Jersey Shore, but not much more. One year my father did really well, and we got to go to Disney World. He didn't want my mother working—he was one of those old-fashioned men who believed the wife stayed home—so money was often tight. Our house was in constant need of repairs, and my father spent all his free time working on it."

"That says nothing about why you barely have a relationship with them."

My lips trembled. "You'd have to ask them. It's not from my lack of trying, at least in the beginning. Once I came out, they backed away. All the way to Texas. It wasn't even a discussion. One day they told me the house was sold and they were leaving for better work opportunities for my father, where they didn't have to put up with the high crime, high taxes, and all the welfare people in the city. If I wanted to come, I was welcome, but since I was eighteen, they made it perfectly clear I'd be on my own no matter what." I forced a smile. "As welcoming as that invitation was, I turned it down."

"I'm sorry."

I hated the sympathy in Nash's eyes. I wanted fire and lust.

"How often have you seen them?"

"I made one trip, the year after they left, but they'd developed a social circle of like-minded people where a gay son didn't exactly fit in. After listening to enough jokes about immigrants and gays and why their agenda is destroying the country for the real patriots, I decided I was better off staying put. They didn't try and change my mind."

"It's their loss," he said softly. "And my gain." Nash's grin came and went like the wind. "Even if you don't know about wine."

"Is that a challenge?" The knots in my stomach loosened. "I'm a fast learner. Teach me." I set my beer on the counter and pointed to the empty wineglass.

He poured a small amount. "Swirl it gently." He showed me how, and I followed his lead. "That allows it to breathe and opens up the flavors of the grapes. Sip it slowly, letting it rest on your tongue before swallowing."

This was a whole lot better than the two-dollar bottles we used to smuggle into parties in high school. "It's good."

He chuckled. "You don't have to say you like it on my account." He set the wine on the counter and walked to the refrigerator, opened it, and pointed to the six-pack of Heineken with one bottle missing. "Feel free."

"After I finish my wine."

I opened the oven, peeking in to make sure the garlic bread didn't burn, and Nash tipped his head and sniffed. "That smells amazing."

"I told you Gladys is a good cook. And she likes you, so we both reap the benefit."

"She does?"

"Yeah. She thinks you're a good influence—someone stable, who'll treat me right. Not like Oscar. She couldn't stand him." I didn't bother to tell him Oscar had shown up again.

"I'm not sure about the good-influence part."

"Oh, I am. You're the good one. I'm bad." I looped my arms around Nash's neck. "Like, right now I'm thinking, I know you have a nice table and all that, but I've never eaten lasagna in bed."

He licked his lips. "Me neither."

"I'll get the bowls."

An hour later, we'd demolished half the tray and all the garlic bread. Nash brushed the crumbs next to him off the bed. "I'll be feeling these all night long."

I took his bowl. "Stop being such a grouch. We can just change the sheets."

"Huh. The cleaning service comes tomorrow and usually does it, but that works."

Obviously, Nash wasn't the type to do his own laundry. "I hope it won't strain your back."

Shooting me a deadly look, he narrowed his eyes. "Is that a way of calling me old?"

My smile was sweet. "I would never." And fluttered my lashes.

Nash grunted and stripped the bed, moving the covers and pillows to the floor. He shook out the king-sized sheet and crawled over the bed, ass in the air to tuck in the corners. I joined him but wasn't much help as I was too busy touching him.

"You're not letting me finish," he growled, the third time he pushed my hands off his butt.

"Listen. You're gonna stick something so pretty in my face, I'm gonna want to touch it. That's how it works."

Nash didn't respond, instead flipping me over and under him. "This is how *I* work." Unsmiling, he leaned in close, and my breath caught. He ran his mouth down and across my cheek. "You've undone me."

Trembling, I held on to his shoulders and let my lips and tongue show how much I wanted him. He groaned, my hands on the button tab of his jeans, when the bell rang.

"Ignore it," he panted. "It's probably a mistake." He pulled my shirt off, and I tugged his over his head and ran my hands over his chest. God, I wanted to lick him from head to toe.

"What're you thinking?" He kissed me and tugged at my lip. "You have a look in your eyes…"

"How good you're going to taste."

The bell ringing had stopped, but now someone began knocking insistently on the door.

"Goddammit, who the hell is it?" Nash stomped out of the bedroom, and I waited for a second to catch my breath, then followed him but stood at the far end of the living room while he threw open the front door. A beautiful woman strode inside, her long, dark hair swishing around her shoulders.

"What took you so long?" She smoothed her hands over his chest.

"Julia, what the hell are you doing here?" Nash side-stepped her and crossed his arms. "I told you I had plans."

"I know. But I had dinner with my girlfriend who lives nearby, and when the car passed by and I saw all the lights on in the apartment, I figured you were home."

I stepped into the room, and she caught sight of me. Her jaw dropped. "What? Who's this?"

"I'm Ethan."

Her eyes narrowed. "Nash. What's going on? He's not dressed. Are you…did you…oh, my God." Her mouth opened wide.

"Am I what, and did I what?" Remaining unflappable,

Nash strolled over to me. "If you barge into my place and start firing off questions, be sure you're ready for the answers. Ethan is my date."

"Date? Him? Y-you're gay?" she whispered.

"You can say it loudly. I have nothing to hide. No, I'm not gay; I'm bisexual."

"B-but you…we have sex."

I didn't know whether it was confusion or horror in her eyes, but whatever it was, Julia obviously had no idea Nash was into men. And I wanted to know more about her and Nash. How long they'd been together, and why she didn't know they were no longer together.

"That's what bisexual means, Julia. I'm attracted to men *and* women."

"You never said—"

"I didn't have to. We weren't dating. It was never serious between us. I'm with Ethan now."

We hadn't discussed exclusivity, but a thrill ran through me when he made that statement.

"This is why you told me we shouldn't see each other anymore? For him?" Her lip curled. "Have fun with your boy toy. While it lasts." She whirled on her stilettos—I had to admit I was impressed—and stormed out of the apartment. Nash huffed out a sigh, and I sat on the couch.

"So…she sounded fun."

Nash grimaced as he took his place next me. "*Fun* isn't exactly the word I'd use. Julia and I work together. She's a brilliant attorney."

"And she's beautiful."

"Yes, she is."

"You had a thing."

Nash ran a hand through his hair. "Our thing was to get together whenever one of us felt like it and have sex. There was no promise of anything more, or that we were exclusive. She knew she was free to see whomever she wanted."

"And so were you."

"That's right. We weren't in a relationship."

I knew it was a risk—we'd only had sex a couple of times and a few kisses—but I had to put the question out there. "What about now? Are you seeing anyone else besides me?"

"What do you think?" Nash retorted, his eyes growing stormy.

"I-I don't know. That's why I asked."

His lips curved in a smile. "I need all my wits about me to keep up with you." He ran his knuckles down my cheek. "I'm not seeing anyone else. I don't want to."

I wet my lips. "Me neither."

"Good." He leaned in close. "Now let's go to bed."

But I held off. Was I here simply to be a boy toy? I wanted a real relationship, and if that wasn't possible with Nash, I had to make a decision.

"What are you doing this weekend?"

He blinked. "Nothing. Why?"

"I have to work on Saturday until four, but do you want to go out and see a movie? Or maybe to a museum on Sunday?"

He took my hand and played with my fingers. "I haven't been to a movie in years."

"We can do both. A Saturday night movie, and Sunday go to a museum or something else. Brunch and maybe the Cloisters?"

"Why this sudden need to go out and do things?"

I pulled my hand from his. "Because I'm not here only to have sex with you—to be your 'boy toy' like Julia said. If that's what you want, maybe you *should* find someone else."

Maybe I was stupid for being so demanding so early on, but I knew how easy it would be to fall for Nash. I had to protect myself.

"Is that what you think?"

"Give me a reason not to." I lifted my chin and met his eyes. His jaw tensed, and my heart sank as I mentally prepared to walk away and say good-bye.

"Action or rom-com?"

I let out a *whoosh* of breath and smiled. "Rom-com."

"I'll get the tickets for the movie and meet you at your job." He held out his hand. "You can pick what we do on Sunday."

I took it, and this time let him pull me to standing. He slipped his arms around my waist, and I liked that we were the same height, so I could kiss him easily.

"Thank you," I murmured against his mouth.

"Don't thank me yet." He palmed my crotch, then pulled down my pants and briefs. "I haven't even started."

"Keep going," I panted, painfully hard.

"I plan to, bossy," he growled and sank to his knees, rubbing the rough bristles of his cheek over my dick. "On and on…"

"Shut up and suck me already—*oh, God*." I moaned when his hot mouth closed over the head of my cock and he began to tongue the hell out of my shaft. "Nash, oh God."

He hummed, increasing his pace and suction. I buried my hands in his hair, urging him on.

"There, yeah, harder, oh God, fuck…" The familiar tingling began in my heels and shot up my legs to curl in my belly. "Nash, I…I…" My voice failed me, and I dug my fingers into his shoulders and came as my hips pumped fast and furious, sending my dick deep. Nash surprised me by taking it all and swallowing. When I'd softened, he sat back, licking his lips, and I joined him on the floor and kissed him, tasting myself on his tongue.

I undid his jeans and reached inside to grasp his huge erection. "Can't let this go to waste." I played over the sticky slit and bent over, my head in his lap, and slid his rigid shaft past my lips. He twisted his fingers in my hair, holding me in place, and I let him thrust, loving the way he moaned and writhed beneath me.

My mouth filled with his hot come, and I drank him dry. When he released me, I lay resting on his thighs, his fingers stroking my face. If someone told me this was heaven, I'd believe them because nothing could be more perfect.

"You taste better than any wine."

He kissed me.

Hand in hand, we walked out of the movie theater on West 84th Street on Saturday night. "What now?" Nash asked, his fingers tickling my palm.

"Are you kidding? I'm hungry. It's seven o'clock, and I'm starving."

"You polished off more than half the popcorn," he teased. "Don't think I didn't notice."

"Okay, Captain Kernel-Counter, but that was a snack. I need *food*." I waggled my brows. "Gotta keep my strength up for later."

He reddened, and I leaned into him. He'd just slipped an arm around my waist, when I heard his name being called.

"Nash? Is that you?"

We turned to see Alex holding hands with a man. Another couple stood by their side.

"Alex? What're you doing here?"

"Uh, I live here. I mean, not here, but in Brooklyn, and last I heard, we're allowed to cross the bridge after dark. Hi, Ethan."

I snickered. "Hi."

"Sooo," Alex grinned. "You guys on a date?"

"Brilliant powers of observation, there, Dr. Stern." Nash

folded his arms and arched a brow.

"Top of my class, baby. Ethan, this is my husband, Rafe. Rafe, you remember Nash, and this is Ethan…I'm sorry, I don't know your last name."

"Moreno. Ethan Moreno. Nice to meet you, Rafe."

"S-same, Ethan." Rafe spoke softly, in direct contrast to the bubbly Alex.

"What're we, chopped liver?" the tall, dark-haired man hovering in the background growled with a smile. "I'm Micah, and this is my husband, Josh."

I shook hands with them, noticing the wedding rings as well as the high-quality clothing they both wore.

"Nash."

I watched them all shake hands, feeling a little out of place. I was the odd duck out—younger and certainly not in the same social strata.

"Do you work with Alex in the lab, Nash?" Micah asked.

"No, I'm a financial analyst—a numbers guy. I'm eyeballs deep in the hospital's budget and help decide funding allocation. You're a doctor?"

"Yes. A neurosurgeon."

Feeling a bit inadequate, I tensed, and Nash tightened his hold on my waist. "Don't," he murmured, then spoke to the rest of the group. "We were about to have dinner."

"Us too. Why don't we all go together?" Alex's bright gaze swept over our little crowd. "We were thinking sushi. Momoya is our favorite."

Rafe took Alex's hand and squeezed it. "Maybe Nash and Ethan want to be by themselves, instead of us barging in on their d-date."

Nash looked to me. "It's up to you. I'm fine either way."

Much as I'd have liked to be alone with Nash, this would be a good test for me to see if I could fit into his world. We had all night to be by ourselves. "Sure. It'll be fun."

Nash took my hand. "Then let's go."

Josh pulled out his phone. "I'll try and see if I can get us a table."

We arrived at the restaurant, and Josh had come through with only a minimal wait time. We were escorted to a table for six tucked in the corner and given menus and water. Nash's thigh pressed to mine.

Alex said, "I met Ethan at the Gucci store. He helped me pick out your present." Alex nudged Rafe. "You were spot-on too, Ethan. Rafe loved it, and so did I. No kids makes for a great intimate birthday celebration."

Rafe blushed and rolled his eyes. "You're impossible. But I did enjoy the experience. Thank you very m-much."

"What do you do, Ethan?" Micah perused the menu.

"I'm a sales associate in the men's department at Macy's Herald Square." I waited for the raised eyebrows and the questions to begin as to how I was with a man like Nash.

Josh sipped his water. "We buy our twins most of their clothing there. They have everything, so it's one-stop shopping. I love it. In and out."

"How did you two meet?" Micah asked.

The server approached, and we decided to order a bunch of rolls, sashimi, and appetizers and share. Micah and Alex ordered beers, but I decided not to. When the server departed, I answered. "On the 2 train."

The four men stared. "You're kidding." Micah laughed. "Who talks to someone on the subway?"

"Apparently, me," Nash responded mildly. "I was seated, and Ethan came barreling in and wouldn't stop talking."

"Sounds like someone else I know," Micah said dryly, fixing Alex with an amused look.

"You know you love me." Alex blew him a kiss, and Micah snorted with laughter.

"I've known you too long. You're like a barnacle. I couldn't get rid of you even if I tried."

"Well, then that makes you the rusty old ship, doesn't

it?" Alex's eyes twinkled, and everyone, including me, laughed.

The friendship between all these men was something I'd always wished for but had never managed to achieve. Between school and work, I had little downtime for play.

"Are you still thinking of moving on to one of the luxury boutiques, or staying where you are?" Alex asked.

"I talked with my manager and Nash, and it makes sense to stay at a large organization like Macy's and make as many contacts as possible, then see about moving into a management role, or a buyer role, which is ultimately where I'd like to end up."

"If you're as spot-on with everything as you were with your choices for Rafe, without even meeting him, I'd say that's a perfect plan." Alex's blue eyes lit up. "Here come some of the appies. I'm dying of hunger."

"You ate almost all the popcorn and half my T-Twizzlers, plus your Milk Duds." Rafe's lips twitched. "I'm sure that's why Dylan comes home on a sugar high every time you two spend the day together."

"Eh"—Alex waved his hand—"you only live once."

"So you all have children?" I'd never been around young, gay married families before. It was a dynamic I'd never thought about.

Josh smiled. "Micah and I have nine-year-old twins, Jacob and Rachel. And Alex and Rafe have Dylan, who's almost nine, and Sari, their fourteen-month-old."

"Dylan's at a sleepover with Micah and Josh's twins at their friend's house, and my mom is watching the baby." Alex crunched on a spring roll. "She lives right near us."

"We're all in the clear. It's nice that the kids all get along." Micah speared a piece of sashimi. "They love visiting their friends as much as we do."

I took a gyoza and put it on my plate. "What kind of law do you practice, Josh?"

"Family law, for the most part. I love the adoption process the most, but I handle divorces and all kinds of law if my clients need it."

Nash remained quiet for most of the dinner, but when we said good-bye to everyone outside the restaurant, he surprised me. "Thanks for inviting us to dinner with you. Next time we'll have to do it in Brooklyn."

Alex's eyes twinkled. "Good luck getting Micah to cross the bridge. He's a borough snob."

"I am not. We'd love to come. Pick a time." He made a face at Alex, who stared at him.

"Wow, you must be something special. Micah doesn't like anyone."

"Well, we are pretty awesome." I snickered. "Just ask us."

"I wish we could hang out and chat," Alex said, "but we have to get home and let my mom off the hook." Alex hugged us both and whispered in my ear, "Good for you."

Micah and Josh shook our hands. "We're going home to walk the dog and enjoy a little peace and quiet."

From the gleam in Micah's eyes, I wasn't so certain how quiet their apartment would be.

When they left, Nash took my hand and squeezed it tight. "Feel like walking a bit?"

"Yeah."

Hand in hand, we strolled up 80th to the park, passing other couples out on a beautiful summer evening.

"I had a really good time tonight," Nash mused as we waited for the light to change.

"You sound surprised."

"At myself, yeah, I am. I spent most of my life alone, thinking that's how I wanted it to be." He played with my fingers, then entwined his with mine, making our two hands one.

"And now?"

"Now I'm wondering if it isn't too late for me to change."

We crossed the street and turned down 72nd to head back to the 2 train.

"If you want my opinion, it's not."

He kissed my cheek. "Your opinion is the only one that matters."

Why did he have to be so damn cute and lovable? God help me, I was crazy about this man.

CHAPTER ▶ 17

Sunday found Ethan and me exploring the Cloisters and enjoying a magnificent view of the Hudson River. When we left, he nudged my shoulder.

"So? What did you think?"

"It was incredible. I can't believe I've never been. One building reminded me of France, yet there are distinct Spanish influences in another. And the artwork is gorgeous."

"I think it's one of New York's hidden gems. It's so peaceful, you can't imagine it's really here, in the city."

I kissed his cheek. "Let's go have lunch."

After our meal, I had no desire to crowd into the train to go home, so I called for a car. During the ride, Ethan remained surprisingly quiet, and I tugged at his hand.

"What's wrong?"

He shrugged. "Nothing. But I've spent every night at your place. I have to do laundry, get my mail, prep lunch, and stuff like that. I should go home."

I wanted to snap at him and tell him no, that he belonged

with me, but I didn't have that right. It had only been a few dates, and though I felt closer to him than anyone else, I had no right to be so possessive and greedy of his time.

"Sure. If you want, the car can drop you off at your place first."

He nodded and stared out the window as the car flew past the river. Each mile closer to Brooklyn brought me closer to a night alone. I didn't want that.

I wanted Ethan.

I said nothing until we drove down Flatbush. "Can I ask you a favor?"

"Sure."

"Would you mind if I hung out at your place while you do what you have to?"

Surprised didn't begin to describe his expression. "Huh? Why?"

"Because I don't feel like sitting home alone. You'll be here, and I'll be there, and that's…silly."

"Yeah? I guess I have to say yes, because I know Nash Roman doesn't do silly things."

His shy smile did something funny to my chest. "No? Am I so predictable?"

Ethan's brows rose, and he grinned. When the car pulled up to his apartment building on Bergen Street and we got out, I pulled him close and planted a kiss on his soft, yielding mouth. He clung to me, and after a few moments, I pushed him away.

"How's that for being predictable? I've never kissed anyone in public before."

Ethan touched his lips, then winked. "You're a fast learner."

I trailed behind, waited while he got his mail, and followed him upstairs, but we were stopped before we could make it past the first floor. A door creaked open.

"Ethan? Is that you?"

He turned and shook his head. "Yeah, Gladys."

"Just checking. You got the boyfriend with you?"

"If you mean Nash, yeah."

He met my eyes, and a red blush crept over his cheeks. "Sorry," he whispered. "I know she's a lot to handle."

I climbed the two stairs between us and pressed up behind him. "So are you."

I heard rapid footsteps and turned to see Ethan's landlady below us, her worn face beaming. "Good. You have fun. And Pete's gonna change your lock today, so I have the new key. Make sure you pick it up. You don't gotta worry."

"Okay, I will. We'd better get going."

"Sure, go ahead, don't mind me. I remember when we was young, me and Pete couldn't wait to get home neither. We're going out food shopping. Gonna be gone the rest of the day."

"Oh, for God's sake," Ethan muttered, and it was a struggle not to lose it on the steps. Luckily, we made it to his apartment before I fell onto his couch, laughing.

"She's something else."

"That's for sure."

Several minutes passed before I managed to speak. "I hope we don't disappoint her." I wiped my eyes.

Ethan opened up the mail and tossed it aside. "Bills. Blah." His green eyes sparkled. "And I don't know. The laundry machines in the basement might be fun. They make a ton of noise. No one would ever know what we were doing." He started to sing "You Spin Me Round," and instead of being shocked at the thought of having sex with Ethan in a dingy basement, a thrill shot through me.

"Maybe so."

His face brightened, and he joined me on the lumpy sofa. "Well, well. Have I created a monster?"

I grasped him by the nape. "*Rawr*," I growled, then kissed him. Ethan responded with fervor, pulling me down on top of him, but something struck me, and I released him. "Wait."

"Why?" he whined, eyes hazy with desire. "I was only kidding. We don't have to do it downstairs. Right here is good."

"Why did you need the locks changed?" Ethan couldn't meet my eyes, and I waited.

"It's nothing."

"So much nothing that Gladys—who seems like a pretty tough cookie if you ask me—said you don't have to worry. About what don't you need to worry?"

I had my suspicion, but I needed to hear it from Ethan.

"On Thursday, before I came to stay at your place, Oscar showed up."

"Oh? What did he want?" My restraint was admirable.

"The usual—I should take him back, he loves me, blah, blah." His expression was uneasy and my gut tightened. "Then Pete showed up with a bat, and Oscar got the message and left. End of story."

My bullshit detector went off. "And that's all? He didn't get aggressive?"

"Oscar talks a good game, but he'd never hurt me. When he tried to kiss me, I kneed him in the balls."

I must've misheard him. "He kissed you?"

"*Tried to*, I said. But he didn't, and then Pete and his friend the baseball bat escorted him out."

I growled. "And you didn't think to say anything to me?"

"Like what?" He raised a brow. "I can take care of myself. I don't need a protector."

"Are you sure about that? This guy is giving off stalker vibes."

Scowling, Ethan scooted away to the far end of the couch. "I'm fine. It's all under control. I mean, I could say the same thing for you and that Julia woman."

I narrowed my eyes. "What does that mean?"

"She showed up at your apartment like she owned the place. And you." He leveled grim green eyes at me. "Are you sure you were just casual?"

"There was never anything between her and me. We'd settled that, I thought."

Ethan set his jaw. "Yeah. We did, and I believed you. Now you have to trust me."

"I do." I shifted closer. "I'm not worried about you being with him. I'm worried for your safety." I cupped his cheek. "Stay with me tonight?"

"Why? So you can protect me?"

I leaned in and kissed him. "No. So I can hold you all night long."

Ethan's smile fit over my lips. "That's something I can get behind."

"Bring your laundry. I'll have it sent out."

Ethan shook his head, a devilish light entering his eyes. "No. Let's go downstairs. Don't tell me you aren't getting hot thinking of fucking me while the machine spins."

Again that dark thrill sparked something alive in me I'd never known existed, but I hung back. "What if someone comes to do their laundry while we're…"

"In midcycle?" His laughter rose between us. "I'll lock the door."

"Fuck, Nash. I know you think it's hot." Ethan's pants lay at his ankles, and he spread himself open. I grew hard, and before I knew it, I was sheathed, lubed, and inside him. "So good," Ethan moaned as I sank in all the way. "More."

The sounds of people walking past us on the street, only feet away from where I had my dick inside Ethan, was a turn-on I'd never expected, and I swelled thick and hard inside his delicious ass. He writhed and groaned, clenching around my shaft. I forgot the fear of being caught and lost myself in Ethan. Holding him down against the thumping machine, hearing his whimpers and cries as I pounded into him, was a heady, all-powerful experience. His velvet heat squeezed me, and I gave up caring if anyone heard us.

"Come on, that's it." I drove in deeper.

"Nash, please. I can't take it."

"Yeah, you can, and you will," I gritted out. "Take it all." Two more hard thrusts and I was there, my climax ripping me to pieces, and I gasped for breath. At the same time, Ethan wailed long and hard as he came, jerking and shivering. I held on to him, whispering, "Look at you. So perfect and amazing."

"Love it." He sighed. "Love you."

I froze, unsure if my ears were playing tricks on me, and chose not to respond, in case it was a mistake. Leaning in close, I kissed the back of his sweaty neck. "I can't believe I just had sex against a washing machine. Me. I don't even do my own laundry." I slipped out of him and got rid of the condom, then pulled my pants up.

"You do me just fine." Red-faced and breathless, Ethan swept the hair off his face, took a roll of paper towels from the sink area, and wiped off the machine. "Can't leave any evidence."

My face grew hot. "I hope no one heard us."

A cocky grin spread across Ethan's face. "You were pretty loud."

"Me?" I scoffed. "That was you screaming for more."

"I'll be doing that again later." Ethan winked, and God help me, I couldn't wait.

Those words he'd moaned played over and over in my head as we ate dinner, and again in bed as he moved over me, riding me into a wild oblivion of lust. Long after Ethan had drifted off to sleep, I held him and wondered whether I even knew what love meant.

"So about later…" Ethan said the next morning as he sat at the kitchen island, eating a bagel. "I'll go to my place first after work, and then I'll meet you here after you get home."

"That seems silly. I can tell the doorman to let you come up. They have a key behind the desk you can use." It all came so naturally with Ethan. Where I used to bury myself in work and prolong my time in the office to have as little downtime as possible, now I looked forward to coming home, and laughing over dinner, and to the welcoming arms holding me tight in bed.

What the hell was happening?

"Oh…okay, if you're sure."

I grabbed the bagel from his hand and took a bite. "I'm sure I want you here when I get home."

Ethan's eyes sparkled. "Did you just steal my bagel?"

"What if I did?"

"Just so you know, I'm keeping a list of your transgressions. For later."

"Tell me more." I took him by the elbow and kissed his smiling mouth. "Sounds intriguing."

He brushed our lips together. "It's better to be surprised." And with a wink and a hard squeeze of my ass, he popped the remainder of the bagel into his mouth and grabbed his bag. "Ready to go?"

"Yep."

We got on the train, but our usual seats were taken, so we held on to the pole, side by side.

Ethan said, "You know, if we hadn't sat together, we

would've never started talking." He stared out the window. "How crazy is that? It has to be fate."

"*We* didn't start talking," I pointed out with a smirk and a slight poke to his shoulder. "You did. If I recall, I was already in the seat, minding my own business, when you almost fell in my lap."

"Hmph," he sniffed. "A mere technicality."

Having fun on the 2 train during the morning rush had never entered the realm of possibility, yet here I was, teasing with a man I didn't know existed six months ago.

Now he was always on my mind.

At 34th Street, Ethan adjusted his bag. "I'll see you later."

I squeezed his arm. "Bye. Have a good day."

The doors slid closed, and he disappeared into the throngs of humanity surging left and right on the platform.

Twenty minutes later, I was in my office, sipping my third cup of coffee while reading through the morning announcements, when my phone buzzed.

"Yes?"

"Your father is here to see you."

I raised my eyes to the ceiling. Here I thought it would be a quiet Monday morning. I sighed. "Send him in."

Of course, he didn't wait for me to respond and had opened the door to my office and walked in while I was still talking. "Good morning." Without asking, my father sat across the desk from me and took a sip from his stainless-steel coffee mug. "I hope you had a pleasant weekend."

"Very. Can I help you? I haven't started on the Ahmed funding allocation yet."

My father waved a hand. "I'd hardly expect you to, considering it was only announced last week and it's an enormous undertaking." He paused. "I do hope we can work together on that, as I have some specifics."

I tipped my head. "I'm sure we can figure something

out. Eventually. So why are you here?"

He laughed. "I see you inherited my bluntness." When I remained unsmiling, he cleared his throat. "I meant what I said last week. I'd like to try and work on some kind of relationship with you. I'm willing to do just about anything."

"Why? Why are you so intent after all these years to make things right between us, when you couldn't have cared less before?"

"That's not how I see it, but I don't want this to degenerate into another finger-pointing argument. This is the closest we've gotten to each other, and I won't ruin it." He sighed and rested his elbows on my desk. "It's as you said, Nash. All these years have passed, and I know I hurt you. I can't go back and make it right. And I'm sorry. I was wrong to leave you behind. I was wrong not to make more of an attempt to see you, instead of focusing on my career. I allowed myself to get buried in the work because it was easier to think that as long as I paid support and sent birthday and Christmas cards, you wouldn't forget me. But instead, you grew to hate me."

Hearing him put it so bluntly, I winced. "How should I have felt?"

"I-I don't know. I guess I was wishing for the impossible instead of doing what was needed to make it happen."

For the first time, my father's mask slipped, and he wasn't the arrogant, brilliant doctor I'd become used to turning away. I saw his hurt and pain.

"What do you want from me?"

"A chance. I'm not getting younger, and now we're in the same city. We're both older and hopefully wiser. I was hoping…can we try to move forward?"

I opened my mouth to automatically tell him to leave me alone, but what purpose would that serve? My mother was dead, and all I had was a head full of blame and a heart full of hate. My life was in such upheaval lately with Ethan at the center, that an attempt at starting over with my father might lead me on a new path instead of circling around and around, caught in a never-ending loop of loneliness. Maybe I'd marinated in my anger long enough.

"How?"

Cautious joy lit my father's eyes. "We can have dinner—any night you want. How about tonight? Diana and I would love to take you out. Celebrate new beginnings, our relationship, the new baby."

"Okay. I guess we all have new beginnings to celebrate."

Shit. That wasn't supposed to come out, but I couldn't pull the words back.

"What? You're moving into the CFO position, I hope? I know you're better than—"

"Stop." I frowned and shook my head. "No. I've already said I'm not about to push Roger out. I'm not angling for his position. I'm happy where I am." When I saw him prepare to argue with me, I shook my head again. "Look. If you plan to have this conversation with me as part of a reconciliation, it's going to be a short-lived one."

"Okay, okay." He raised his hands. "What is it?"

"I'm seeing someone."

"Julia, Diana's friend. Yes, I know. That's wonderful. I met her at the gala. Bring her along."

"It's not—"

My father's phone rang. "I need to take this. It's Mrs. Ahmed. Nash, please let's continue this. I can't tell you how happy I am we've made this progress." He hit the screen. "Elizabeth, how wonderful to hear your voice.... Yes, we're on for lunch..." Still speaking, he walked out, leaving me frustrated.

I wanted to bring Ethan, but could I do so if my father thought I was dating a woman? Should I? And how would I explain who Ethan was to me, when I wasn't sure myself?

CHAPTER ▶ 18

When I entered Nash's building and approached the concierge sitting behind the imposing marble desk, anxiety knotted my stomach. What if they wouldn't let me in? I'd been with Nash when he'd left instructions for me to be given the key, but they could easily forget.

"Hi, I'm, uh, Ethan. I'm here for the key to 10D, Nash Roman's apartment?"

My concern was for nothing as the man handed over the key with a heavy black-metal tag on the end. "Yes, sir. Here you are."

"Thanks." I breathed a sigh of relief.

Once inside, I set my bag on the floor and put the key on the counter. I kicked off my loafers and wiggled my toes with a groan of satisfaction, then proceeded to lie on the sofa and curse myself for my stupidity the previous day. I hadn't thought too hard on it because every time I did, I wanted to be sick.

"I can't believe I said that." That, meaning *I love you,*

while we were having sex. My face burned. "I'm such a fool." I huddled into a ball of embarrassment. "Hopefully he didn't hear." A distinct possibility, since we were going at it so hot and heavy at the time. And despite my foolish words, I smiled at the memory.

Who would've thought the quiet, standoffish Nash would let go so gloriously? Originally, I'd meant it as a joke, but I saw something in his face that made me think he'd be into it. And boy, was I right. His hesitation melted away, and he was on me like a second skin. I loved it.

I loved him.

Those dreaded words materialized before I could catch them. But God help me, it was true. I was in love with him. Every part—the quiet sternness when he was being overprotective, and his gentle sweetness that made me melt because I would've never expected it. I loved coaxing out the teasing humor he kept hidden. And I loved how fiercely he wanted me and how he never held back when we were in bed. I happily bore the marks of his mouth and hands, secretly reveling in every sore, aching part of my body he left in his wake. No one had ever made me feel as needed and desired.

My phone rang, and it was Nash. "Hey, what's up?" It was unusual for him to call during the day. Occasionally, we'd text, or sometimes when I wanted to tease him, I'd send suggestive memes.

"I have a favor to ask. It's more like a question, but…"

"Nash. What is it?"

He huffed out a sigh. "My father. He…wants the two of us to try and start new."

"Which is good, right?"

"I'm not sure, but I told him I'd try. Thing is, he wants us to have dinner tonight—him and his wife and me."

Of course he would. My insecurities wormed their way to the surface. "That's great. I'm happy for you. And don't worry. I can just go home, and we can see each other another night—"

"Will you be quiet for one minute?"

I bit my lip at his low growl. *God.* Even annoyed, the man was a sexy beast. "What?"

"I'd like you to come with me."

If he'd asked me to run naked through Times Square, I couldn't have been more surprised.

"*Me?* Why?"

"I…I just…I just want you with me. Please, Ethan? I need someone who's going to be there for me. Someone on my side."

Good-bye, heart. You belong to Nash now.

Suddenly shy even though I was alone, I cast my gaze downward. "I'm on your side, you know that. I don't think…I don't know if I belong there."

"You do. You belong with me. Where I am."

Did he even realize that exposing his pain was ripping my heart in two while at the same time making me fall even more crazy in love with him?

"Is your father okay with you bringing me?"

"Why wouldn't he be?"

I rolled my eyes at his naïveté. "In case you don't realize it, I'm a man. I'm sure he's expecting you to come with a woman."

"I've long ago given up any notion of needing to impress my father or living up to whatever expectations he set for me. I do what I want."

"And that includes shocking him when you show up with a man?"

"That has nothing to do with it. If he can't deal with us, that's his problem. He's made a reservation for seven at Gramercy Tavern."

A restaurant I'd always heard about and wanted to try, but under the circumstances, I wasn't so sure this was the right time.

"Please, Ethan?"

It might end up being a huge mistake, but I couldn't say no. "All right. What time should I be there?"

"Make it six forty-five so we can have a drink at the bar first."

I smiled. "Fortification?"

"Not at all," he responded with a husky chuckle that sent an indecent throb of hunger through me. "I'd like a little time alone with you beforehand."

"I-I'll see you then."

My head fell back on the pillows, and a long *whoosh* of breath escaped me. "Better take a shower. I got a feeling I'm gonna need to look my best and be on my toes."

At six forty, I walked into the Gramercy Tavern, soaking in the sights and sounds of one of the city's finest restaurants. Wesley had once eaten here and couldn't stop raving about the duck he'd had and some lobster-and-squash dish.

"You're not at Applebee's anymore, Ethan." I touched my Gucci tie. I belonged here as much as anyone.

"May I help you?" A young woman stood by the front door, and I smiled at her.

"Yes, I'm meeting someone. I'm not sure if he's here yet."

"Ethan?" At the touch of a hand to my shoulder, I turned to see Nash.

"Found him."

"Come with me." He took my elbow and steered me toward the bar. "What do you want to drink?"

"A beer, I guess?"

"Heineken?" At my nod, he ordered my beer, and a Scotch and water for himself. "That's not the suit you wore this morning." His appreciative gaze swept over me.

"No. I went home first to change. The suit I wore was old, and I'd gotten a tuna stain on the tie. I wasn't going to meet your father and his wife for the first time wearing that."

"You look good no matter what you wear. Or don't."

I held a hand to my ear. "Was that you making a joke? Again? Two in one month? Are you sure you're the same grouchy man I met on the 2 train?"

To my surprise, Nash didn't have a snarky response at the ready. He cupped my cheek, his thumb playing over it. "No. I'm not."

My heart thumped. "What happened?"

"Not what. Who. You, Ethan."

I fought not to swoon because I'd end up on the floor. "Me? And here I thought I was too much to handle."

"You'll never be too much to handle, because I can't get enough of you to hold."

Over the rush of joy singing through my veins, I did swoon and leaned into Nash, rubbing my cheek to his. "You can hold me now all you want."

Nash set his glass on the bar. "I wish I could, but unfortunately, it's showtime. My father just walked in."

My stomach dive-bombed to my knees, and I stiffened. Nash put a hand on my back. I placed my untouched beer next to Nash's drink.

"Hi, Dad, Diana."

When I faced the man, he made a valiant effort not to appear surprised.

"Nash." He waited expectantly, his icy-blue eyes, so like Nash's, laser-focused on me.

"This is Ethan Moreno. Ethan, my father, Dr. Martin Roman, and Diana, his wife."

"Dr. Roman, nice to meet you." I held out my hand, and

to give him credit, despite the granitelike face, there was no hesitation in his grip. "Mrs. Roman." She responded with all the warmth missing from her husband's greeting.

"So nice to meet you, Ethan. I'm so glad we can all get to know each other."

"Dr. Roman, your table is ready. If you'd like to follow me?" The hostess waited, and Nash and I took our drinks before trailing behind her to a corner table. I pulled out the chair for Diana and sat across from her. Nash took the seat next to mine, facing his father, who couldn't stop staring at him.

"This is one of our favorite places," Diana said, placing the napkin on her lap. "Have you been here before, Ethan?"

"No, never. It's a little above my pay grade." I figured I might as well put it all out there right from the start.

That got Dr. Roman's attention. "Do you work at the hospital as well, Ethan?" He cocked a brow.

I was pretty sure he knew the answer, but I had nothing to hide. "No. I'm a sales associate at Macy's Herald Square in the men's department."

"Oh, I love Macy's. I shop there all the time." Diana's effusiveness didn't rub off on her husband.

"Is that how you two met? Did you sell Nash a suit?" Dr. Roman's brows drew together.

"No, Dad." Nash took over. "Matter of fact, we met on the 2 train."

A busboy came by with the breadbasket and filled our water glasses. The server took Dr. Roman's wine order.

"Interesting."

Diana's eyes grew wide. "That's incredible. I think it's sweet and such a New York story."

Dr. Roman didn't appear to feel the cuteness and frowned. "I thought we'd be seeing Julia tonight. From what I'd heard, the two of you have been together quite a while. Very nice *woman*."

I didn't miss the emphasis. Nash's jaw tightened, and I reached under the table to squeeze his knee, but he paid me no attention.

"Go ahead, Dad. I know you have something to say."

"Don't be so defensive. I'm just wondering how you go from dating a woman to a man. And the times we've met Julia, she seemed perfect."

"Perfect for whom?" Nash pressed his lips together. "I'm bisexual. I've been dating men and women my whole life. Something you would've known had you been around."

Diana lowered her gaze, then met mine, and I hoped my smile was enough reassurance that she understood I wasn't the enemy.

"I don't want to start off dinner with an argument. I'm surprised. You can't blame me."

"I don't know why there has to be any blame assigned," Diana said firmly. "I knew Nash wasn't coming with Julia. She and I spoke this afternoon." Once again she met my eyes. "She told me she went to Nash's apartment the other night, and he was there with a man. I assume it was Ethan. You told her he was your date."

"And you didn't think you should tell me?" Dr. Roman broke in, a scowl on his face.

"No." She lifted her chin. "It's not for me to speak about anyone's life. I don't decide when and if someone decides to come out. They do." What I could only describe as a gentle fierceness sparked in her eyes. "It's up to Nash whom he tells and when."

"Thank you, Diana." Nash tipped his head to her, then addressed his father. "When you left Mom and me and moved away, I cried every night, thinking it was my fault. As I grew older, I vowed to never let anyone get close enough to hurt me again. And the fact that you never made any real effort to see me only reinforced my belief that people weren't to be trusted. That I could and should be on my own. You don't even know my favorite color or food. Why would I tell you about my personal life? The doorman in my building and I have a closer relationship than you and I."

Dr. Roman passed a hand over his face. "I thought…I tried the best I could, but I will take responsibility and admit I didn't do the right thing. I said it in your office, but it bears repeating. I'm sorry. Meeting Diana has made me realize how wrong I was and how important family is. I've made a lot of mistakes in my life, Nash, but losing you all these years was the worst one. All I want to know is that we have a chance at some kind of relationship. I hope." For the first time since we sat at the table, Nash's father acknowledged me. "If Ethan makes you happy, so be it. I'm no one to judge, considering what people say about my marriage to Diana."

"What?" I asked, then immediately wished I could take the question back. "Sorry. Ignore me."

A frosty smile, so reminiscent of my early days with Nash, touched Dr. Roman's lips. "No, it's fine. I'll tell you because if you and my son are serious, which I assume you are because he brought you tonight, you should know the extent of gossip and innuendo that might be coming your way." His expression softened. "Diana worked for my hospital in Wisconsin."

"As a nurse?" I knew I was being nosy but I couldn't help my curiosity.

"No. Nurse's aide," Diana responded with a wink. "The one you call for the bedpan."

Well, that was certainly unexpected. Maybe Nash and his father were more alike than they thought.

"I noticed her on rounds and pestered her to have dinner with me. She was the first woman to turn me down."

Diana broke in. "I'd heard the stories about doctors and nurses…and nurse assistants. I refused to be gossip fodder in the hospital."

He chuckled. "I wouldn't take no for an answer. I can

be rather persistent when I want something."

"Sounds familiar," Nash murmured.

"Yeah." I grinned. "Like father, like son."

"Is that so? Funny, I thought someone else was the persistent one." Nash raised a brow but placed his hand on mine. Ridiculously happy, I turned my palm up and laced our fingers together.

Dr. Roman continued, "Diana was hesitant because she'd heard stories about me."

"Stories?" Nash raised his brows. "Really?" His voice was heavy with irony.

"Not all of them were true. I wasn't a saint by any means, but I wasn't out with a different woman every night either. Before I met Diana, I'd been alone for two years. I've told her everything, including what happened with your mother. She knows the ugly as well as the good. We have no secrets." He met Nash's eyes, and I watched their interplay.

"I'm glad to hear that."

The server brought Dr. Roman's wine, and Diana sipped her water with a shake of her head. "I do miss my Pinot Noir. The baby is due in six months, and we'd love to have you in his or her life, Nash. Even though there's such a big age difference, you're still going to be the only big brother they have to look up to." For the first time, her cheerful demeanor cracked. "My family wasn't thrilled with my marriage to Martin. They still don't approve."

"Why is that?" Nash's brow furrowed.

"Because he's much older and, let's face it, he's so wealthy. They feel like he manipulates me, that he's controlling because of the power imbalance." Her pretty eyes turned sad, and her mouth drooped. "They didn't come to the wedding, and they never responded when I told them about the baby. It hurts, but I can't let them upset me."

Dr. Roman touched her cheek. "Little do they know, I'm putty in her hands. Diana rules the roost in our house.

Our marriage is an equal partnership, and I could no more control her than she could me."

Out of the corner of my eye, I saw Nash's thoughtful gaze. To me, their marriage seemed like a strong and happy one, and I hoped Nash saw it that way as well.

Our server stood at the table. "Can I take your orders? Our seasonal menu is featured on the first page."

At the $165 price listed, I gulped. Diana gave her order first, and Dr. Roman followed. Nash looked to me.

"I shouldn't have had such a big lunch," I said weakly.

"You're a very bad liar," Nash murmured. "Please."

Perhaps sensing my unease, Diana cut a piece of bread and handed it to me as she addressed Nash. "I'm so happy this evening is turning out so well. It's Martin's birthday next week, and I planned to take him out to dinner, but now I can truly say it's a family celebration by including you and Ethan."

That was her subtle way of letting me know she was paying for the dinner, and while I appreciated it, I still hated lugging around this inferiority complex. Would I ever be able to let it go? I decided to order from the same menu as everyone else.

"Tell us something about yourself, Ethan, aside from where you work." Dr. Roman fixed me with his version of Nash's intensity. "Where did you go to school?"

"Fashion Institute of Technology. I wasn't about to be a designer, but I was always interested in the fashion world and up-and-coming trends. I took their business and marketing classes."

"I love Fashion Week here and in Los Angeles. It's so exciting, don't you think?" Diana said. "So much going on. It's like a Broadway show for each designer."

"I've never been to Fashion Week," I admitted. "It's my dream one day to be able to attend. Initially, I thought about leaving my job to work for one of the luxury houses, hoping to get an in to become a buyer, or at least work with them, but it's a very closed-off industry. Nash and his friend recommended I stay with a large company like Macy's for now, to be able to make those contacts on a wider scale and network with a broader spectrum of buyers."

As I spoke, Dr. Roman's expression changed from skeptical to understanding—was I imagining it?—and I could feel some of that initial coolness ease. "That's a wise decision, Ethan. It's best to surround yourself with as many opportunities for advancement as possible. Don't limit yourself to what you think you want because you might miss out on what you need."

Nash's surprised face mirrored my emotions. "Thank you, Dr. Roman. I really appreciate the advice. I'm planning to do just that."

His nod was brief. "You're welcome. And I think we can dispense with the formalities. If you're close enough with my son for him to introduce us, please call me Martin."

"Thanks, Dad," Nash responded quietly, and while I knew Nash's hurt and betrayal was a slate that wouldn't be wiped clean after one dinner, I hoped he would eventually be able to let go of the decades of anger.

I said the same to him as we undressed that night for bed. I finished first and climbed into bed, watching him hang up his suit and put away his tie.

"It turned out to be a very nice evening, don't you think? Diana is really sweet, and your father thawed some toward me."

His smile was wry. "I had my doubts. I was certain it would be a night of listening to his excuses, the same overused words over and over again. But then I thought… what's the point of holding on to grudges anymore?" He got under the covers, brushing his feet over mine. "If I continue to push him away, it's me who'll be missing out on a new baby brother or sister and the chance for a family. My mother is gone, and I doubt she'd want me to spend my life steeped in recriminations and regret."

"I'm glad you feel like that. There's always time for a second chance if you allow yourself to take it."

Nash put his arms around me. "How're my chances for getting lucky tonight?"

I pulled him to me for a kiss. "One hundred percent. And I'm thinking we're both lucky."

CHAPTER ▸ 19

The week passed with me buried in paperwork and meetings. The Ahmed donation was the main subject of the board meeting I normally didn't attend, but because Roger and I worked so closely, I was forced to sit through.

As we left the conference room, I joked, "This only reinforced why I have no desire for your job. I'm happier to stay in my office and deal with numbers rather than all those egos."

He joined me in laughter. "It's a skill that takes years to hone, trust me. They don't teach you Bullshit 101 and Advanced BS in school."

Speaking of bullshit, I spied Julia by the elevator. Roger glanced at me. "Not that I poke into people's private lives, but were you two…a thing?"

"No. At least not in my mind. Why?"

He shrugged. "Just some gossip I'd heard. All I can say is it's better to keep business and pleasure separate."

I gave him a quick nod. "I'm doing just that. I'll have

those numbers for you later. I have an appointment."

Ethan and I had taken to seeing each other at lunchtime during the week when he could take a proper lunch break, and today we were meeting at a deli on West 38th Street. As I entered the bustling restaurant, I spotted him already sitting at a table and hurried over.

"I hope you haven't been waiting long."

"Nope. Just sat down and was contemplating if I should have the corned beef or the pastrami."

"You can have a two-meat sandwich. That's what I'm doing. It's the best." I scooped some of the coleslaw they gave for free onto my little plate.

"And here I thought you only enjoyed one kind of meat." His eyes twinkled, and a rush of heat traveled north and south simultaneously.

"You're going to get me in trouble."

With deliberation, he took a pickle, put it between his lips, crunched it, then moaned. "So good."

"Will you stop? I don't need a *When Harry Met Sally* moment here," I hissed.

"Sorry." But he chomped on the pickle, his eyes alight with laughter.

"No, you're not." I leaned in closer. "And I envy that pickle."

The harried waiter stopped by, and we ordered our sandwiches and black-cherry sodas.

"How's work going?" I asked Ethan. "You have a sale going on? I got an email this morning."

He sighed. "There's always a sale somewhere. I think there are two weeks out of the year where we don't have one going on. Anyway, I was thinking…"

"Always a dangerous thing," I snickered. Our sandwiches were plunked down in front of us, along with two glasses of ice and our cans of soda.

"Ha-ha. No. I'm serious. By the way, remember Diana

said it was your father's birthday? I think you should get him a present."

Damn. Not what I expected, but he was right. "I-I agree. Thanks for reminding me." I chewed my sandwich. "What do you think we should get?"

Surprise brightened his face. "Oh…well, a small leather accessory is always nice. Or you could ask Diana what he likes." He took a bite. "Thanks for including me in the present."

"First of all, it was your suggestion. Second, you come with me as a package deal."

Ethan's eyes grew soft. "Yeah? Is that how it works?"

"I'm hoping."

A faint blush tinged his cheeks, and I remembered his words in the laundry room. I hadn't been able to get them out of my mind. "I'll send her a text and ask her, and then maybe after work we can go shopping and have dinner?"

"I'd love that."

I love you.

Startled, I blinked, and shoved the sandwich into my mouth. What the hell was I thinking?

But I knew.

Even still, knowing it in my heart and admitting it in my head were two very different things.

Ethan glanced at his phone. "I gotta go. If I clock in late, I'll get docked pay." He pulled out his wallet and gave me two twenties. "Here. Take this. I'll see you later." I knew better than to say no. Pride was something I understood, and Ethan refused to let me pay for everything. I never wanted him to feel like I ran the show, or that because I had more money than he did, his opinion didn't count as much as mine. Diana had mentioned her family assuming a power imbalance in her marriage to my father, and I was ashamed to admit I'd drawn the exact same conclusion. Now that Ethan and I were in a similar situation, I understood. The last thing I wanted was for him to suffer from inadequacy when he'd given me so much.

"I'll meet you in your department around six thirty." He was working late today.

With a wave, he was gone. I finished my lunch, paid the bill, and returned to the hospital. On the way in, I met Alex.

"How's it going, Nash? I gotta tell you, Rafe loved meeting Ethan. Maybe we can all get together again soon."

"Maybe so."

"Wow. An answer instead of a grunt. I'm honored."

We entered the elevator.

"As you should be." My lips twitched.

"And a joke too? My God, is the world coming to an end?" Alex exclaimed in mock horror.

"It might be if you keep this up," I growled.

"Ahh, there's the crabby Nash we know and love." Alex patted my cheek. The doors opened, and I walked out, Alex trailing behind me like a golden-retriever puppy, all smiles and bouncing blond hair. "Things are good, huh?"

"Yes, Alex. Things are good." Once inside my office, I closed the door, and he sat down. "We had dinner with my father and his wife a few days ago." Alex's big blue eyes widened, but surprisingly, he remained silent. "It was…very nice." I had no idea why I'd become so chatty and needed to share my feelings, but I replayed the evening to Alex, including how Diana and Ethan had connected.

"As someone who has zero relationship with my own father, I'm really happy for you. How are you feeling about the situation as a whole, going forward? You managed to be civil to each other and promised to try, but do you think he's going to follow through?"

I clasped my hands on the desk. "I think…it's up to me, and the signs are there. The night started off strained, but as it progressed, I thought, why was I angry? The past can't be changed, but I have the opportunity to alter the course of my future." Alex nodded as I spoke. "And with a new baby on the way, and Ethan and me…it just felt right to move on."

"Ethan and you what?" Alex couldn't seem to stop grinning. "Don't think you can slip that in and not expect me to ask."

I sighed. "Of course not. But honestly? I haven't a clue. He's the first person I've ever shared so much with. The first real friend I've had."

"Hey," Alex piped up. "I'm here too, ya know."

"I know. And believe me, sometimes I wonder why you bother."

"Don't be an idiot," Alex replied with a roll of his eyes, and a ridiculously happy feeling settled in my chest. "But I'm glad you realized Ethan is the guy for you." When I didn't respond, he frowned. "You do realize that, right?"

"Can I tell you something? I'm not really sure what to think, and I need someone's opinion."

Uncharacteristically solemn, Alex hitched his chair closer. "Lay it on me."

I could pretend to be the big old badass, but in truth, I was as lost as the six-year-old kid whose father walked out on him all those years ago. I licked my lips and swallowed. Hard. Talking about private times wasn't in my wheelhouse, but then neither was falling in love.

"Ethan and I were…together. And he said he loved me. But"—I put my hand up when I saw Alex bounce in his seat—"I know he didn't mean for me to hear. It was spoken in the heat of the moment."

"Yeah. Those hot moments," Alex mused. "You get so carried away that you lose all sense of place and time and just feel. All your truths come out spontaneously." He blinked, and a sheepish smile curved his lips. "Trust me. I know." His eyes narrowed. "Don't tell me you're going to be stupid and deny you're in love with him too."

I rubbed my face. "It's so fast. I-I haven't had time to

think about it."

"The heart doesn't operate on a schedule. And you don't think about love. It simply…is. Just ask yourself what your life would be without Ethan in it." His phone beeped. "Gotta go. I'll talk to you later."

After he left, I sat at my desk. I didn't go through my emails or finish reviewing the reports I had waiting. I thought about what Alex said and what I'd be doing tonight—and every other night—if I didn't have Ethan.

A little past six thirty, I walked through the main floor of Macy's and spotted Ethan at the men's fragrance counter, in conversation with a man I recognized from the bar the first time I'd kissed Ethan. I walked up behind him and leaned in close.

"Hi."

He whipped around, and a big, beautiful smile broke out over his face. "Hey."

"Who's your friend?" Not that I was jealous, but I was curious if they'd dated.

"Oh. Uh, this is Clay."

I stuck out my hand. "Hi, Clay. Nash. Nice to meet you."

Clay's handshake was firm. "Same. Ethan was telling me you're looking for a gift for your father? Cologne is kind of pedestrian, so how about a facial and massage? I also work at a spa, and we're seeing almost as many men come in as women. My husband and I get a couples massage once a month together."

"My father getting a massage?" I rubbed my chin. "I'm not sure. I should've checked with Diana if he's into that."

"Oh, he is," Ethan said with a nod. "I spoke with her, and

she said he's so overworked, she thinks it would be perfect."

"You spoke with her?"

"She stopped by this afternoon. Bought him a few cashmere sweaters." Ethan winked and straightened my tie. "Don't worry. I gave her my employee discount."

Not to bash Macy's, but I knew my father's taste ran more to Madison Avenue, so this was more likely Diana wanting to establish a connection with Ethan rather than supplementing my father's wardrobe. Considering how close they were in age, I understood.

"Then I think that's a great idea."

"Wonderful," Clay said. "I'll get the information to Ethan."

"Sounds good. Thanks." I took Ethan's hand and tugged, eager to be alone with him. "Ready for dinner?"

"Starving."

But from the look in his eyes, I knew we'd be ordering in. I nudged his shoulder as we exited the store through the men's department to get to the train station.

"So…Diana, huh?"

He shrugged. "She came in and wanted to talk about the dinner. She was so happy that you and your father seem to be on the road to reconciliation."

"You helped me see that it was the right thing to do."

"Nah." Ethan shook his head, his hair flopping over his brow, and I pushed it off his face to keep his bright eyes in view. "It was there. You knew it all along."

We entered the train station, and Ethan tapped his phone to pay and huffed as I swiped and reswiped my MetroCard until it worked.

"Time to level up, Nash, and go full tech," he teased, waving his phone in my face.

"I already leveled up." My smile left no misunderstanding, and when I finally made it through the turnstile, Ethan linked his arm through mine.

"If you can say something as sweet as that to me, you know I'm going to reward you when we get home—I mean, back to your place."

"You can call it anything you want, as long as you're there with me."

No seats were available, so we held on to the pole the entire ride, chatting about our day. I told him more about the massive donation enabling the hospital to set up a foundation.

"It's still in the preliminary stages, but so much good work can come out of it—academic chairs at universities, scholarships, so much research." I paused, thinking of all the work already done and yet to come. "It's mind-boggling. I swear, at the board meeting, Mrs. Ahmed treated my father like a god."

"I guess he is to them. Even though her husband died, he lived longer than anyone predicted."

At Grand Army Plaza we exited the train and walked the few short blocks to my building. I pushed the door to enter the lobby, when I heard a shout.

"Ethan!"

We both turned to see a man walking with purpose toward us. Ethan's jaw flexed, and he gave me a push. "Go inside. I can handle this."

"Who is it?"

"Ethan," the guy yelled again, closer now and drawing the stares of people walking past. "You better talk to me."

"Is that Oscar?" He was big and beefy, with short brown hair in a buzz cut.

"Please, Nash. Let me talk to him. I don't want you involved."

"You've got to be kidding. You think I'm going to leave you out here with him? He could have a gun or a knife."

Ethan shook his head. "Oscar isn't like that."

"Anyone is like that." I planted my feet. "I'm staying put."

I watched Oscar approach, eyes dark as a thundercloud, mouth pressed tight. The flush of anger rose over his cheeks.

"This your new boyfriend?" Oscar gestured toward me with a balled fist. "Got yourself a sugar daddy?"

"Go home." I took a step forward. "Know when it's time to walk away."

"Yeah? You think 'cause you have money you're better than me?"

"Oscar, please. Just leave me alone," Ethan implored. "I told you to stop. Don't make me get a restraining order."

I ignored Ethan and addressed Oscar directly. "What goes on between Ethan and me has nothing to do with money. It's about respect. I would never look at another man or cheat on Ethan. I'm better than you because I don't hurt the man I love."

And because I knew how painful it must be to see Ethan and realize what you once had was now lost forever, I gentled my voice. "Leave him alone. We're happy. Go find someone else to be with. I understand how hard it is to let go, and I've cut you some slack. But not anymore. I won't tolerate you stalking Ethan, and I'll do whatever's necessary to protect him. It's finished between you two, Oscar. Don't do anything foolish to fuck up the rest of your life. Ethan told me you have plans. That'll all go to shit if you get arrested over a man who doesn't want you anymore. Is it worth it?"

Our gazes clashed, and then Oscar's shoulders slumped and I could see the fight drain from him. He dipped his head, and without another word, walked away.

I turned to Ethan. "I don't think we'll be hearing from him again."

Rooted in place, Ethan slow-blinked. "Love?"

I took him by the elbow and led him through the lobby and up to the apartment, where I closed the door behind us.

"I heard what you said in the laundry room."

Ethan's face flushed pink. "Oh."

"Yeah. Oh." I backed him up against the door and rested my cheek on his. "And I thought to myself: where the hell would I be if I didn't have you?"

"Certainly not having sex on a washing machine."

"Wise-ass."

"You love it."

"Yeah. I do." I cupped his jaw. "And you." I heard his sharp intake of breath. "I love you, Ethan. I thought I wanted only one thing in life—to be left alone—but I was wrong."

"You? Wrong?" Ethan teased, his smile rivaling the brightness of his eyes.

"Yes. There are two things I want—you and me. Together."

CHAPTER ▶ 20

"That was very romantic." I kissed him back, pushing his jacket off, then undoing his tie.

"I can be romantic." Nash kissed my face and neck. "I can't think about the right words. I can't think of anything at all except how much I want you."

We kicked off our shoes, stripped out of our clothes, and ran to the bedroom. Eager to feel his naked skin on mine, I pulled him next to me. "I only wanted to be the most important thing in someone's life."

Nash bit my ear and whispered, "You're my everything."

I ran my hands along the curve of his spine and cupped his ass. When my fingers brushed his hole, he groaned and trembled. I pushed him so he lay under me. His beautiful dick rose up thick and strong, and my mouth watered in anticipation, but not to suck him off. I licked a path from his neck to his stomach and nuzzled his groin, inhaling his gorgeous scent.

"You smell so good. So real. So mine."

Nash choked when I spread his legs, and hummed with pleasure as I ran my nose along the cleft of his ass and kissed his hole.

"Ethan." His head thrashed on the pillow.

I answered not with words, but with my tongue and lips, pouring all my heart, desire, and love into my touch. Nash bucked, his hand wrapped around his shaft, and I had to hold his thighs apart to delve deep.

"Ethan, Ethan, my God," Nash shouted, his eyes rolling as he came. It was a beautiful sight to see, and I sat and watched him spiral out of control. His chest heaved, and when he finished, he motioned to me. "Come."

I snuggled in next to him, and he grasped my erection and took me from root to tip in a firm up-and-down stroke, while I sighed and flexed my hips, thrusting slow and lazy into Nash's fist. My climax knocked me under like an ocean wave, and I struggled to catch my breath. We lay quiet, a perfect peace between us.

"Thanks for dealing with Oscar."

"I feel sorry for him."

"Why?" I struggled to sit up.

Seeing Nash so relaxed, face flushed, his hair messy and hanging in his eyes, my heart hurt from all the happiness it held. A happiness I never dreamed possible.

"Because he doesn't have this." He carded his fingers through my hair, and I might've purred like a cat. "He had everything when he had you, but threw it all away for a random nobody. I can't imagine how much that hurts."

I snuggled into him and kissed his neck. "What happened to the grouch I used to look forward to seeing on the morning 2 train?"

"Was I really that bad?" It was either my snort of disbelief or the sky-high arch of my brow that caused him to shake with laughter. "Okay, okay. I get it. I know I was. But I didn't know."

"About?"

He pulled me tight. "Anything. Everything. You. Me. Us."

"That makes perfect sense." I kissed his shoulder.

"Are you making fun of me?" Nash's warm chuckle rumbled in my ear.

"Maybe." My stomach growled. "Let's order dinner. I'm starving. Then we can pick out that present for your father. I don't want you to forget."

He propped himself up on an elbow. "You realize I probably would have. Thank you. I know he wasn't the friendliest at dinner, but you handled yourself perfectly."

As we showered, I thought about what Nash said, but I didn't bring it up again until we'd ordered and were having a drink. I took a sip of my beer from its frosted glass.

"About what you said earlier—that your father wasn't the friendliest to me. You know my parents and I barely speak."

Nash's eyes softened with sympathy. "When was the last time?"

"Christmas. I always call them. It's enough."

"You know I'm here to support you."

"Yeah. I know that. But you know what? It's not the same situation with your father. He's been trying to have a relationship with you. Mine never did, and I don't need them to be happy."

The buzzer sounded, and Nash gave me a kiss. "As long as you need me."

"I'll always need you." I patted his ass. "Now go get my sushi. I'm hungry."

Try as I might to avoid it, working on a Saturday was occasionally a must if you were in retail. Before I had Nash, it hadn't been too big a deal, but now? I was so not happy, and I couldn't stop grumbling as I got dressed, while Nash watched me from the bed.

"It's not too bad—only until three. I always request the morning shifts, and Wesley is happy with that. He knows he can trust me, so he comes in a little later, around noon."

"Don't apologize." Nash stretched and held his pillow closer. "I need to catch up on sleep, since someone kept me up late every night this week." His lips tugged up in a lopsided grin, and my heart turned over.

"Am I already hearing complaints?" I finished knotting my tie.

"If you weren't going to work, you'd be in trouble right now." He raised a brow.

"My kind of trouble." I leaned over and kissed him. "Meet me in the city, and we'll go to dinner? Or do you want to eat in Brooklyn?"

He cupped my cheek for a deeper kiss. "I don't know. Alex has been bugging me about dinner again, so maybe we can get together near here."

"I'd like that. He and his husband are so nice."

"I'll text him and see if they're free. I know they have babysitting concerns."

"Okay. Let me know."

"I will."

One last, long kiss, and I had to pull away from him before I said to hell with work and jumped him.

I grabbed my wallet, phone, and keys, and gulped a cup of coffee. The train was empty on a summer Saturday morning, and I was at work early for once. I met Clay walking into the employee locker area.

"Hi, how's it going?" He clocked in first, then me.

"Good, even for a Saturday morning."

"Yeah. It sucks, but at least it's not that often. It was nice meeting Nash." He nudged me. "Wasn't he the guy from the bar when we went to dinner that time?"

Recalling that hot, dirty kiss in the men's room, I knew my face flamed. "Yeah."

"Yeah?" He cackled. "That's all I get? You meet a guy on a train and tell me you hooked up in the bathroom. Now it's obvious you two are together. That's some crazy shit right there."

When he put it like that… "I know. It's pretty wild."

"But things are good?"

We rode the escalator to get to our respective floors.

"Yeah. Really good. The reason I'm not liking early Saturday morning shifts now."

"That's awesome. I'm happy for you. Maybe the four of us could go out sometime." Clay's smile was bright, and I knew how happy he was for me after all the shoulder crying I'd done with him.

"Yeah. How's Duncan?"

"Great. He's got a new assignment. Some buy-and-bust detail. Not too happy about it, but the life of an undercover detective isn't for the faint of heart."

"I hope he stays safe. See you later? We can have lunch together if you can."

"I'll text you."

I got off at the mezzanine, and Clay continued to the first floor. Once I'd logged in to the register, I began the morning sweep of the floor, straightening out the tables and shelves. I worked my way toward the dressing room, dreading what I'd find, my fears warranted when I saw the mess the evening shift had left.

"For Christ's sake," Ernesto muttered, joining me. "Do they just not give a damn?"

"I know." I glanced over my shoulder at him. "Hey, you're on with me today? Great. We'd better clean this up. I gotta tell Wesley when he comes in that the evening crew is not doing it. Look at this shit."

We each took a pile of clothes left on the racks that should've been put back on the shelves.

"This is crazy, man." Ernesto frowned. "It's that Devon guy, I bet. The one who came from the Kings Plaza store? I don't know what they do over there, but this is the big time. You can't be pulling your low-level shit in the flagship store."

"You're right. It's only the two of us until Wesley comes in at noon, but we can get the area looking good before opening."

I was glad to be on with Ernesto, who had a good attitude and was a hard worker. Together we cleaned up the mess and had our area looking almost perfect when the first customers arrived. The sales were slow but steady, which I preferred. Occasionally we'd get busy, but the two of us made a good team. We handled the line, and I pushed the new store credit-card sign-ups to Ernesto. We got a little bonus for each sign-up, and I knew, being a Christmas hire, he needed to prove they should keep him on board.

We were in a bit of a lull when I noticed two well-dressed men standing in a huddle by the escalator, each with an iPad in hand.

"What's that about, do you think?" Ernesto asked as he rang up a sale. I was behind the register, retagging a return.

"Don't know, but they definitely look like they're from corporate or maybe one of the designers."

Ernesto's big brown eyes widened. "Yeah? Damn." He straightened his tie. "I look all right?"

"Yeah, you look great. Why are you worried?"

"I want so bad to be full-time with you in the men's department. I'm afraid 'cause I was a Christmas hire last year, that they're always looking for a way to get rid of us." He chewed his lip. "It's so slow in swimwear sometimes, I'm always waiting for them to tell me to leave."

"You do great. I told Wesley too."

"Yeah? You did?" His hopefulness was heartbreaking.

"Thanks, man. You don't know how much I need this job. My sister, she's gonna have a baby, and the bastard guy walked away from her. I told her he was no good. Now it's just me, my mom, and her. And my mom's on SSI, so it's gonna be up to me to step up and take care of everyone."

God. You never knew what someone was going through. I squeezed his arm. "I get it. Don't worry. I'll make sure to put in a good word with Wesley for you."

"Thanks, Ethan."

I rehung the shirt and approached the two suits. "May I help you gentlemen with anything?"

One man was in his early forties, the other about ten years older. Both were beautifully dressed—the younger man in a navy-blue tropical wool suit with a blue-and-white-striped shirt and bright-blue tie, while the older wore a charcoal-gray wool-and-silk blend with a gray-and-yellow bow tie. The older man's smile was friendly.

"Is Wesley here?"

"Not yet," I answered. "My name's Ethan, and I'm a senior sales associate. Wesley comes in at noon. But maybe I could help you if you tell me what you need."

"We're a little early. We're from Hugo Boss. We're here to see the layout since we haven't had an on-site in almost eight months. We'd like to know the level of inventory you have at the moment, how quickly the products move, and which are the fastest and slowest sellers. Normally we wouldn't show up on a weekend, but we're doing final run-throughs for Fashion Week, and Wesley said he'd show us around the space."

Fashion Week wouldn't be until September, but I knew the prep for it was a massive undertaking. It was a dream to be able to speak with these men, but I tried to keep my excitement at bay. "While you wait, I can tell you that Boss sells more than any other midprice bridge line. Customers—mainly men in their late thirties and forties—come in specifically for Boss. We've had to place calls to the stock room every week for additional suits and sports jackets in sizes over 44 regular. During the holiday, the Boss tuxedos and black suits sold out in the first shipment you sent us."

The men looked to each other, and the one in the blue tie made notes while Bow Tie said, "Thank you, Ethan. That was very helpful. How long have you been working here?" I had the feeling he was in charge.

"Four years."

"So you must have a really good handle on the merchandise."

I didn't want to sound braggy, but I also didn't want to let an opportunity slip by to impress people from a brand I truly understood and liked. "To be honest, I'm not that up on swimwear and athletic wear, but I try to watch corporate and sportswear. I figure I have to know my merchandise to sell it, so I make it a point to purchase something every season from the collections I like. Boss tends to be a perennial favorite, as you can see by the tie I'm wearing. I know it's older, but—"

"It's from the 2014 collection, if I'm not mistaken." The younger man met my startled gaze with a smile. "Ten years ago I was living in a tiny studio in Chicago, working at Dillard's in men's sportswear, living off ramen, and reading up on anything I could get my hands on to figure out how I could move up in the industry. If you want it, trust me, you'll get there too."

Wesley appeared on the escalator and greeted the two men. "Jack, Thomas, good to see you both again."

They shook hands, and I knew my time was up. "Nice to meet you both. I'd better get back to work."

"I'll be with you in a minute," Wesley told them, then walked away with me. "I hope you had enough time to speak with them."

I stared. "You planned this?"

His eyes twinkled. "I did. I stayed downstairs, walking around, hoping you'd have enough time to impress them with your knowledge." He wrinkled his nose. "I swear if I had to get sprayed by any more cologne, I'd need to take another shower."

I put a hand on his shoulder. "You did this for me?"

"I'm not that altruistic. I'm getting too old to be on my feet all day and deal with rude customers, shoplifting problems, lost stock, and innumerable other issues. I'm tired, Ethan. I'm sixty-four years old, and I've been working since I was sixteen. I want to have a life outside of this." He waved his hand in the air. "It's time for me to turn it over to someone else. You."

"Me?" I didn't know what to say. "You're quitting?"

"Retiring. Johnathon and I want to travel, and he's talking about buying a place, maybe in Portugal or Spain, where he can write."

All this information coming at me fast and furious made my already muddled head spin. "You're really serious."

"I am. Now I have to talk to Jack and Thomas. Thomas is the New York head buyer for Boss suits and sportswear, and Jack is his assistant." He lowered his voice. "That could be you in a few years." He patted me on the shoulder and walked away.

Ernesto came running up to me as I wandered over to the register in a bit of a daze. "Dude. What happened? Who were they?"

I watched Wesley laughing with the two men as he led them to their part of the floor. I smiled at Ernesto.

"The future."

CHAPTER ▶ 21

"Tonight?" Alex asked. "Damn, I'd love to, but my mother is going to a Broadway show with her girlfriends, and we don't have another regular sitter."

I frowned. "Oh. Okay, I guess I should've realized you can't make spur-of-the-moment plans." I heard a muffled voice in the background.

Alex said, "I already know what the answer is, but Rafe wants me to ask if you and Ethan would like to come over for dinner. We can order in and watch a movie. But you probably wouldn't be interested in that."

"Because?"

"Because I know how much we enjoy a night out without the kids when we get the chance. And much as we love them, I don't think you and Ethan are at the point where you're interested in sippy cups, bath time, and putting a fourteen-month-old to bed."

I thought about an evening spent with a potentially crying baby and a little boy bouncing between us. Spilled drinks and nonstop chatter. But…in less than six months, I'd have a half brother or sister, and if things continued on a positive path with my father, I'd be having one-on-one infant-time myself.

"Don't put words in my mouth, Dr. Stern. We'd love to come. And we'll bring dessert."

"Uh…you're kidding. Wait, no, of course you're not. You're Nash. You don't have a sense of humor."

"I have you as a friend. That requires a certain level of comedic awareness."

"Awesome sauce." Alex whooped so loudly in my ear, my brain rattled. "Come by around seven. The kids will have eaten, and it'll be closer to Sari's bedtime."

"Sounds good to me. Ethan's at work until three-three thirty, so he'll have time to unwind a little before we come over."

"How's his job going? Has he made any headway on moving up?"

It wasn't something I liked to push Ethan on. I figured if he had any news, he'd tell me.

"He hasn't said anything, and I'm letting him set the pace. I don't want him to think I'm pushing him to get a better job because I'm ashamed of what he does."

"He's sensitive about that, huh? I get it. He's got pride."

"That he does."

"All right, then, I'll let you go. I have to get the house in a semi-ordered state. I'll text you our address. See you tonight."

"Thanks."

"Hey, Nash?"

About to disconnect the call, I paused. "Yeah?"

"I'm really glad you called."

"Me too."

I set the phone on the kitchen counter and poured myself a cup of coffee. Without Ethan's smiling face or his laughter ringing out in the air over one of his silly television shows, the apartment seemed empty. Lifeless and without color.

Like I was before I met Ethan.

I finished my coffee and scrolled through the computer, looking for a local bakery where we could pick up a cake and some cookies for the children. I decided on Butterly Bakeshop and called, making sure they had their blackout cake. The times I'd eaten with Alex and he'd ordered dessert, it was always chocolate.

The door burst open, and Ethan ran over to me. "Guess what?" He dropped his bag on the floor. His green eyes shined bright, and a flush of excitement pinked his cheeks.

"What?" I closed the laptop.

"Two guys from Boss came in today, and I talked to them. They were really impressed with me. And then Wesley said he'd deliberately come in late because he wanted me to meet with them first. And then"—he flung his arms around my neck—"then he told me he's going to retire and he's recommended me for the manager position."

I held him tight. "That's terrific. Exactly what you were looking for—a step up."

"I know. I know." He nodded rapidly, the words tumbling out of him in his excitement. "I can't believe it. Of course, it's not a guarantee, but Wesley's worked there so long, and they respect his opinion. And the men from the company were very nice—not obnoxious at all like the sales associates in the boutiques. The younger one said he'd been where I was, and I should just keep working hard and pushing for what I want and I'll get it."

Remarkable that this man chose me to share the most important news of his life. *Me.* A man who didn't recognize happiness until it hit him in the face. I wanted to give Ethan everything he'd ever dreamed of.

"I know you can get something you want right now."

I kissed his cheek and pulled him by his tie. Our noses touched.

"Yeah?" His breath hit my lips, and then his mouth covered mine as I undid the silk knot at his throat. "Tell me."

I shoved the suit jacket off his shoulders and watched him undo the buttons of his shirt. "I'd rather show you."

Still kissing and holding each other, we walked to the bedroom, where we both undressed. I ran my hands over his fit, muscled body, and Ethan cupped my ass, nestling our erections together, tingles of delicious friction shooting through me.

"Can't wait." Ethan's hips rolled hard, his cock hitting my belly and leaving a sticky mess against my stomach. "All I wanted this afternoon was to come home and be with you."

I nuzzled his shoulder and bit the firm biceps muscle lightly. "Funny, that's all I wanted too." I teased the cleft of his ass, loving the jerk of his full dick. I continued to play with him until he squirmed.

"Nash, come on." His eager hands tugged me to the mattress, and he took my mouth again in a bruising, heart-stopping kiss. I pinned his arms above his head as I took control, demanding his tongue, sucking it greedily when he gave it to me. My cock leaked furiously, and I spread the liquid over my fingers and slid them inside him. He gasped and arched into my touch. "That's it. Oh, yeah."

"You like that?" I smiled in satisfaction and spread him, teasing along the nerve-rich opening, while kissing his mouth, down his neck, then sucking on his nipples.

"Love it."

"Show me. Show me how much you love it." I reached over to the nightstand and grabbed a condom, ripped the packet with my teeth, and with Ethan watching and panting, sheathed myself. "Ride it." I laid on my back and gripped my dick then groaned as Ethan fit himself on me and sank until I had fully penetrated him. "God, you're amazing. It's never been this good."

With a catlike grin, Ethan tipped forward, his muscles tightening further around my shaft. "I know. I promised you the best, and I'm going to deliver."

I flexed my hips, holding him at the waist, pistoning up into him. Ethan moaned and grabbed the headboard, rising and falling over me. His position thrust me deep into the snug confines of his ass, and I gripped his rock-hard dick, rubbing him from root to tip. His face filled with wonder as I stroked him faster.

"Oh God," he mumbled. "Oh…oh, fuck." Ethan tensed and shot a heavy stream through my fingers. He shook and trembled, squeezing my throbbing dick in his tight passage, and I let go as the backdraft of my climax rocketed through me.

"Jesus," I finally managed to breathe when I came to awareness, and found Ethan sprawled on top of me, face buried in my neck. His skin rippled under my fingers, and I kissed the top of his head.

"By the way, we have dinner plans."

"Yeah. Right here in this bed."

I snorted and slung an arm around his neck. "I hate to disappoint you, but that's not what I mean. I spoke to Alex, and he invited us over to his house. They can't go out because they don't have a sitter, and I said that was okay. If you don't feel like it, we can change plans."

"No. Don't do that." He raised his head and shifted off me, my dick slipping out of him as he nestled by my side. I dealt with the condom and faced him.

"You're sure? Maybe you want to go out and celebrate."

Ethan's feet slid between mine. "I told you early on I wasn't a partier. It was Oscar who liked going to the clubs. Don't get me wrong, I like to dance and have fun, but when I'm with someone I care about, I don't need to spend the night surrounded by other people when I only want to be alone with the person who means the most to me."

I rubbed my cheek to his. "So does that mean you want to stay home and do it another night? I'm sure they'll understand."

His head shake was definite. "No. I like them. Alex is a good friend to you, and he gave me some good advice when we went to dinner at Balthazar. I think it will be nice. They have two little kids, right?"

"Yeah, and one of them is a baby."

Ethan chuckled. "Well…that'll prepare you for big brotherhood. Speaking of, Diana said now that the morning sickness is over, she's feeling good."

Interesting how Ethan and Diana had connected so fast. I knew they'd texted, but this personal information was something you shared with a good friend.

"Looks like you've become pretty close. I didn't know."

He chewed his lip. "Yeah, well, she doesn't really have many people to talk to or friends here. She confided in me that all the wives she's met so far are much older than her or, if they're her age, they make these subtle digs about how much older your father is, insinuating she's with him for the money or she's just a trophy wife. Stuff like that. So I'll send her funny memes and also tell her to ignore the haters, but it's hard for her."

I winced hearing those words because I knew they weren't much different from what I used to think about her.

"I'm sorry that's happening to her. I should make more of an effort to reach out to her—say hello and ask how she's doing. Friendship isn't going to happen overnight. I'm not as quick to open up."

"Don't I know it." Ethan's lips pressed to mine for a brief kiss. "She'd love that." He jumped up. "What time is dinner? I can take a shower, right?"

"Yes, we can." I grinned and followed him into the

bathroom, where he turned on the water. We stood under the stream, and from the gleam in Ethan's eyes, I knew what he wanted. What I needed.

"Face the wall," I whispered but held him to me a moment longer and kissed his wet lips. "Spread your legs."

A slow smile crept over Ethan's face. "Ohh, I love it when you get all bossy. Remind me to get some handcuffs. We can have some real fun."

A flare of something dangerous fisted deep in my belly at the thought of Ethan laid out on my bed, and an answering fire leaped in Ethan's bright green eyes.

"Turn around."

I dribbled body wash over his broad shoulders and sudsed him up, massaging the smooth ass cheeks and the cleft between. He wiggled and widened farther. "Come on. I know what you want. I want it too."

Steam rose in the shower stall as I sat on the cedar bench that flanked its walls. Ethan's pink hole called to me, and I dipped my tongue inside. His moans and sighs echoed in the small space as I licked where I'd just been with my cock. Ethan jerked himself off at a slow, leisurely pace, and I held his hips steady, pushing in as far as I could.

"Fuck, Nash. Too much."

I ignored him, my efforts growing demanding and harsh, his ass clenching under my hands. "Come on," I grunted. "You love it."

Ethan cried out. "Please, oh God." A keening sound came from his lips as he came. His legs grew unsteady, and I pulled him to my lap, effectively trapping my stiff cock between his ass cheeks. His shifting was all I needed to get off, and my orgasm was brief yet satisfying and sweet.

"That was perfect."

"Mmm, you're perfect."

"Let's rinse off and get out of here."

Once that was done, I turned off the water, and we dried

ourselves and walked naked into the bedroom. I watched him dress in a dark-green Henley and a pair of artfully ripped black jeans. Ethan was one of those men who looked as gorgeous fully dressed as he did naked. At my encourage-ment, Ethan had brought over some clothes both for work and casual so he didn't have to leave at night. He'd go to his place to pick up his mail and check out his apartment, but I'd become increasingly dependent on opening my front door and seeing him there.

Yeah, I was a greedy son of a bitch who wanted him with me all the time.

He played with his hair and caught my eye in the mir-ror. "What?" He raised a brow. "Still thinking about those handcuffs?"

Damn. I'm losing my Iceman touch.

My face burned, but I laughed it off. "Not exactly." I sat on the bed. "What would you think about moving in here?"

He stopped fiddling with his waves and turned to face me. "What? You want me to live here? With you?"

"Well, it is my apartment. I wasn't planning on moving out."

For the first time since I'd gotten to know him, Ethan was at a loss for words. "I-I don't know…I'm not sure."

More curious at his hesitation than hurt by it, I pointed at the bed. "Tell me why."

The mattress dipped as he lowered himself to sit, and I waited for him to gather his thoughts. He brushed at his hair several times before puffing out a breath, and I could picture the thoughts swirling in his head.

"It's not that I don't love you and want to be with you, so if that's what you're thinking, forget it."

"I wasn't, but it's nice to hear."

Ethan's smile was quick but nervous. "It's…I don't…I can't afford it," he blurted out. "I love the apartment, and it's a dream being here with you and everything, but I don't want to live in a place so far above my pay grade. What I can contribute wouldn't make a dent in the monthly payments or your mortgage."

"I don't have a mortgage."

He waved his hands in the air. "See? I've never known anyone who didn't have a mortgage. And I bet the monthly carrying charges are in the thousands."

"Yes, but—"

"No buts. Come on, Nash. You know I barely make forty thousand dollars a year, and that's before taxes. I can't justify living here. It would mean living off you."

"So you're letting pride keep us apart?"

"It's more than that. Diana said that everyone thinks she's your father's trophy wife. They assume she's with him for the money."

"I see. It's not pride, then, but fear of what other people think." While I understood where he was coming from, I didn't like it. "Didn't you tell me you were the one who told Diana not to care what others think?"

He reddened. "I guess it's easier to give advice than take it."

"To turn it around, people will talk about me as well. It's not only you. They'll think because you're younger, I'm only with you for the sex and that I'm paying all your bills."

"Yeah. See? They'll think you're my sugar daddy."

I brightened. "Really? I've never been in that position. It might be fun."

"Yeah, well, not to me."

I took his hand. "I don't mean to make light of it, but I have to tell you, I don't give a damn what people think. I never have."

He drooped. "I don't either, but all my life I've worked hard for everything I've gotten. No one ever handed me anything. But if I lived with you, everyone, especially the people you work with in the hospital, are going to assume what you said, and I hate it. That's all they'll think about when they meet me."

As much as I wished I could dismiss that, it wasn't fair of me. Ethan's feelings were valid.

"Okay, so we can go as we are for now, but I want to revisit this in six months."

Ethan held out his hand. "Deal." He leaned in close and kissed me. "Nothing will be different except I'll have six more months of loving you."

I held him close. "That sounds pretty damn good to me."

We picked up the cake, cupcakes, and cookies and arrived at Alex and Rafe's house around seven thirty. Alex answered the door holding his daughter, a replica of him down to the big blue eyes and curly waves.

"She's so cute. Looks just like you, Alex." We walked inside, and Alex set her on the floor. She grabbed his leg.

"Don't let that angelic face fool you. She can be the spawn of the devil when she doesn't want to go to bed. Like now."

Rafe waited a few steps farther into the house with a young boy at his side. That would be their adopted son, Dylan, whose mother had died.

"We brought goodies. And some for the kids too." Ethan held up the bag. "I hope the kids have room for a cupcake or maybe cookies?"

"Ohh, Daddy, can I see?" Not waiting for a response, Dylan ran to Ethan.

"Sure."

"Hi, Dylan. I'm Ethan. Want to show me where the kitchen is? Then I can take stuff out of the bag and you can pick what you like first," Ethan whispered loudly. "The perks of being the big brother."

"Yeah. This way." Ethan and Dylan walked away, and Rafe waved to us. "Let's all go to the kitchen. The kids finished dinner a little while ago, so this is perfect timing."

Sari toddled after her brother and Ethan. "Daddy. Want cookie."

"Don't worry. You'll get one."

The spacious limestone had tall ceilings and beautiful pine floors, somewhat visible even with all the toys scattered around. We passed a large front room with a fireplace, and the next was a wide-open space that flowed into the kitchen. A glassed-in sunroom led to a small backyard, and I saw a cat sleeping on top of a picnic table.

Ethan and Dylan sat at the huge center island, and I watched as Sari stood by her high chair at the end.

"Up," she directed Ethan, who did as told and put her in, making sure she was buckled in securely.

"You're a natural, Ethan," Alex joked.

"Happy to help out, but I've seen enough meltdowns in the store to know that parenthood isn't my thing. But she's a real cutie, I have to admit."

On that we were in agreement. I'd never had the urge to create a mini-me, but considering how my life had done a 180, who knew?

"Did you guys adopt or use a surrogate for your daughter?" Ethan's brows shot up, and embarrassed, I made a clumsy attempt to backtrack. "I'm sorry. That was really nosy of me."

"Nah." Alex's smile put me at ease. "It's fine. We found a great woman who was willing to be a surrogate, and Rafe and I decided we'd each donate and let it be a surprise whose sperm fertilized the egg."

"I think it's obvious whose genes she's inherited." Rafe gave us a taste of his dry wit. "And I don't only mean looks-wise. She'll keep after you and won't relent until you give her what she wants."

"Aww, but babe, I'm so worth it, don't you think?" Alex fluttered his lashes, and it was so typically him, we all couldn't help laughing.

"Daddy A, cookie." Sari pointed, and Alex fixed her with a semi-stern glare.

"Not the way you ask for something. Try again."

"Can I have, please?"

"Much better." That earned her a kiss on her cheek.

"This looks amazing. And from our favorite bakery. We get the kids' birthday cakes there." Alex pushed the box of cookies to Sari. "Take one, honey, then it's bedtime. Just one."

She pushed out a big lower lip, but the cookies were too enticing for an argument. "This one." She chose a rainbow cookie and chomped on it, the chocolate smearing over her face.

Dylan had his face in a chocolate cupcake, and Rafe handed him a napkin. "All is right with the world now that dessert has arrived. Sit, guys. Ethan, we have Heineken for you."

"That would be great, thanks."

Alex took a bottle from the refrigerator and gave it to Ethan. "What do you want, Nash? We have wine, white and red, or Scotch."

"Red wine is good."

Alex poured out three glasses, handed one to me, then Rafe, and held his own up. "To new friends and friendship. *L'chaim.*"

We toasted, and I heard meowing at the back door. Rafe opened it, and the big orange tabby strode inside without even stopping to acknowledge our presence, and tail up, headed for the stairs.

"He's ready for bed." Alex snorted. "Tired out from his

napping in the sun all day."

Rafe set his wineglass on the island, wiped the little girl's face, and picked her up. With a sigh, she settled into his shoulder. "I think someone else is ready for b-e-d."

"I'm ready to relax after a long day, myself." Ethan stretched.

"You worked today? Must've been a madhouse." Alex sipped his wine. "Good thing I bought you a six-pack."

"Saturdays always are. But it was worth it."

A whimper emerged from the little person Rafe held.

"Don't tell any good stories until I finish with Sari," Rafe called over his shoulder as he mounted the steps.

Alex checked his watch. "Dylan, are you finished? Go brush your teeth."

"Okay, okay. Dad, Jacob asked if I could FaceTime with him, Rachel, and Lily tonight."

"Okay, sure."

"Yay." He pounded after Rafe, and Alex faced us with a wry smile.

"My life—bedtime schedules and playdates."

"But you love it, right?" I asked him, curious to hear. Not that I was thinking of a family.

"I wouldn't trade it for anything. I have everything I've ever wanted. Now about dinner, what were you guys thinking?"

I looked to Ethan, who shrugged. "Doesn't matter to me. I'm fine with anything. I'm starving, though, not gonna lie. I barely had time for two slices of pizza my buddy bought for us."

"How about Thai? We can do a bunch of noodle dishes. Or there's a place that does great lobster rolls and fries."

My stomach growled, and Alex and Ethan laughed. "It all sounds good to me."

"Okay, Hangry Harry. Let's do Thai since that'll come quickest. I'll order some Pad Thai and curry and a bunch of appies." He tossed me the remote. "Pick a movie, whatever you want." He started placing our food order.

Ethan snatched the remote out of my hands. "Oh, no. He'll probably put on the news or the stock market, something boring like that. I'll choose."

Alex cackled. "He's got your number, Nash."

Ethan found something vaguely *Spiderman*-looking, and I murmured, "Boring, huh? I'll show you boring when we get home."

"Looking forward to it," he shot right back.

Rafe rejoined us. "So what made the busy day worth it, Ethan?"

A huge grin lit Ethan's face. "I met the head buyer and his assistant for the Hugo Boss brand and had a great talk with them. Then my manager announced he's retiring, and he's recommended me for his job. It's exactly what I was hoping for."

"Wow, congratulations, Ethan." Alex raised a glass and closer to him, Rafe shook Ethan's hand.

"That's wonderful. I'm sure you're thrilled."

"I am. I almost can't believe it."

"I can," I stated with conviction. "They recognized a good thing when they saw it."

Ethan's smile was sweet. "Thanks, but I don't have the job yet."

"Speaking of not letting things go, how're you two doing?" Alex winked at me. "I hope you realize what a good thing you've got."

I nodded. "I've been called many things in my life, but a fool isn't one of them."

"Are you two planning on living together?" Alex met my startled gaze with a shrug. "Hey, if you can ask about my sperm, I think I can ask that."

"You have such a way with words, Alex." I tipped my head to Ethan, who stared into his beer bottle. "That's up to Ethan."

"It's complicated," Ethan replied. "Yes, of course I want to live with Nash. I'm there most nights as it is, and my apartment barely feels like home anymore."

"And?" Alex screwed up his brows. "I'm not hearing any obstacles."

"Alex." Rafe's quiet warning stopped him from prying further.

"Sorry." He ducked his head as if embarrassed, but I knew Alex. He wouldn't shut up so easily. And I was right. He only managed to wait a minute before continuing. "All I'm saying is, if you love each other, nothing should stand in your way. Cut out the toxic people and surround yourself with those who care about you. And if what's stopping you, Ethan, is what I think it is, don't let others' opinions shape you. Live your life, and to hell with everyone else. That's what we do."

The evening was a success, and with a promise to have our next get-together at my apartment, we returned home after midnight. Ethan had remained quiet, and after undressing for bed, I pressed him.

"Are you upset by what I said? I don't want you to feel rushed. I know this whole thing between us has been pretty quick. It surprised me too because I've broken every one of my rules. Don't talk to strangers on the subway. Don't let anyone know who you really are. Don't fall in love because you'll only get hurt. But I'm not regretting a single moment. Are you?"

"I could never regret being with you."

Ethan kissed me, and as the familiar hunger rose, a chill ran through me.

Why did his words sound like a good-bye?

CHAPTER ▶ 22

I might not have officially moved in with Nash, but we did all the coupley things people who lived together did. On Sunday we had brunch, then went food shopping, and after putting everything away, took a walk in the park and the zoo, where we laughed at the antics of the red pandas and otters. Nash even tagged along when I went to the library to check out some books on leadership and goal achievement.

When we returned to the apartment, I flopped on the sofa. "Ugh. I don't want to go to work tomorrow."

"It's been a good weekend, hasn't it?"

"Yeah. A great one." I sensed Nash giving me my space about moving in, and I appreciated it. "But I have to go home tonight."

His face shuttered. "Why?"

"Because I've been away all week, and I need my clothes. And I have to check my mail and see what died in my fridge. I still live there, you know?"

His jaw worked. "Yeah, I know." Pacing for a bit, he

finally stopped. "Can I come with you?"

"Why?"

"I don't know. Do I need a reason?"

"No. Of course not. If you want to, you can." I checked my phone. "We can go now."

"Up to you."

I didn't comment. If his feelings were hurt, he should say so, but he wouldn't because that was Nash. And I wasn't going to push him.

We walked down Flatbush to my street, and he followed me up the front steps. Not surprisingly, Gladys popped out of her apartment the moment I stepped inside.

"What's wrong? Why are you here?"

Puzzled, I leaned against the banister. "I live here. Why should something be wrong?"

"I thought you were living with the boyfriend. I mean, I know if I could stay in one of those bee-youtiful apartments where he lives, I wouldn't be living here. And I own the place."

I glanced at Nash, whose lips twitched.

"Trying to get rid of me?" I asked Gladys.

Her face turned serious. "Never. Me 'n' Pete were saying how quiet it's been since you started staying with Nash. But that's life, ya know? Sometimes things happen when you least expect it, and you gotta deal with it, even if it wasn't planned."

That sounded ominous. "Is there something you're not telling me, Gladys?"

Her shrug was noncommittal. "Nothing really."

I didn't believe her. I sensed something was up, but maybe she didn't want to talk with Nash there, since she didn't know him too well.

"Anyway, I came to check on the place, pick up my mail, and get fresh clothes."

Gladys pursed her red lips and frowned at Nash. "You

ain't asked him to move in yet? He's not gonna wait forever, ya know. Guys like Ethan don't grow on trees."

And Nash gave her his most Nash-like answer. "We're weighing all the options."

"I'll stop by on my way out, Gladys." That was the easiest way to end a conversation. I mounted the steps, but of course I should've known that wouldn't prevent her from finishing what she wanted to say.

"That tells me nothing. Listen. You're no youngster, and if I were you, I'd make sure Ethan knows how you feel about him. He's had enough of guys who don't know how to treat him right."

We continued up the steps and into my apartment. The air smelled stale, and I threw open a window, then proceeded to throw out everything in the refrigerator that had spoiled in the week since I'd last been here. Nash remained quiet and sat on the couch, looking as out of place now as he had the first time he'd come.

I was angry with myself, but I didn't know why. I had a great guy, a promotion on the horizon, and new friends in Alex and Rafe. My life was finally moving forward, but I was still the same inside. I didn't want to stay here alone, yet I was unsure what it would mean to live with Nash and give up all my independence.

"I'm just going to check the bathroom."

Nash nodded. "Whatever you need to do. I'm fine as is."

In the tiny space, I pulled out my phone, knowing there was one person who really understood where I came from. I sent a text.

Can we meet for lunch tomorrow? I need to talk.
The response was immediate.
Of course. Everything okay?
I think so. I want your opinion.
Okay 12:30?
Sounds good. You pick the place.

smile emoji

Upon my return to the living room, Nash had his eyes closed and was breathing deep and evenly. I grinned to myself. I'd cut short his sleeping late on a Sunday by jumping on him at seven this morning and initiating sex.

No regrets at all.

"I'm awake." Eyes shut, his lips tugged up. "I know you're standing there."

"You're cute to look at when you're all relaxed. Not like the grouch-face I used to see every morning on the train. That was what I called you before you told me your name."

At that, he opened his eyes. "Grouch-face, huh?"

I sat next to him. "Yeah. I mean, you were hot as hell with that stone-cold stare. I used to think about what you'd be like in bed."

Heat blazed from his eyes. "You did?"

I licked my lips. "Mmhmm. You'd be all bossy and demanding. You'd like me to be on top. Oh, and you'd be hung like a horse and love it when I sucked your dick."

"Okay. Enough," he choked out, and I fluttered my lashes, trying my best to look innocent.

"You asked."

"Want to know what I thought about you?"

I snickered. "I bet I can guess."

Nash remained serious. "Yes, you were gorgeous, and who wouldn't want you? But it was more than that. I was caught first by your eyes. Then your mouth…you were such a smartass, but I couldn't help but wonder how you'd taste because your lips looked so soft."

I blinked, and Nash gave me that sweet half smile with a touch of wicked promises.

"Every time the train careened around a corner and you slid near, I wanted you to stay pressed up against me. When you reached your stop and left me, I ached. Do you know why I was so afraid to kiss you?"

Stunned by his words, I could only shake my head.

"Because I knew once I did, I'd never want to stop. And I was right." Soft and warm, his mouth covered mine, and I lost myself in him. "I don't want you to stop either."

I cupped his cheek. "I'm going to pack some stuff, and before we leave, I have to pick up the mail."

Nash's relief was evident. "You're coming back with me? I wasn't sure."

"I don't want to sleep without you anymore."

Diana was already seated when I rushed into the restaurant. "I'm sorry," I panted. "I got held up."

She waved a hand. "Don't worry. I have nothing else planned for the day. I can walk back with you. Tell me what's wrong? Your text sounded ominous."

I smiled in reassurance. "No, nothing like that. I was feeling unsure, but then Nash told me what he thought about when he first met me."

"And he made you feel better?"

I blushed, recalling how after our mutual confessions in my apartment, we'd gone home to his place and had such intense sex, we didn't make it to the bedroom. The moment we stepped through the door, Nash had stripped me naked in the living room, and we went at each other on the couch, even forgetting to close the blinds. Good thing his apartment faced the park. We only had to worry about peeping birds and squirrels.

"Yeah. He did."

"So what was the issue? Did you resolve it?"

The server came by to take our order. I chose a Caesar salad with chicken and Diana had salmon. Once he left, I picked up the conversation. "Nash asked me to move in with him. And when I didn't say yes right away, I think he was upset. Like he was afraid I wasn't with him for the long haul."

"Aren't you?" Her expression was frank. "You love him, right?"

"Very much. And I've told him. It's not that."

"But there is something." She sipped her water, her gaze never leaving my face. "And I think I know. You're afraid of what people who don't know anything about your relationship are going to think and say behind your back and even to your face. They'll believe you're with Nash for his money and social status and that all you have to offer him is your youth and sex."

My cheeks burned, but as expected, she understood exactly where I was coming from. "Yeah. I don't want people gossiping whenever they meet me. More for his sake than mine."

Our food came, but neither of us began to eat.

"Why? From what I've seen and heard, Nash can take care of himself. I'm sure he doesn't care."

"He says no, but I'm also very aware that he's extremely quiet about his private life. Having me could be a liability for him personally."

"I doubt he sees it that way. I was in your exact position with Martin, and I had the same doubts. Martin has much more of an ego than Nash and didn't care a whit what people thought. He still doesn't. Either way, I believe Nash is the same. All that matters is that he loves you and you love him. If people talk—and they will because they love to gossip—there's nothing you can do to stop it. You and Nash know the truth, and that's what matters." She picked up her fork to eat, and I did the same. "Sorry, but this little kicker inside me needs to eat."

We finished our meals, and when the check came, I tried to take it, but she frowned. "My treat for being my friend. I don't have many here." She gave her credit card over, and the server returned almost immediately with her receipt.

"What about Julia? You two seemed pretty tight."

Her pretty eyes clouded. "I thought so too, but she's been odd lately, and I haven't seen much of her."

We walked outside, and she hooked her arm through mine. "I need to get Martin some fresh T-shirts and socks, and I also want to look at baby clothes, so I'll come with you to the store."

"Sounds good."

I led her to the section to shop for Martin and took my place on the floor. I was ringing up a customer and chatting with them about their son's upcoming wedding when I saw Julia riding up on the escalator. For a moment she glanced around, her gaze sliding over people before settling on Diana. Her jaw set, and she marched over there. I finished with my customer and keeping my eye on Julia, called Wesley over.

"See that woman? She used to date Nash, and she was friends with Diana until recently."

Wesley darted a quick look and frowned. "You think she's here to make trouble?"

My smile was grim. "Well, I don't think she's here to decide between boxers or briefs. I'm going to keep an eye on them."

"Do that. I can take care of the customers. It's not too busy."

I strolled over to within earshot, careful to keep behind Julia, but it didn't matter. She made no attempt to keep her voice down, and as she was talking about me, I stuck my head in the racks of bathrobes and listened.

"I can't believe he's gay. Diana, why didn't you tell me?"

"It's not your business."

A rude sound escaped her. "It's ridiculous. I knew there was something off about him. He was okay in bed, but nothing special."

"Julia." Diana's exasperation was evident in that single word. "I don't want to hear this. Please stop. Nash and Ethan are both friends of mine—for God's sake, Nash is Martin's son. Besides, you never cared before if Nash saw someone else. You always said he was nothing more than a hookup. It was only recently…oh. *Now* I get it." Her lips tightened. "Ever since that huge donation from the Ahmed family and Martin being given such an important position, you began to show a lot more interest in Nash."

"Don't be ridiculous, Diana. I can't believe you don't see how wrong Nash was. He used me," she hissed. "He used me as a cover so no one would suspect he was gay. I can't imagine your husband is okay with this. I'm sure he wants his son to be normal."

I couldn't help it. I had to stick my nose into the conversation. "Being gay is normal, Julia."

She whirled to face me. "Listening in? Be careful what you might hear."

"I could say the same for you."

"Nash is only fooling around with you to stick it to his father. I'm sure you know that a man doesn't care who sucks his dick, as long as he gets off." Her eyes narrowed, and I wondered how this pretty woman could have such an ugly tongue.

"A blowjob is just the tip. So to speak." My smile was wicked, but my words hit their mark. "Nash and I have more in common than merely sex. We're living together. He loves me, and I love him." Her brows flew up, and I could see she was genuinely shocked and hurt, so I took a page from Nash's book and spoke to her the way he had to Oscar, trying to be kind. "Please leave us alone. You're a beautiful, intelligent woman who deserves to have someone love her. It's not going to be Nash." Dismissing her, I directed my attention to Diana and took the shirts and sweaters she held. "Is this everything? I'll ring you up."

"Thanks, Ethan. Julia, I think you should go back to work."

Shiny-eyed, she left without a word, and Diana put a hand on my arm. "Did you hear yourself? You said you and Nash are living together."

"I did?" I chewed my lip. "I guess I was trying to get my point across. I'm still not sure."

"Aren't you? You're not the type who says things he doesn't mean."

Together, we walked to the register, where I scanned the price tags, but Diana wasn't finished. "Ask yourself, what are you afraid of? I think you'll find your answer."

I handed her the bag, and she kissed my cheek and left.

The rest of the afternoon passed quickly, and then I returned to Nash's place. Instead of hanging out in front of the television, I wandered around the rooms, remembering the first time I came to this apartment and how intimidated I'd been seeing the expansive marble lobby, high ceilings, and shining floors. Not a speck of dirt would dare to invade the residence of Nash Roman, and I smiled. Feeling inadequate in my perfectly respectable clothing, I'd immediately wanted to run and change into something more luxurious, befitting such a beautiful home.

It was only five, and Nash wouldn't be here until seven. I had too much on my mind to sit and wait for him, so I took the key and left the building, determined to walk off the funky mood I was in.

It wasn't overly warm, and there was a light breeze. I turned on Flatbush and headed toward downtown, deciding along the way to go to my apartment. When I arrived, Gladys and Pete were on the stoop, talking to a couple in their thirties. I'd never seen them before and was about to continue on my way when Pete called out, "Don't think I didn't see you there, Ethan. Get over here."

"Okay, I'm coming." I laughed and shook my head as I

walked over to join them. "I didn't want to butt in on your conversation."

"You're part of this in a way." Gladys took my hand. "Ethan, this is Sophia and William Hernandez. They're thinking of buying the building."

Dumbfounded, I gawked at Gladys first, then Pete, and finally the Hernandezes. This must've been what she didn't want to talk about yesterday. "Oh. Uh, wow. Cool." I addressed the couple. "Are you from the area?"

"Yeah," William answered. "Not far. Grew up in Brownsville, and I work out of the 6-9 Precinct in Canarsie. I was a probie, and Pete was my rabbi. Taught me everything I know. When he mentioned he was thinking of selling his house, I told him I was interested."

"I didn't know you and Gladys wanted to move."

Gladys tucked her hand through my arm. "I made some meatballs. I'll give you some, and we'll talk."

Pete walked the Hernandezes to their car, and Gladys led me to their apartment, where she plunked me in a kitchen chair and took the seat opposite me.

"So you know Pete's got an aunt who lives in Florida."

"Yeah, Margaret. I remember."

"Well, she's tried to deal with it on her own, but her Alzheimer's is getting worse. She can't live by herself. The doctor's talked to Pete and said she needs someone to be with her all the time. Margaret helped raise Pete, and he feels responsible for her. So we're gonna sell the house, move down there, and take her in to live with us. Both of us will look after her."

"And the apartments?"

"I know Willie and Sophia want more space than the small apartment we have 'cause they want kids. They're gonna renovate."

"So they won't be renewing the leases."

Pete entered the apartment. "You're right. They want

the whole building for themselves." He fit his bulk into the chair between Gladys and me. "I hope you're not upset with us, Ethan. You know you're like family to us, and we want to stay in touch. But I gotta take care of Margaret. And you've got Nash now."

I did. But there was a huge difference between staying with Nash because it was where I wanted to be, and having no other place to go. That, however, wasn't Gladys and Pete's problem. It was mine, and I couldn't be angry with them.

"Of course you have to do what's best for you and your family."

Gladys turned fierce. "You're like family too. The son we never had. I'm gonna miss you—and just when you might become a big shot at the job. I was already bragging to the girls at church how proud I was of you. They're all tired of hearing me talk about you, but I tell them they're just jealous because my Ethan treats me right."

"I don't have the job yet."

She waved her hand at me. "*Pffft*. They'd be crazy not to give it to you."

I blinked at the burning in my eyes. "Don't worry, I'll still get you the employee discount. No matter what." My attempt at joking failed miserably.

"I don't care about that, and you know it. If I had my way, I'd stay here, but you gotta do what's right for the people you love." She hugged me hard. "It's gonna be all right. Lemme give you some meatballs to take home with you."

It was useless to protest, and since Gladys's meatballs were pretty amazing, I didn't say no. She let me go and began to pull out plastic containers.

"I'm just going to get some more things from upstairs."

"Take as long as you need." The aroma of tomato sauce and garlic filled the air when she removed the lid from the giant stockpot.

Pete walked with me to the door. "She was real broken up about leaving. What made the news easier was knowing you got someone good in your life now. Once we get settled there, we'll give you our address. And if you ever need anything, you let us know. You always got a place with us, no matter what. No questions asked."

Too choked up to answer, all I could do was nod. He understood. Pete might be gruff and rough around the edges, but inside he was a teddy bear of a man, the kind of person who'd be out there, without ever needing to be asked, shoveling his neighbor's sidewalk when it snowed.

"Pete, come here. I need you to help me," Gladys called out, and he squeezed my shoulder.

"Gotta go. The boss is calling." He winked and hustled inside while I trudged up the stairs.

Inside, the tiny box of a room didn't know it, but its days were numbered. It had served me well in the years I'd lived here, and as I packed up some more clothes to bring to Nash's, I could look back and know I wasn't the same person who'd come here with stars in his eyes.

Gladys met me on the stairs. "Here." She handed me a shopping bag. "Take this. I gave you some garlic bread and salad. I know you like it. And we ain't leaving for a coupla months. Pete's gonna fly down in a week or so and look for a place, and once that happens, I'll go ahead and be with Margaret until he sells this and makes everything final. He'll take the car and drive it to Florida."

"You've got it all figured out."

She gave me a hard hug around the waist. "You do too. You just gotta realize what you've got is what you've always wanted."

I kissed the top of her head. "Thanks. I'll see you soon. And thanks for the food."

I called for a car, too tired to trek with a heavy bag to Grand Army Plaza, and thought about Gladys's words.

"What you've got is what you've always wanted."
She was right. I was getting in my own way by refusing to enjoy what I had. When Nash came home, I'd make sure to tell him I wanted to move in. We'd celebrate with meatballs.

Of both varieties.

I laughed, and couldn't wait. Suddenly, everything looked brighter.

It had been a whirlwind day of meetings, necessitating my poring over balance sheets and budgets until my eyes started crossing. When threes began to look like eights and I'd gotten four different answers for the same column of numbers, I knew it was time to stop.

That time, however, didn't arrive before five o'clock, and I decided enough was enough and it was time to call it quits. Gone were the days of staying late, using work as an excuse, when the truth was, I'd hidden in my office because I had nothing waiting for me at home. I didn't need quick, unsatisfying sex. Now I had Ethan.

Or did I?

After our discussion, I couldn't be certain if he wanted to stay or if he still struggled with the age and money gaps between us. My phone buzzed, and seeing Diana's name pop up, my brow furrowed.

"Diana?"

"Yes, hi, Nash."

"Everything all right?" A sudden fear hit me that she was calling me with bad news either about herself or my father, and I didn't want to hear either.

"Yes, I'm fine and so is your father. I had a checkup the other day, and the doctor said it's all looking good."

Relief rushed through me. "Good. What can I do for you?"

"I saw Ethan today for lunch and afterward went shopping in Macy's. While I was there, Julia came in. She said some very nasty things."

"Like?"

"Like Martin would prefer if you weren't seeing Ethan, which is not true. And that you were together only for the sex."

My face burned at the thought of my private life on display. "Jesus." I scowled into the phone. "This is so embarrassing and infuriating. She had no right to accost you."

"She said that to Ethan as well. The last part, I mean. But it's my belief that Julia only started pushing your relationship when she discovered you and Martin were related. She figured if the two of you were together, it would elevate her status."

"I think you're right. It all fits. Neither of us was ever interested in a serious relationship until my father received the award, and things ramped up after the pledge from the Ahmeds. That's when she began to make an effort to have dinner more often, get me to stay the night. She was the one to push me into going to the gala as a couple.…I can't believe she had the nerve to confront you, especially in a public place. And Ethan. This was exactly what he was afraid of. The outside gossip affecting our relationship. How was he when you left him?"

"I wouldn't worry. Ethan held his own and was kind to her. He told her that you two loved each other, and she should find someone who'd love her."

"That's a whole lot nicer than I would've been."

Diana's laughter rang in my ear. "Yes, I'm sure. I just wanted you to know that Ethan stood up for the two of you and sounded very sure of your relationship."

"He should. I asked him to move in with me."

"He told me. I understand his hesitancy and can't say I blame him. People can be cruel, especially when it seems like one person holds all the power because of money or status."

"That's not the case with us, and he knows it."

"But sometimes you form an opinion before you even know the person. I think you might've thought that about me, but I hope your opinion has changed." I knew exactly what she meant, and my heart sank.

"I did, which was wrong of me. And I see now what you mean and how easy it is to make assumptions about people."

"Ethan might know in his heart that your relationship is solid, but the head takes a while to catch up." She hesitated. "Forgive me if I'm butting into your private life. I hope you know I'm in an awkward place here, technically being your stepmother when I'm younger than you. And though I'd like to be friends, I understand the resentment you might have."

I sighed and pushed my fingers through my hair. "I don't resent you. But I can't say I think of you as a stepmother, either."

"How about just a friend, then? I'd be happiest with that."

"I think we can try."

"Good. I want things to work out for you and Ethan. From what I saw at dinner, you care about each other. Give him time to come to terms with having a partner who has so much more than he does. Once he realizes there really is no power imbalance because of your bank account, it will work out."

"Thanks, Diana. I appreciate the talk and the warning about Julia."

"Are you going to say something to her?"

"I'm not sure yet," I answered grimly. "I probably shouldn't because this is a workplace, but I can't let her malign Ethan and spread rumors about our relationship."

"I'm sure you'll figure it out."

"Talk to you soon. And again, thank you."

"You're welcome."

The call ended, but I didn't move, instead staring at the walls of my office for too long. The intelligent thing to do would be to ignore Julia and her nasty tongue, but I knew her, and she'd continue to spew vicious lies about Ethan unless I put a stop to it.

Julia's office was located on the same floor as mine, and I strode down the hallway to her office. Her startled secretary feebly attempted to stop me.

"Nash, wait, she's on the phone."

"It's fine."

Without breaking stride, I pushed open the door. Indeed she was on the phone, shoes off, skirt hitched up, long legs up on her desk, giving me a bird's-eye view of her black silk panties. Her brows rose, and a grin lifted her red lips.

"Aaron, I'll have to call you back." She set the phone in the cradle, and I swear she spread wider. "Like what you see, darling?"

"No. Cover yourself, Julia."

"Why? It's my office. I can do what I want. There used to be a time when you were interested." In one fluid motion, she left her desk and wrapped her arms around my neck. "I remember you licking me and how good it felt."

I detached her clinging arms. "Stop it. You're better than this." Her refusal to listen was pissing me off. "I told you we were over. Stop obsessing over me."

"Don't flatter yourself. You weren't the only one sharing my bed."

I'd tried. Now she'd pissed me off. "Then what the hell are you accosting Ethan for at his job? If I was just another lay, walk away and leave us alone."

"You were with a man," she hissed. "How do you think that makes me feel?"

"No different than if it had been a woman. I've always had men and women as sexual partners."

"So you were sleeping with men too when you were with me?" Her red lips formed an O.

"Occasionally."

She paled. "You should've told me."

"Why? We weren't exclusive. You just said you've slept with other men too."

"It's different." Her gaze was defiant.

"No. It's not. I don't like your insinuations, but if it makes you feel better, we always used a condom. And we all get a full medical checkup every year right here in the hospital." I tipped her chin so she would meet my eyes. "You're not in love with me. You only wanted me because you hoped to capitalize on my father's power."

"And you were using me as a beard because you like men."

My anger spiked. "You're being ridiculous. I didn't need a beard. I've never made a secret of my sexuality, and I had no need to hide it. I chose not to bring it to work for this exact reason. The speculation and ugly comments. Work and personal life should remain separate. Now, we can choose to be civil to one another and move past it, but I'm not going to tolerate you taking your anger out on Ethan or Diana."

She pulled away from me. "Fine, whatever. I don't care. Seems to be a pattern in your family. You and your father both like them young."

If she wanted me to take the bait, I refused, and without another word, I walked out, returned to my office, and decided I'd had enough of the day.

"I'm off, Madeline." I waved to my secretary, who stared at me, slack-jawed.

"Nash? You're leaving for the day?"

I laughed. "Yes, unless you think I should stay. And you should go home as well."

"Lately you've been leaving early."

I winked at her. "Lots of things are going to change around here."

The trains, however, did not cooperate with my eagerness to get home, due to a sick passenger at Fulton Street, where we were held up for almost thirty minutes. Hoping the Wi-Fi would work, I sent Ethan a text to let him know I was stuck. It took well over an hour to get home, but I finally made it, and the most amazing smell greeted me when I opened the door.

"I'm home."

In a frilly apron and with a bandanna to match holding his hair off his face, Ethan welcomed me with a kiss.

"Hi."

"Mmm. Tomatoey. I never knew how much I'd like someone greeting me in a cute little apron. You look—"

"Delicious? Tasty? Good enough to eat?" His eyes twinkled.

"The last one's never been a problem and is a personal favorite of mine." I pulled him into my arms and kissed him hard, leaving him breathless.

"That was nice. I should wear this every day."

"I don't care what you do or don't have on. Just seeing you here when I open the door makes it all worthwhile."

"Oh. That was really sweet." Ethan's eyes grew soft, and he chewed that luscious bottom lip for a second. "I'm sorry if I've been a pain in the ass about moving in."

Even in that ridiculous outfit he had on, I couldn't tear myself away from touching him. "Let's talk." Hand in hand, we crossed the living room to the sectional, and I kicked off my loafers before sitting. "You weren't. I might've been a little too eager to get you to agree to something you weren't ready for. I'm not sure of the right way to do things, since I've never been in this position. You can tell me if I'm being too pushy, and I'll stop."

"Do you want to?" Ethan asked, more somber than I've ever seen him.

"Honestly? No. I don't want to think about you anywhere but here with me." I rubbed my cheek to his. "I spoke to Diana. She told me what happened at work. With Julia."

He grew stiff, but I held on tight. I wasn't going to take the chance he'd run.

"She was very angry." His lips moved against my skin. "I felt bad for her."

"Why? Julia wasn't nice to you."

"Because she lost you. She let you slip away."

"That's where you've got it all wrong. You can't lose what you never had. And Julia never had me."

If I thought Ethan would find my words comforting, I was wrong.

"I don't want to 'have' anyone. That makes it sound so calculated and like it's all a game. What I feel for you is as far from a game as anything could be."

"I didn't mean to make light of it." This was a side of Ethan I never imagined when we'd sat next to each other on the train. When we'd first begun talking, I thought he was nothing more than a smart-mouthed party boy. Wickedly good-looking but all flash and no substance. Every day spent with him proved how wrong I'd been. "It's the same for me. I hope you know. That's why I wanted you to move in with me. This isn't take it or leave it, though. If you want to stay in your apartment, that's okay. I'm not going to make you choose."

"Gladys and Pete are selling the building. I went by today, and they told me. They're moving to Florida to take care of Pete's aunt."

"The new owners aren't going to renew the leases?"

He shook his head. "They want to make it a single-family or something like that."

"So you'll have to move."

"Yeah." A smile flirted on his lips. "Maybe it's a sign. Like the universe is telling me not to let pride get in the way of what I have. There are other ways I can contribute."

My hope grew, but I didn't want to interrupt Ethan.

"I talked to Diana. I figured she, better than anyone, would understand my position. And she said that people will always gossip and be negative and that I have to ignore the haters."

"Diana's a smart lady."

"I know. And I agree. My biggest concern isn't for me; it's you."

"Me? Why?"

"Because you're such a private person. I know you're not going to like people talking about us. And there's so much—you being with a man, and me being more than ten years younger and working as a salesperson. I can only imagine the things they'll say. *Did you hear they met on the train? He must be great in bed, why else would someone like Nash be with him?*"

"*Hmm*, you're probably right."

Ethan lifted a shoulder. "See?"

I couldn't let him sit in his pot of misery any longer. "And so what? Who gives a fuck? We know the truth. You're damn right—you are great in bed. You turn me on like no one else has, *ever*. But…you're also a sweet, kind, loving person. A wonderful friend. What's wrong with that? The thing is, I don't owe anyone an explanation for why I'm with you. The only person I have to prove anything to is you."

"There's nothing to prove. I'd be with you even if you didn't have all this." He swept his hand in front of us, and I grabbed hold of it.

"And I'd love you no matter what. We can work out the

living arrangements the way you want."

His eyes sparkled. "*Hmm*. Any way I want? Does that include wearing your ties, because I spotted some beauties in the closet. You know that's what first caught my eye when I saw you on the train. I thought who the hell is this gorgeous god wearing basic boring navy but the most beautiful Hermès tie on the subway, and how can I talk to him?"

I snatched him closer and kissed him hard, finally knowing what forever tasted like. "You can borrow anything of mine you want. You already own my heart."

Six months later

"I've never been in a hospital before."

Nash gave me a quick, strained smile. "It's been a few years for me as the family of a patient. I was with my mother when she passed away."

I grabbed his hand as he walked past me. "At least this is for a better reason."

Nash's hair stuck up in all directions, a direct result of him constantly running his hands through it. "God. Ten hours of labor? Diana must be going through hell."

We'd gotten the call from Martin at eleven p.m. and rushed to Mercy Hospital. Martin was all for Diana having a C-section to make it easier, but she refused, saying she wanted a natural birth. Nash hadn't stopped pacing since a nurse had come out close to two hours earlier to say Diana was doing fine and it shouldn't be much longer.

Two hours seemed like a damn long time to me, but

what did I know? I'd called into work to take the day off and was assured the staff would have it under control. I was a little nervous, as my promotion to manager of Men's Designer Sportswear had only become official a month ago, and I hoped that taking time off already wouldn't be held against me.

"She's young and strong, Nash, and she has the best doctors."

Another forty minutes passed, and my stomach growled. I'd only had a few cups of awful vending-machine coffee. "Sorry."

Nash took the seat next to me just as the door to the waiting room opened. A woman around fifty stepped inside, carrying a tray of coffee and holding a bag. "Nash. I thought you and Ethan might want some breakfast."

He jumped to his feet and took the coffee from her. "Madeline, you're a godsend. Thank you."

I'd never met Nash's secretary in person but spoke to her almost daily. I stood and waved, giving her a tired smile. "Hi, I'm Ethan. It's nice to finally put a face to the name."

"At last!" she exclaimed and gave me a hug. "I'm so thrilled to meet you."

Nash handed me the coffee. "Not like she hasn't been nagging me to bring you to the office, but I keep telling her your schedule is different now that you're a manager."

I sipped the hot coffee. "I don't have the luxury of leaving in the afternoon anymore. I usually stay until five thirty or six now."

"And I'll meet him at the store, since it's on the way downtown," Nash explained as he dug into the bag and pulled out a bagel with cream cheese and handed it to me, then took the other one for himself. "Madeline, thank you so much."

"You're welcome. I figured you'd be hungry. And Ethan, thank you for all the discount codes and coupons. I can't stress enough how helpful that was at Christmastime."

"My pleasure. And here." I set my coffee on the table and dug into my pants for my wallet. I extracted my card. "Take my cell number and call or text me whenever you see something you like, and I'll do my best to get you the best deal."

"You're so sweet, thank you. Any news on Mrs. Roman?"

"We're still waiting. They're hoping soon."

"Well, I'd better get to my desk."

"I'll let you know when I hear something. And thanks again, Madeline." Nash held the door for her.

We finished our bagels, and I'd taken the last sip of my coffee when the doctor stuck his head inside.

"Congratulations, Mr. Roman. You have a sister."

With a wondrous expression, Nash looked at me, and I kissed him on the cheek. "I was right. I told Diana she was going to have a girl. Oh, I'm gonna have so much fun dressing her."

"Wow. A sister." Nash sat with a dazed expression. "It didn't really hit me until now." He tossed his cup into the trash. "Let's go and see if we can get a look at her."

As soon as we came into view, we were beckoned by a nurse. "Mr. Roman, come with us."

I followed at his side as we were taken to a room in the labor-and-delivery area. All smiles, Diana sat propped up, with a little face swaddled in a blanket next to her and Martin hovering at her side.

"Nash. Come meet your little sister."

He met his father's eyes. The two had become if not close, at least friendlier, and we'd have dinner with them once a month. I knew Nash still grew impatient with his father's insistence that he could be more than Roger's deputy, but they'd reached the point where they could have an enjoyable evening without growing angry about the past. Martin was pleasant to me, although I was still uncertain whether he accepted Nash having a male partner. Nash of course remained supremely unbothered about his father's opinions and told me I should feel the same. If only it were that easy…

Nash washed his hands and approached Diana gingerly.

"Don't worry, Nash. She won't break."

He laughed. "I might. I'm so nervous I'll drop her."

I couldn't help taking a slew of pictures of Nash with the baby, and my heart did some funny jumps when he bent his head to kiss her forehead and she waved a fist in the air, accidentally booping his nose.

"What's her name?" Nash asked. "You were too superstitious about telling anyone before she was born."

Martin cleared his throat. "Her name is Cassandra."

My breath caught, and I stared at Diana. "I remembered Cassie was your sister's name, and Martin and I both love it. And Nash? Rose was your mother's name, and I'd love to honor her memory, as well as have Cassie's birth be a new beginning for all of us. I'm hoping it's okay for us to have Cassandra's middle name be Rose."

"Y-yes. I-I think that's beautiful."

I blinked, hoping I didn't start bawling. "I didn't think you'd remember. I haven't thought about her in a very long time. She was so young when she died."

"Cassie's going to have two overprotective big brothers to watch out for her," Diana joked, watching Nash smile into the baby's face.

"Thank you, Diana, Dad." Nash handed the baby to Diana. "Now I think you should get some rest."

"Were you two here all night?" Martin inquired, taking a seat by Diana.

"Yes. And we're going to go home and go to sleep." Nash peered at him. "You should too."

"I'm fine. I don't want to leave Diana. She's been through an ordeal."

"You need rest as well."

Diana said, "Thank you, Nash. That's what I've been saying." Then to Martin, "You've already got me a private nurse, which I don't need. I'm fine."

"I don't want to leave. I can take a nap in my office later."

I completely understood why Martin wouldn't want to go home.

We took the train, and it was early enough that we managed to get our two-seater together in the first car. I poked Nash. "So, how does it feel?"

"I'm not sure. It's wild to think I have a sister. She's so little and innocent. I don't want her to ever get hurt."

"Impossible, but I get what you're saying. All you can do is be there for her. I'm sure that's why your father is insisting on staying."

Nash's brow furrowed. "What do you mean?"

"He knows he messed up royally with you, so he's probably overcompensating by trying to show he can be that devoted father he never was before."

"You're probably right."

"Do you resent it?"

He took his time answering. "No. I'm glad he realizes how bad he screwed up. I don't want Cassandra punished for something that happened almost forty years ago." His smile was tender. "And while we're at it, let's talk about her name."

"I was as surprised as you. Cassie died so young, and my parents stopped talking about her. I only mentioned her once to Diana. I didn't think she'd remember. And giving her your mother's name was sweet, don't you think?"

"Yes. Diana's a good influence on my father. I don't think he and I would have the relationship we do now if it wasn't for her." He nudged me. "He told me he's very impressed with you."

Shocked didn't begin to describe my response. "Me? What're you talking about?"

Nash chuckled. "You know he admires go-getters, and when you officially got the promotion, he decided to help behind the scenes."

"I'm not following. I know Diana basically bought the baby her whole wardrobe at Macy's—there's nothing yellow, green, or white left in the store."

Nash rolled his eyes. "It's way beyond that. He has several friends on the Macy's board, and being who he is, couldn't help but drop your name in conversations. The response he's been given is that you're 'up-and-coming and one to watch.' "

I struggled to keep my composure, as it wouldn't look right to do backflips and cartwheels on the train. Never mind that I'd probably pull something important, as I hadn't been able to get to the gym in a while.

"Me? One to watch? I-I didn't know anyone knew my name outside of my department, and certainly not any members of the board." I pinched my eyes shut for a second, unable to wrap my head around the thought that someone would do that for me. "I thought your father basically tolerated me, and only because you care about me and he doesn't want to jeopardize the relationship building between the two of you. Don't get me wrong. He's nice enough, but I always had the feeling he'd be happier if you were with a woman."

"My father..." Nash sighed. "My father is a study in contrasts. You're probably right that he'd prefer I be married to a woman and have children, but he can see how happy I am and that it's because of you. In his eyes, he's helping because he's going to do whatever he can to make you as successful as you can be. But if you don't want him butting in, you'll have to tell him."

"And if I'm okay with it? My field is so competitive, and to get ahead is accomplished by who you know as much as what you know. I'm not ashamed or above accepting a helping hand." I searched his face. "Are you annoyed?"

"Not at all. I think it's nice that he wants to do this for you." He paused as the train screeched along the curve of the track. "My history with my father doesn't have anything to do with you."

"Sure it does. I'm your partner, and if you told me he hurt you and you couldn't see him anymore, I'd tell him thanks but no thanks." Nash's face registered surprise, and it tore at my heart that he could still be so uncertain about himself. "You're my priority."

That unexpected, sweet smile sent a pang of longing through my chest. As tough and hard an exterior as he portrayed to everyone else, the real Nash hadn't moved far from that hurt and broken child, still suffering from his father's abandonment. I swore I'd never let anyone—myself included—disappoint him again.

"You're mine as well, Ethan."

"And we couldn't have done it without this baby." I patted the hard plastic seat. "Who would've ever thought that the dirty, ugly, number 2 train could be a matchmaker?"

Nash took my hand. "I'll be forever grateful that it led me to you. The number one and only man of my heart."

I hope you've enjoyed reading Nash and Ethan's story, but it isn't over yet. You know I couldn't let these men get away without having them baby-sit Nash's little sister, Cassandra Rose. Be prepared, because you can only imagine how funny that's going to be. DATE-US INTERUPPTUS is their story and you can read it here:

https://dl.bookfunnel.com/og1gu5g2vb

If you have a moment, I hope you'll leave a review. Reviews are truly the lifeblood for an indie author and I appreciate them more than you know.

I'm sure you're also interested in reading about Alex and Rafe, and Micah and Josh. You'll first meet Alex in *Memories of the Heart* as Micah's wise-ass best friend— some things never change!

When you download *Date-Us Interruptus* and subscribe to my newsletter, you will get *Memories of the Heart* FREE!! Alex and Rafe's story is *One Step Further* and you won't want to miss it. I hope you enjoy them all. These were some of my first self-published books and the characters will always hold a special place in my heart.

FELICE STEVENS writes romance because what is better than people falling in love? Her favorite part of a romance novel is that first kiss…sigh. She loves creating stories of hopes and dreams and happily ever afters. Her stories are character-driven, rich with the sights, sounds and flavors of New York City and filled with men who are sometimes deeply flawed but always real.

Felice writes gay romance because she believes that everyone deserves a happily ever after. Having traveled all over the world, she can safely say that the universal language that unites people is love. Felice has written in a variety of sub-genres, including contemporary, paranormal, and she has a mystery series as well. You can find all her book listed on her website.

Felice is a two-time Lambda Literary Award nominee and the Lambda award-winner in Gay Romance for her book, *The Ghost and Charlie Muir*.

BOOKBUB
https://www.bookbub.com/profile/felice-stevens

NEWSLETTER
https://tinyurl.com/y85e69ab

READER GROUP
https://www.facebook.com/groups/FelicesBreakfastClub/

FACEBOOK AUTHOR PAGE
https://www.facebook.com/felicestevensauthor/

INSTAGRAM
https://www.instagram.com/felicestevens

TWITTER
https://twitter.com/FeliceStevens1

WEBSITE
felicestevens.com

* 9 7 9 8 8 8 8 9 4 9 0 0 8 1 *